Five Days to Be Mine

Mercy Denton

Contents

AUTHOR'S NOTE

Welcome back to the Sinful Delights Series. If you're new here, an extra welcome to you!

I hope you enjoy Mara and Evan's story. Some things I want to share before we begin:

This book takes place in Canada and is written in Canadian English, some words may look different to you. If you find what you think is an error aside from that, you're welcome to drop me a screenshot here: mercydenton@gmail.com

Five Days to Be Mine is about instant love and not waiting when you find the one you click with. It's about exploring kinky play with consenting adults who are in their thirties and know what they like and what they might like to try.

That includes: squirting, light role play, rope, anal sex, a lot of orgasms, public play, consensual spanking and a primal take down scene that's been carefully negotiated.

The MC, Evan has an ex that was toxic and caused a lot of mental anguish. The FMC has a father who was financially and emotionally abusive to her and brief mentions of those themes appear in this story. If you choose to read, I hope you fall in love with Mara and Evan like I did.

Please consider leaving a review. Reviews help indie authors get noticed!

Happy reading,

Mercy

1 MARA

DECEMBER 23RD

Eating out makes me uncomfortable.

I always feel like everyone stares at me, silently judging me for eating too much or eating at all.

But this place, Sinful Bites, is more about the experience than the food, and so far, the experience has made me squirm. And it's not because it's a restaurant where you can play with your food or play while you have food in a kink-friendly way. No, I'm not squirming in the 'I'm going to combust because my panties are soaked' way, but because the antics of my bosses are making me seriously uncomfortable.

Who wants to see their fifty-something-year-old boss naked?

Not me. Even if he isn't hard on the eyes, it feels kind of ick.

I could have happily continued to work with Kyle Wilson without seeing him sport a leather vest, revealing his chest and in a pair of leathers. He is holding a leash.

On the end of that leash is my other boss and floral designer to the stars, Sabrina Wilson. She's topless, and her lacy thong doesn't hide much.

"Come on, Mara, don't you want to put a cherry on me?" Sabrina asks me from below the glass table.

I know I'm blushing as I shake my head.

"I will!" Matt, my co-worker, picks a cherry from the bowl and places it between Sabrina's just-the-right-size boobs.

Kyle leans down and takes it between his teeth, then Sabrina kisses him hotly, and I turn away.

I love my bosses.

Meeting them changed my life for the better, but seeing them like this is just too much.

It was luck that I started working with them right after I graduated college, but that was almost a decade ago. The shine has worn off.

They are floral designers known for their elaborate sculptures and displays that grace celebrities' homes. They have been featured in magazines and are often called upon to be judges for any reality TV show that deals with design. Working for them, looks awfully good on my resume.

But it's not just the work experience I've gained that's changed my life. They introduced me to the lifestyle.

One night after work, we had gone to celebrate Jenny's birthday, and Sabrina, having had three more cocktails than she should have, mumbled, "Sorry girls, I have to let my Dom know, and he's going to be pissed." I sat there, frozen because this classy woman, who is super confident and successful, didn't just say, Dom.

As in, her Dom. It's not because I think people with Doms should look a certain way. I mean, Sabrina is one of those people that floats through life. Like, she doesn't belong with us mere mortals. So to find out she had a Dom, like something out of a romance book, made my head spin.

Clearly reading the fear on my face, she ordered herself a coffee and explained what Jenny and Matt, the other floral designers on staff, knew: that she and Kyle were in a D/s relationship and had been for years.

That was the first time I saw a crack in Sabrina's mask like she was terrified of what I'd say now that I knew.

"I don't want you to quit over this, Sabrina; as you know, it doesn't affect our work."

That was true because I would have never guessed.

Sabrina is typically the one who goes out and meets her clients, while Kyle is the one who supervises us in creating their elaborate visions, but he's right there beside us, getting dirt under his nails, literally.

So when I asked, "Can you teach me about the kink stuff?"

Sabrina hugged me in relief.

Over the next few months, I went with Kyle and Sabrina to munches and a few play parties. I went out with a couple of Doms, but the experiences weren't great; they left a sour taste in my mouth.

Exactly like this experience is making me feel, tonight.

Maybe kink just isn't for me.

I reach for my water, then take a canapé off the plate.

Beside me, Kyle has Sabrina's head on his lap, and he's feeding her something wrapped in pastry and rosemary.

Jenny is running away from Matt.

At the table across from us, a serious-looking group of burly men aren't amused as Jenny keeps backing into their space. They keep sending menacing looks our way.

"What are you doing, Jenny?" Sabrina calls.

"Playing keep away! He has to get me if he wants to feed me another bite."

"Oh, this is fun! I'll play too!" Sabrina pushes up off of Kyle's knees and runs around the table.

A tall man with broad shoulders, wearing a charcoal suit with a purple shirt, strides over to us.

"Your activities are bothering our other guests. Play equipment is set up in the dining room tonight if you'd rather go there." He has a quiet air of authority, a stern expression on his face.

"Sorry!" As Matt grabs her, Jenny giggles and, this time, does bump the next table, spilling their drinks.

The man in the suit raises a hand, and immediately, a staff member comes over to clean up the table and refresh the drinks with profound apologies.

"The dining room is through those wooden doors," the man says to our party. "Can I get anything else sent to your table?"

"More of these things," Sabrina says, holding up the pastry wrapped bite.

"Of course,"

"You're the best, Evan."

He flashes her a model-worthy grin, and I stare at how his wide smile suddenly transforms his face.

The smile doesn't quite meet his eyes; it's the smile you use with a customer, but it's effectively cool and calming.

His gaze shifts to me. "We have a whole menu of non-alcoholic drinks."

"That's okay," I say quickly, grabbing my water glass.

Sabrina pats my arm. "Mara doesn't want anything too sweet."

My face burns. I can't believe she said that aloud.

Evan's gaze narrows on me, but one of the men at the next table calls him away.

"I didn't want you to feel pressured," Sabrina says, squeezing my shoulder.

"Mara, did you think of giving Ryder another chance? He's a great guy, and I know you two will hit off," Kyle interrupts.

"I don't think he's a great guy," I swallow, embarrassment making me clench my fist closed nervously.

Ryder is a friend of Kyle and Sabrina's, and they set me up with him.

At first, he seemed the type of Dom I was looking for: someone who didn't want any strings, was soft and wanted to give a good round of impact play and go for takeout after the play session ended.

But on our second date, he said, "I'll only top you if you lose ten pounds."

I deleted his number that evening and have avoided the question of him whenever Sabrina or Kyle brings it up.

"I want to go play!" Jenny says, grabbing Matt's cheek and kissing him noisily.

Matt returns her kiss. "Then let's go play, my brat,"

Jenny giggles and gives us a wave.

The two make their way to the back of the cavernous restaurant to the pair of wooden doors.

As dark as it is, the glass tables in different sizes, with the overhead lighting that is just the right tone of yellow, makes the place warm and cozy in a professor's library kind of way.

Kyle reaches for another pastry on the plate and feeds it to Sabrina.

"I want to see what's behind the doors, but I don't want to leave Mara," Sabrina says.

Matt looks over and gives me a grin. "Mara, you could come back and play with us."

That's it, I'm going to have to quit my job.

It's a job I love, and I'm good at it, but I know after tonight, there is no way I can work alongside the Wilsons anymore.

"I'm not in the mood to play. Thank you for bringing me here, though. This place is wild."

Across from me, a man is spoon-feeding his partner hot chocolate while pulling on a chain connected to her right nipple.

The hot chocolate spills off the spoon, and the man is now leaning across, licking it off his partner's skin.

"It's our pleasure. We couldn't think of a better way to reward our staff for a successful year." Kyle claps me on the shoulder while Sabrina stares at me as if she's calculating something.

"Mara, you're so talented. Wendy Svennson asked for you to be her designer specifically. It's time you take the lead on a project."

I struggle for words. This is what I want more than anything: to create stunning pieces out of flowers, to make people happy.

"Thank you."

Sabrina flashes me a smile. "You deserve it! We'll talk about it when we get back in the studio. Now come play!"

"You two can go ahead. I'm fine here by myself."

"Oh, I don't think you'll be by yourself for long," Kyle smiles above my head, and I turn, a sinking feeling in my stomach.

"We'll leave you," Kyle pulls Sabrina up by the arm, and they stand.

"Ryder, glad you could make it," Sabrina says.

I stare through the square glass top table at the floor. I know my face is bright red.

"You'll keep Mara company, won't you?" Kyle brushes my shoulder. I look up at him. His exaggerated smirk makes me feel awful, like I'm the butt of a joke.

"Of course I will. A pretty girl like Mara shouldn't be alone on this festive night."

Sabrina giggles. "I need another drink, Sir."

"Hey, Mara," Ryder says, touching my shoulder.

I reflectively jump. I didn't want to talk to this Dom, to this guy who told me I had to lose weight. I've heard that my whole life. It's getting old.

"Hi, Ryder." I am definitely going to quit. I can't believe they didn't take no for an answer, and this guy is here.

"Good! See, our Christmas matchmaking is a success! Are you surprised, Mara?" Sabrina asks.

"Definitely," I murmur.

Sabrina leans down and hugs me. "You deserve to be happy."

"Come on, my beautiful woman, let's get you that drink. Have fun, you two," Kyle says as he leads Sabrina away.

"How have you been, Mara?" Ryder takes a seat across from me.

I tense, grip the arm of the chair as if i could dislodge the tension in my body by gripping the wood.

"This is a surprise."

I don't know how I get the words out. But they are measured and calm, and in the back of my mind, I'm proud of myself for not screaming at this guy and causing a scene.

"I hadn't heard from you since our last date. I thought we'd hit it off."

He bites his lip, raising his eyebrows as if he's puzzled. His skin is super fair, his pale eyes look hollow.

I kind of want to throw something at him.

I can't believe Sabrina did this to me.

I told her that I didn't want to go out with Ryder, that I didn't call Ryder back after our last date, thinking he'd take the hint.

"Mara, talk to me." He takes my hand off the armrest and holds it in his.

"There's nothing to talk about. I'm not interested in seeing you." I try to take my hand out of his, but he holds it tighter.

"Okay, it doesn't have to be a long-term commitment. You like to play. Let's do that."

"Ryder, you're a nice enough guy, but you're not for me."

"Mara, you must understand, I play tennis and ski."

Whatever I was expecting him to say wasn't that. I burst into a startle laugh.

"I hike and swim. What's your point?"

"You do?" Ryder's eyebrows will fall off. They've climbed so high on his face.

"Yeah."

"My point is, if we're going to see each other, even casually, I need someone who can keep up with me. I didn't mean anything when I said I'd only top you if you lost some weight."

"Oh, you didn't?" I manage to squeak out the words, keeping my voice level.

"No, take it as a friendly suggestion. Look, if you need to aim for a smaller goal first, we can do that. Lose three pounds, and we can play. Agree to it now, and I'll take you back to my room."

"No, thanks." I pull my hand out of his clammy grasp, rage rolling through my veins.

"Mara, it would be for your own good."

"To be with you?" I can't put enough credulousness in that word.

Ryder retakes my hand and claps the other one over it. "Yes, to have someone who can motivate you to your goals."

"You have no idea what my goals are!" I snap my hand away again.

"Come on, Mara, one night, and we can discuss it tomorrow."

I stare at him, shock waves holding me to my chair when all I want to do is run out of the room. I'm frozen with humiliation and disbelief.

Ryder leans forward, and I twist my hand out of his, shaking my head.

"No, Ryder, not interested. Leave me alone."

"Aww babe, don't be like this. Come with me. We can get a start on that play."

"The beautiful woman said no. I suggest you leave now," the commanding tone belongs to Evan Brennon.

I hadn't even noticed he approached our table. His expression is stern, fury clear on his face.

Ryder glares at him. "This isn't any of your business."

"This is my business. This establishment is mine. I won't let consent violations go unchecked. She has said no more times than she needed to. Javier will escort you out."

A bulky man with a shaved head appeared on Evan's right.

"No, I'm good, thanks."

Javier claps a thick hand on Ryder's neck. "Let's go, buddy."

"Come on, this is ridiculous."

"You're not welcome at Sinful Bites again," Evan says.

"Mara, tell them it's a mistake!" Ryder shouts.

I feel the eyes of the room on us and shrink back in my chair as far as my fat body will let me.

"Look at me," Evan's voice is sharp and cool. His tone sends a shiver of heat down my spine.

I meet his rich brown gaze. He raises an eyebrow.

"No, it wasn't a mistake."

Javier grunts and leads Ryder away.

Evan leans down and squeezes my arm. "Good girl. May I join

you?"

The warmth in his tone as he gave the praise has my heart racing.

I tuck my hair behind my ear and shrug. "It's your place."

"That's not what I asked. I asked your consent to join you."

He stares at me so intently that I can't look away from his gaze, even if I want to.

"I think I would like that," I say.

"Good. Evan Brennon." He holds out his hand.

"Mara Cotter."

"So, how's your night been?"

I laugh at the smirk on his face.

"It just got better."

2 EVAN

"You didn't have to do that." Her laughter evaporates as suddenly as it came.

All I want is to pull this woman into my arms and hold her.

"This is my place, and I am responsible for what happens inside."

Mara tilts her head. "Not according to the waivers we signed, where we acknowledged all risks and assumed personal responsibility. I can look after myself."

"Assuming all risk doesn't mean putting up with douchebags," I say. "Can I get you a drink?"

I noticed throughout the night that she only drank water, and she'd been here with the Wilson's for hours and hasn't eaten a single thing.

Mara glances down, then quickly meets my gaze and looks away. She shakes her head.

"We have great mocktails," I offer, in case she doesn't want anything alcoholic.

"I..." The direction of her eyes floats behind me.

I smile at my head server as she carries a full tray of drinks to the table in the corner.

"Tell me, Mara, or I'll have to punish you," I lean in slightly, blocking her view of the tables beside her.

"Why, for choosing something sweet?" She juts her chin out, as if daring me to tell her that she can't eat something with sugar. The attraction I've felt for this woman ever since she walked through the door of my restaurant racks up another notch.

"No, for not being honest. I saw you eyeing the tray as Chantel passed you."

"We aren't in a scene," she smiles.

Is that a hopeful note in her tone, or am I just being hopeful?

I test the waters by offering my palm out flat. She tentatively puts her hand in mine, and I close my fingers around hers.

"You're right. We aren't in a scene. Not yet," I raise my hand, signaling Chantel.

"What can I do for you, Mr. Brennon?" Chantel says.

"What two mocktails have been the most popular tonight?"

"Holiday Mule and VanCityLights."

"What's in the VanCityLights?" Mara asks.

"Vanilla syrup, passion fruit puree, a splash of grapefruit juice, a dash of bitters, club soda and a drizzle of maple syrup."

"Sounds great," Mara says.

"Please also bring us a full appetizer tray."

"You got it, Mr. Brennon."

"I'm not hungry," Mara moves her fingers out of my hand, and I let them go.

"I notice you haven't eaten anything tonight."

"I was planning on grabbing something at home."

"My chef would be personally offended," I say with a smile but my tone conveys I don't find this funny.

"Then your chef needs thicker skin," Mara smiles shyly. But she puts her hand back in mine, and my heart skips a beat.

"Why haven't you eaten anything?"

"The Wilsons are great. They're just a little over the top. They judge me no matter what I eat, and I didn't want to put myself through that tonight. I wanted to have a good night."

"By starving yourself?"

Mara takes her hand away from mine and pushes out of her seat.

I grab her arm and tug it gently. "No, stay here, pretty girl, and talk to me."

"I'm not starving myself. I know I have to eat, and I do. I also know I'm fat."

"Mara-"

She raises a hand to stop whatever might come from my mouth.

"No, but I'm *okay* with my body. I've done a lot of work on myself to accept that this is the size I am, and I am definitely not going to lose ten pounds, so some wanna-be Dom can top me."

I stare at her. Her eyes are ablaze with anger, her pink lips are set and she's crossed her arms. But her shoulders are back and she meets my stare unflinchingly. It's a don't-fuck-with-me stance I appreciate.

"That guy?"

"Yes."

"He didn't."

"Oh yes, he did. But on second thought, he dropped it to three."

"I wish I told Javier to be rough on him."

Mara shakes her head but flashes me that quick smile. It lights up her whole face.

It's now my mission to make her smile like that as often as possible.

"What I'm not okay with is being the centre of attention because they always make it about the food. How much I'm eating, what I didn't eat, or in their opinion, what I should eat."

"That sounds like a horrible work environment." I offer my hand again.

"Tell me about it," Mara places her hand in mind.

I rub along her thumb to her index finger. She sighs, and relaxes a little.

Chantel, one of our servers, approaches our table and gracefully lays down the appetizer plate and a tray with drinks.

"A club soda, Mr. Brennon."

"Thank you, Chantel." I accept my drink with a smile.

Mara takes a sip of her drink. "Okay, this is good."

"Good. If they are so awful, for one, why do you work with them and two, why did you come tonight?"

"The first one is they gave me my start right after college. I'm a floral designer, but I do want to work independently. That's not in the cards, not yet. And secondly," she leans forward, her luscious breasts spilling onto the table, "Evan, have you seen this place? I wanted to see it. I was eager to discover something different."

I laugh, loving how my name sounds from her lips. "It is a unique experience."

"How did it come to be?" Mara sets her drink down, and offers her hand to me.

I raise my eyebrows, liking the gesture and hold her hand in mine. It's my turn to squirm slightly, but I hope to cover that up by taking a canapé from the tray and holding it to Mara's plush lips.

"Evan, I don't need anything."

"Allow me the pleasure of feeding you," I insist gently.

She parts her lip a little and bites the pastry. Her eyes widened, and she brings her fingers to her mouth in the most delicate way.

"That's amazing!"

"I know," I pluck one off the tray and drop it into my mouth unceremoniously, and Mara grins.

"This place is my revenge of sorts," I say with a shrug, but the truth is, I am damn proud of Sinful Bites.

"How so?" Mara's tone is all curious. She twirls a finger through her curly hair, and the gesture makes me want to run my hands through that hair.

"I married my ex at eighteen. It was a dumb thing to do even though I thought the reason was good. She made me feel like a freak when she found out I wanted to spank her and do kinky things to her. She said I'd never be successful if people found out what a kinky bastard I am. This place made me my first cool million."

"Impressive," Mara says. "Not the money, but the fact that you used her rejection as spite. Well, and the money, too," she laughs shyly, ducking her head.

"Spite is a beneficial emotion if you're focused enough," I comment.

"Did you just up and decide one day to open a restaurant where people could be naked and kinky?" Mara tilts her head. Her clear, blue sky eyes glow with interest.

"Hugo Hotel was in the market for a new restaurant to give their guests a memorable experience because they had cut ties with the old restaurant here. They needed something to fill the space. A lucky encounter led to meeting the Hotel's CEO, and my big mouth made did the rest of it. My brothers helped me get it off the ground and rolling," I dance my fingers along her palm.

She gives me that sly grin, revealing a dimple in her cheek and grips my fingers lightly as as she copies my move. "How many brothers do you have?"

"Three. Noel, Theo, and Hunter. I'm the second eldest."

"I always wondered what it was like to have siblings. I'm an only. I have a stepbrother but he's older than me, we didn't grow up together."

"Mostly, it's a headache," I smile at her, taking another canape off the appetizer tray.

This time, she doesn't hesitate and opens her mouth for me right away. "Good girl."

She blushes, her round cheeks tinged pink. I'm half-hard for this woman.

"Thank you," she says softly.

It's been a long time since I have felt an instant attraction to a woman, and never in this way.

Looking at Mara only makes me want to study her more.

Her eyes are a deep blue, her curly hair frames her face in a way that speaks of something fashionable and contemporary, and the way her eyes roam over the place and take everything in tells me she's observant.

The fact that she could put up with the Wilsons for this long tells me she's a saint.

"Did you discover something different tonight?" I raise my eyebrow, leaning forward.

"Hmm, I discovered that burly men like fruity drinks," she smiles. "There is a lot of licking things that I wouldn't think of licking off of chests, and it's possible to be lonelier than I thought during the holidays." Her voice rises on that last word.

She glances at me quickly, then away.

"Are you lonely right this minute?"

She flashes me that smile. "No, at this moment, I'm feeling special by the company I'm in."

"Good," I grin like an idiot, gently stroking the webbing of her right hand. "Give me a second; I have to send my interior designer a message."

"Why?" Mara's brows furrow slightly.

"We chose these high back chairs with arms to give people more opportunities for bondage play. But now I realize I should have gone with a banquet or bench seating because I want to sit beside you and put my arm around you."

Her cheeks turn bright red, and then she giggles, but I'm one-handedly texting Steff, my designer, because I'm serious.

"You can't change your restaurant decor because you want to hug me," she leans back in her seat, shaking her head.

"Yeah, I can. I'm rich that way," I grin.

Mara laughs a fully spirited sound that make her shoulders shake.

I finish texting Steff, and I set my phone aside.

"Mara, would you like to play with me tonight?" I'm not afraid of rejection, and when there's something I want, I go after it.

I want this woman in my bed.

I want to feel her curves with my hands and worship her body like she deserves.

I want to know how she tastes and kiss her until those plush lips are swollen.

She reaches for her drink and takes a sip. "Evan, I don't know."

"We can talk about it until you figure it out."

She rubs her arms, and I lean back, giving her space.

"You're not pressuring me." She says it almost to herself.

"No. Only giving enthusiastic encouragement."

She blushes and nibbles her lip. "You've had orders with Sabrina and Kyle; you must have known how..."

"Unhinged?" I supply.

She shakes her head. "How creative they are before now."

I sigh. "Sabrina is good at making sure the smell of the flowers doesn't compete with the food. See that frame of flowers on the door? The little tiny white with the other flowers? And how they are wrapped with festive glass balls? Sabrina showed me that design, and it's perfect. You can't smell the flowers."

"Us floral designers have all kinds of tricks.The flowers are mini roses wrapped with leather leaf fern around the glass-dropped ornaments."

"Yeah. That's exactly what I wanted, something to light the place up, but nothing that made it smell like walking into a florist shop."

"Glad we met your expectations."

"Working with Sabrina, I thought, was worth it. But after tonight, I don't know."

"Oh! Don't let my interactions with them affect how you do business. I know it's strange, but in a weird way, they are protective of me, and they're showing it."

I take a sip of my club soda, studying her. "How sure are you that you will look for employment elsewhere?"

"Very sure. Why?"

I lean forward, closing the space between us as much as I can with the table between us.. "I'm not cutting my business with them only because of how they treated you, though make no mistake, that is plenty of reason, but because unless I miss my guess, they've racked up a bar tab that they won't pay."

We don't deal with money at Sinful Bites in our daily operations.

The guests are booked and paid for before they come in for their reservation, and usually, the price of the dinner includes the bar package, but on special occasions, like tonight, we allow guests to open a bar tab. Usually, it's charged to their credit card on file with the hotel, but I don't think the Wilsons are staying overnight, and I don't think they are good for their tab.

You get a sense of people after a while, and I heard a rumbling about a supplier not being paid.

The fact that Mara doesn't look surprised makes me more confident in my guess.

"Kyle is fond of betting on sports," she bites out the words, and her face drains of colour. I want to soothe her, to chase away whatever caused that expression to appear. "It's okay, I won't tell anyone what you said."

She shakes her head, sending those curls bouncing. "I believe you."

"I never bet on anything I can't win."

Mara laughs. "You're telling me this restaurant wasn't a gamble?"

I shrug. "My brothers made sure I had a whole team behind me, guiding me so this thing didn't flop."

All of my brothers pitched in, and even Noel, distracted in his grief, still put me in touch with a great team of people to get Sinful Bites from something in my fantasies to the reality it is now.

"You're lucky to have them."

"Yes, I am. So, Mara, what do you want to do tonight?"

Her eyebrows raise in an arch. "Evan, you weren't serious about the invitation to play?"

A sequin covered hip bounces our table.

Sabrina giggles and grabs Mara's shoulder to steady herself.

"Oh, there you are, Mara. We're going to continue to party at home where there aren't so many restrictions," Sabrina says. "Want to come?"

Kyle comes up from behind Sabrina, roaming his hands over her hips; the two other people in their party are behind them.

So quickly I might have missed it, a look of slight discomfort flies across Mara's face.

"No, that's okay, you go ahead."

"Aww, poor Mara, all alone on Christmas!" Her blonde colleague shouts, leaning down to hug her.

Mara shrugs her off. "I'm good, Jenny. Merry Christmas. I'll see you guys after the break."

"You better!" Kyle says, pointing a finger at him. "Remember, you're under contract."

Sabrina laughs, slapping Kyle on his shoulder. "I don't think Mara is going anywhere. She's too timid for that. Merry Christmas!" Sabrina yells.

From my periphery, I see Javier and the other security guy, Paulie, and I subtly shake my head. These guys are going. The place is winding down, and the only table I needed to keep in good graces tonight was the Bear Daddies, who had complained about Sabrina's group when they sat down, and they already got comped another visit.

"Bye, Evan!" Sabrina blows me a kiss.

"Merry Christmas," I say to them.

Finally, they are out, and other than whoever is left in the private dining room, which for this evening was turned into a dungeon, it's just Mara and I and an elderly couple by the far window.

"Did you come with them?"

"No, I took an Uber."

"I'll make sure you get home safely tomorrow."

"Evan, it's okay. You don't have to pretend."

"Mara, I never say anything I don't mean."

Dawn comes by and sweeps away our plates and empty glasses. I smile my thanks at her, then lean across the table and take both of Mara's hands in mine.

"Mara, I'm going to ask you again. Do you want to play with me tonight?"

3 MARA

Evan's touch is warm, and sure. I like how his thumb is making circles along my index finger.

His tone is serious and he hasn't said or done anything that makes me feel like he doesn't mean what he says.

But I've been hurt in the past by guys who aren't really attractive to me but have pretended to be, only to later learn that fetishizing a thick girl was on their bucket list.

I shift on my seat, my cheeks burning with Sabrina's parting comment.

I don't think of myself as timid. At work, I'm efficient and friendly. Though it's true I might let myself be taken advantage of at work, but that has to do with confidence. The extroverted personalities of my employers would make anyone a little shy.

But I hate that Sabrina said that. She's known me for years.

I don't *want* to be timid.

"I want to play with you, Evan." His smile shows off a pair of impressive dimples. It makes me swoon.

"You've made me the happiest man in the place. How experienced are you with kink?" He extends both hands, palms up to me.

"I haven't been in the lifestyle long, but I've played with people before. I've attended munches and kink parties."

"What are you looking for?"

I place my hands in his and take a breath. I want to give him an honest answer. I've always known that I needed something more sexually, to find pleasure, but I don't know if I like casual play or if I want a formal Dom/sub relationship.

"That's a big question." A wave of anxiety crashes through me trying to find words to explain what I want in a relationship and what I don't want. I can't seem to form them to get them out of my head.

"You're right, forget I asked that," Evan grips my wrist. "What are you looking for *tonight*?"

I swallow past a lump in my throat. The thudding of my heart is so loud, I'm sure Evan can hear it. His touch feels so good.

"Escape. Something fun."

"You didn't seem opposed to spanking when I mentioned it," Evan's heated gaze makes me squirm.

"No...I like to be spanked."

"Good. What about sex?" Evan raises an eyebrow and flashes me that grin.

My insides turn to liquid at the question. "Not opposed to that either. Except anal," I rush out the words. "I need to get to know someone, to work up to that."

I tense, expecting Evan to say that he can work me up to it or that I'll like anal with him.

But he runs a finger along my forearm gently. "No anal sex tonight. Do you like your breasts played with?" He says it so casually, it makes me give him an answer without hesitation.

"Yes. But lightly, I don't like impact on my breasts. I'm okay with clamps though."

"I can't wait to feel those gorgeous breasts in my hands." I'm blushing furiously and I shake my head at him. I want to believe him, that his words are true but in my experience, guys say they are attracted to me and it's only a surface thing.

But this is just one night. One play session.

"You don't have to say that."

"Say what?" Evan takes both my hands in his, and squeezes them. His intense gaze is filled with heat and want and it's making me blush.

"That my breasts are gorgeous."

"Ahh, you don't know how to take a compliment. That is a spankable offence."

His tone is serious but playful.

"But it's not true."

"Have you seen your boobs? It's so true."

I laugh, sipping the last of my drink. "You can't think they are gorgeous."

Evan leans back in his chair, and crosses his arms over his chest. "Are you calling me a liar?"

The cool tone sends a shiver up my spine. His expression is serious, his eyes are hard, and I squirm in the chair.

"No...it's just most guys don't think any part of me is attractive."

"Mara, look at me." It takes a lot of willpower to lift my eyes to his but I do.

"I think you're beautiful and I can't wait to get to know you better."

I suck in a breath, his words making me want to bolt out of my seat.

Because when he sees that I'm not anything special, that I'm barely holding my stuff together, he'll leave.

When he gets to know me and realizes that I'm serious about being okay with my body being this size, that I'm not going to go on a diet or an exercise program to change it, he'll leave.

"It's only for tonight." Evan shrugs. "That's what we're negotiating for, tonight. Do you like oral sex? What about vibrators?"

"I'll take as many orgasms as I can get." My voice is thick. I swallow, feeling off-kilter by how easily I talk with this man.

"You might regret saying that by the time I'm done with you."

His words unleash a fresh river between my legs. My heart is in my throat. I can't wait to run my hands down his muscular chest to feel if his lips are going to be as soft as they look.

"What about marks from impact play?"

"On my ass is fine." This is so surreal, it's like I'm ordering groceries or something. Except for the way I'm wet between my legs.

"Good," Evan says. "What about names or honorifics?"

I swallow, meet his eyes briefly and look down. I know I told him that I want an escape, that I want something fun, but I also want to feel cared for and giving Evan a title will help me get into that headspace.

"I...do you like Sir?" I go to touch his arm and hesitate.

He notices and smiles. "Yes. I'm going to like hearing Sir from you. Names, Mara?"

I shake my head. My eyes are closed so tightly they are scrunched up. "Nothing degrading or humiliating. I'm on birth control, but I want you to wear a condom."

"Open your eyes, Mara." His voice has changed to that cool Dom tone.

I inhale, shakily, willing myself to stay in this chair.

Somehow this is happening, and I've come this far. If he's going to run, here is one of the doors he'd run through.

"Yes, I'm going to wear a condom. I'm not in a relationship currently. I have a play partner that's really casual. We get together when she's in town. What about you?"

I laugh. "No, I'm not seeing anyone."

Evan crosses his arms in front of his chest. "Mara, you told me that you like your body. Why are you so quick to brush off the possibility of someone being attracted to you?"

His words freeze me, taking me out of the lovely headspace we were in. I push down the irritation I feel and try not to snap. It's a fair question.

"Because too many experiences have taught me that just because I like my body, men who say they do usually have an expiration date."

"What do you mean?" Evan asks.

I feel tears gather in my eyes and blink them away.

He signals the server.

A moment later, a glass of water is set before me. I gratefully take a sip.

"They'll say they like me and then want me to go on a diet or an exercise program, and when I don't want to, suddenly I'm not attractive to them."

"I hate that you had those experiences, Mara. I'm going to be attracted to you tomorrow morning when you wake up in my bed. I can't wait to play with you. Any other limits I should be aware of for this scene?"

"No, I don't think so."

I sit back in my chair. Evan's eyes roam the length of me, it's not in a judgmental way but in an appreciative way, and my nipples harden as I'm stroked by the searing heat in his gaze.

"I don't like to be scratched," his tone is all serious.

"Okay, I'll keep my claws to myself," the words come out thickly, past the lump in my throat.

"Good. What about aftercare?"

Nobody had ever brought that up before in a negotiation and I bite my lip, not sure how to answer. If I tell him what I really want, would he laugh at me?

"I'm not sure…I don't know how to answer that." I take another sip of water, as if it could cool down the heat I'm feeling.

"What do you need to come down from the scene?" He rests his palm on my arm.

This is suddenly too real. I don't know if I can go through with it.

This kind of thing doesn't happen to a girl like me.

For one brief second, I wish I had left with Sabrina and Kyle.

But Evan stands, comes around to my chair and kneels.

A Dom, kneeling for me? I've definitely stepped into a fairytale.

His palms are warm through the silk of my dress.

"Mara, tell me what you need."

The room reels for a moment. His intensity takes all my breath away.

He rubs little circles on my legs, warmth spreads through my nylon clad legs.

"I like to be reassured afterwards," my voice is so small I doubt he's heard me.

He tilts his head, and oh, he's so handsome.

"In what way?" He presses on my thighs softly, his thumbs brushing across the fabric.

"I need to be told that I'm okay…reassured that I'm not dirty."

Oh god, I actually said the words.

Now I can't talk. My throat is closes up.

"Mara, I can't wait to play," Evan stands, offering me his hand. "Tell me if something crosses your mind. I want to make you feel as comfortable as possible. Do you have a safeword?"

"Can we use red for stop, yellow to pause and green for go?" I push out of my chair, stumbling a bit getting out of the seat.

Evan reaches a hand out and steadies me. "Works for me. Anything else?"

"One more thing." I thread my fingers through Evan's long, slender ones. "I need the lights to be off when we have sex."

4 EVAN

“**N**o.”

I hate seeing her smile leave her face.

She tries to pull her fingers out of my grasp but I hold on to them.

“But...that’s what I need.”

The wobble in her voice makes me want to wrap her in my arms and soothe away her worries.

"Tell me honestly. Is that a hard limit or is it what you want?"

"It's what makes me comfortable," Mara says.

"I want to see you. I want to see every part of you.”

She shakes her head, sending her curls bouncing. “But then you’ll see my body.”

“That’s exactly what I want. I want to see what colour your nipples turn after I am done sucking them. I want to see what colour your clit is. If I don’t see your body, how am I going to worship it?”

My cock twitches at how she blushes.

“Evan, you don’t find me attractive.” The words are spat out. She turns her head from me.

I see the fear that's thick in her aura like a shield, and I want to bat it away.

"You're calling me a liar again? Oh, Mara, your ass is going to be so sore tomorrow."

Her blue eyes drill into mine, her face crunches up in the most adorable way, and then I'm rewarded with that sparkling laughter.

"This is ridiculous. You're..." She shapes her hands like a frame and holds them in front of my face.

"A horrible catch. I work all hours, I have a trail of exes, and I like to be in control."

"One of the city's top bachelors, rich and handsome."

"You left out, 'cold, grumpy and bossyboots.' All things my exes have said."

I sling my arm around her, bringing her close to me.

She doesn't pull away. She places her hand on my chest.

"Bossyboots?" Mara's eyes glow. "That's under that control thing, right?"

"Yeah. And the word used was 'tyrant,' but I'm trying to woo you. 'Bossyboots' feels softer."

"I hate to tell you this, Evan. But bossyboots doesn't make you sound softer. I like that you are straight to the point."

"I value my time. I don't like wasting it. Are you ready to do this, Mara?"

"Tell me what I can expect," her voice is soft, hopeful.

"A very sore bottom, orgasms and great sex. This way," I take her hand in mine. It's clammy.

I know this is it; she's either going to come with me or change her mind.

The way she pushes a stray curl behind her ear is so endearing I wonder if it'd annoy her if I put it back in place.

She meets my gaze. "My expectations, Evan Brennon, are very high."

"I won't disappoint, Mara...?" Her last name slips my mind.

"Mara Cotter. Do you always forget the girl's name?"

"Often. I only check it, when it counts," I smirk.

She laughs, her head thrown back exposing the curve of her neck.

The sound echoes around the now-empty dining room, and I smile. This woman has eased my usual contrariness and I can't wait for this night.

"Good night, Mr. Brennon," Javier nods to me as we walk out of the double-wide doors.

"Good night, Javier."

"One floor down is where I have an apartment," I tell Mara as I press the elevator button.

"You live here?" She ducks her head, as if she regrets saying the words.

"I know, who lives in a hotel? But given the amount of time I spend in the restaurant, it made sense to live on-site. Besides, Julian Madden Hugo doesn't like to take no for an answer. The CEO of the Hugo Empire can be a testy bastard, even if he's a loyal friend."

The elevator cars whirl open. I place my hand on Mara's lower back. I like how it feels there, leave it there, even after the doors close.

"Everything in this place is so snazzy. I feel like I'm on a movie set," she says, touching the leather wall texture of the car.

"I know what you mean."

"You didn't grow up ...?"

"Rich?" I supply. "It's not a bad word, Mara."

She blushes furiously. "Most of the rich people I know are assholes."

She frowns, and I want to know who she is thinking of but I don't want to lead her to any emotional landmines-not tonight.

I laugh. "That has been my experience too. My dad is an inventor. My mom worked as a paralegal. We were brought up in chaos, not luxury."

Mara smiles, and steps a little closer to me. "My mom works for a law firm. It's how she met my stepdad."

"Your stepdad is a lawyer?"

I gently take my hand away from her back, and brush over the soft cress of her stomach, then reach for her hand her fingers slip into mine.

The elevator opens silently, and we step out to a tiled hallway.

I guide Mara past a pedestal table with a vase of white flowers. She stops and touches it gently.

"Gorgeous cymbidiums. You didn't get these from us."

"I don't take care of the decor down here. They're..."

"Flowers, I get it. Not everyone loves them like I do,"

Mara grins, saving me from having to explain. I stride over to the wooden door, and using a keycard, I swipe it through.

"All private and stuff," her voice wobbles a little.

"After you," I close the door to my private wing, and because I need to touch her, I wrap my arm around her waist, wanting to soothe away her nerves.

"I like how you feel in my arms."

"I like it too," she ducks her head shyly.

I nuzzle her neck, liking her scent.

"My stepdad was the mail clerk," her words come out in a rush. "He's a good guy."

I let go of her, and gesture down the short hall. "Right this way."

Mara stops. "This is..Evan...how do you live here?"

I stand behind her, place my hands on her shoulders and nibble her neck.

She giggles and leans against me. "I am one lucky guy," I tell her.

It's true. There isn't a morning when I wake up and don't thank my lucky stars. The apartment is palatial, with wide ceilings and windows that stretch out to the cityscape below.

To our left is a kitchen that's all cool and modern. On our right is a dining room I don't use.

"Here, come sit."

Suddenly, I'm all nervous and feeling shy.

Mara is the first woman I've had in my personal space.

She exhales. "I want to get into the scene, Evan. Where do you want me?"

I turn back to her, taking in the set of her shoulders, the press of her lips. She's ready, and again, I'm mentally fumbling.

From tonight, I know Mara is a little unsure of herself, and maybe has a little social anxiety, but right now, in this moment, she is the confident one boldly claiming what she wants, and damn, does that make her all the more attractive to me.

Because I know this isn't easy for her.

Buying time, I walk briskly past her. "Follow me."

The motion sensors are activated as I walk, and the lights come on in the bedroom area as we enter. We pass a seating area, with a cluster of chairs, and a low chaise lounge -with its high back, it's going to be perfect for my purposes.

"I'm going to get the things I need. You have five minutes. When I get back, I expect you to be naked, with your hands resting on the back of the chaise, so you're kneeling. Do you understand?"

"Yes, Sir." Her eyes drop to the floor.

My dick twitches. I cup her nape, wait until her eyes meet mine, and very softly brush my lips against hers.

She makes the most adorable mewling noise. I resist the urge to kiss her senseless. "Good girl," I rub my thumb across her jawline.

Mara exhales, her whole body heaving with a sigh.

"I'll be right back. Five minutes. Good girl." I rub my thumb across her jawline.

She nods, reaching behind her head to unclasp her dress. I want to watch her take it off, but I sense that giving her time and letting her settle into this moment is the wiser course of action. I'm trying to show her that she can trust me.

In my bedroom, I take off my suit jacket, tossing it on the back of a chair. Entering my walk-in closet, I search through my stash of toys, happy to find things that are still in their packages. I grab two that I need, open them up and give them a wipe with a toy cleaner, setting them to the side to dry.

From my collection of impact toys, I take a soft suede flogger and an oval paddle where one side is smooth with faux fur, and the other is leather that will give a nice sting when I lay it against her ass.

My mouth goes dry thinking about laying this paddle against Mara's round bottom hearing her cry out.

I can't wait to give her an experience that she won't forget tonight because my intent is to have her back for more.

Grabbing the tools I will use, I stride back into the sitting area.

My blood roars in my ears.

Mara is kneeling on the chaise, her hands on the back of the seat, naked.

Her head is down.

I can't tell if her eyes are open from here, but seeing her so openly submissive makes my dick even harder.

Her back is smooth and lovely, with a gentle curve to her generous bottom, which I can't wait to paint with my paddle and soothe with the flogger.

I can't wait to roam my hands over her thighs, feel the curves of her ass and explore those bountiful breasts.

But I stop myself from rushing over to her. I set the toys on a side table, deliberately making them thump.

She doesn't react.

"I love how ready you are, waiting for me like this. How does it feel to know you're about to receive a spanking?"

Her shoulder rises slightly as if she's about to turn her head to me but she stops herself.

"It feels...good, Sir."

"Perfect," I pick up the paddle and smack the hard side against my palm, one, two, three times.

"Five being the most pain, one being the least. Tell me how much these hurt you."

"Yes, Sir," her tone is high and excited.

I grin, I touch her shoulder briefly to let her know I am there, and then I lay the paddle across the centre of her right ass cheek.

"That's a three, Sir."

"Noted," I repeat, bringing the paddle down on her left cheek.

"Three."

"Do you want me to bring you to a five?"

"Yes, Sir. Please."

Oh, how she said that, please, with a note of hope in her voice, it compels me to give her what she wants.

I'm grinning so wide my face hurts as I bring the paddle down with a little more oomph. She jerks from the chaise but doesn't look back at me.

"Is that a five or past that?" I turn the paddle over to the soft side and rub it along her ass.

"No...that's, good, Sir."

"I love hearing that," And for the first time, I caress her skin, my palm against her soft ass, rubbing where I laid the paddle. "Take these for me."

"Yes, Sir."

I bring down the paddle with a snap, watching for her reaction. She lifts her head but quickly gets back in position.

I soothe away the hurt I just inflicted. "Good girl." I land the paddle across her ass, loving how her skin blushes to a pink on impact.

"Oooh..." she lets out soft gasps. "More, please."

I can't deny this willing submissive. I bring the paddle down again, covering her ass.

"Sir!" she gasps out on the last impact.

Her ass has turned a lovely shade of pink. The way her head drops even more tells me she's finding this pleasurable.

"Good girl, Mara," I purr as I dimple my fingers into her tender flesh.

She whimpers at my touch. I slide my hands up, from her ass, to the soft rolls of her stomach, exploring the sides of her breasts.

"I like how your hands feel," she says.

"I love how your body feels under them." I touch her nape, brushing my palm across her spine, along her soft rolls that are below her hips, caressing her ass.

"That feels good," Mara murmurs, her tone syrup.

"Good," satisfaction is evident in my voice. I bring the paddle down, a little higher on her ass, and quicker this time, with four snaps of my wrist.

"Oh! Ouch!" Mara says. "That's good."

"You're a good girl for taking them," I praise.

I lay the paddle down again, the echo of the leather loud in the silent room, her ass turning a darker shade of pink with every thwack of the paddle.

When her breathing changes to short, gaspy breaths, I still. Turning the paddle over, I rub her ass with the fuzzy side.

"Ah! That tingles," Mara says.

"Does it?" I work her over with the fuzzy side of the paddle once more, and then I can't take it anymore. I need this woman in my arms.

Sitting the paddle aside, I drop behind her on the chaise. "Come here."

She turns, her eyes glassy with unfallen tears. I pat my lap. She bites her lip. "Now, Mara."

"Yes, Sir," she says.

She lays herself across my lap, her head down to the floor.

I trace the circle of pink on her ass, with my other hand making small circles on her back.

"This is a lovely ass, Mara."

"Thank you, Sir."

"You're welcome. Remember when I said that lying was a spankable offence?"

"Sir!" her cry of surprise sends all the blood to my cock and I laugh.

"Time for those spanks."

She stiffens for a moment, her breath coming out in a long exhale.

I rub her back and drop a kiss on her shoulder. "What colour are you, Mara?"

5 MARA

My ass, heated from the paddle, is throbbing in a delicious way. My body feels warmed with desire. I want to feel Evan's hand on my ass.

But I hesitate for a second, wondering if this is too much, if i should say thank you and make my exit? Because I could so easily fall for this man. That has alarm bells going off in my bed.

One night, I remind myself, I exhale.

"Green, Sir," I tell him.

Though thoughts of the future are scaring me, this right here, stretched across his lap, my body supported by the chaise and his strong legs, I know I'm safe.

I want more of what Evan is offering.

"Happy to hear it." His hand comes down on my ass in three sharp spanks.

It throws the thoughts of running out of my head, and I moan.

The sound shocks me, and I bite my lip as if I could take it back.

"Yes, that's it, give me your sounds." Evan brings his palm to my ass. The sound of his hand hitting my ass sets off a stream of wetness between my legs.

I moan, low and loudly my body heaving.

"Good girl," Evan murmurs.

The next spanks I feel, and they make me suck in my breath sharply, but he rubs a soothing circle on my ass until I relax into the bite of pain.

His hand comes down hard again, in a snap-snap rhythm. The sharp sting is making my thoughts feel heavy, bringing them to a standstill.

He spanks, he soothes, and I am lost in his touch, hungry for more of his praise.

"It is a very pretty colour, almost red, Mara."

"Thank you, Sir." I can't wait to see how my ass looks.

"You're very welcome. This is a most spankable ass," He brings his hand down, one, two, three, four, alternating between my left cheek and my right.

I close my eyes, feeling weightless, as his hand continues, decorating my ass with spanks, from the bottom to the top of my thighs to the curve below my spine.

I need this so much. It's been a while since I last played with someone.

The spanking lulls me to this almost sleep state. I close my eyes in the twinkling pleasure.

Evan rests his palm against my ass. "Your bum is giving off its own heat."

I giggle, happy and content to be laid across his lap.

"Did that spanking make you wet?"

"You're going to have to see for yourself." I stretch a little, bending my legs.

"I can't refuse such an invitation." I can hear the grin in his voice as he dips a finger into my wetness.

The breath oofs out of me at his hungry touch. I am absolutely boneless as his warm fingers spread my lips and his thumb presses against my clit.

"Can you come for me, Mara, just like this?"

I'm wet enough, and his touch is driving up my pleasure, with every half circle his thumb is making against my clit.

"I ... I want to," I force the words out through a gasp.

"I love how eager you are." His hand comes around my breast. He squeezes it gently and yes, that brings me closer.

So, so close.

"I'm happy to give you what you need." Evan scoots me off his lap, slides off the chaise, and kneels in front of me.

"Now I need to taste these nipples." He lifts my breasts with both his hands.

His fingertips are light and make circles across my big nipples.

Each touch he gives makes me more desperate.

My breasts spill out of his hand, I start to tense, about to make a remark about them being too big.

"They are gorgeous, Mara." He catches my nipple between his fingers and squeezes.

The shock of pleasure darts to my clit.

Evan rises slightly on his knees.

His hands slide down to my waist, and he brings me forward on the chaise, dropping quick kisses between my breasts.

I gasp, as the heat of his mouth covers my nipple.

He sucks it hard, drawing it into the roof of his mouth. A blaze of desire rolls through me and I scream.

The sound echoes off the walls, and I don't care.

His lips and mouth, his hot breath, feel so good.

He sucks so hard I am panting with need.

My hands close around his shoulder, feeling his hard muscles through the soft fabric of his dress shirt.

He lifts away from my nipple. "So tasty,"

"Oh, Sir!" I cry out as he bends his head to the other nipple. This time he takes the tip gently between his teeth and it sends hot shivers up my body.

I can almost come from this exquisite torture.

I squirm, as his hand trails over my stomach rolls, then down between my legs.

This man can absolutely read my mind.

His fingers explore my pussy as he sucks my nipple in long, slow draws.

He's making me wild. I keep running my hands over him, feeling his steel muscles under soft skin, making sure I use my fingertips, remembering he doesn't like being scratched.

"Hmm, if I do this, will that get me your orgasm?" Evan curls his fingers, pressing against my pussy.

"I...yes!" His touch sets off a rocket of an orgasm. My toes curl, my heart thuds as pleasure ripples through me.

I clutch his leg as my body buzzes, the orgasm cascading over me.

I bite my lip to hold back my scream.

His hand is threaded in my hair, his fingers massaging my scalp.

"Good girl, Mara."

I lie there, shuddering, trying to catch my breath, the tingles of pleasure settling in my body.

Gently, Evan guides me so I am sitting.

With his hand on my nape, he brings my lips to his and kisses me.

His need for control is evident in how his tongue dominates mine, in how he tilts my head back, deepening the kiss.

My arms come around him, and my breasts are against his wall of muscles as I'm lost in this deep, lingering kiss.

He tastes so good.

He breaks off the kiss, his rich brown eyes bearing into me.

"You took that spanking so well."

"I needed it," I admit, the words a whisper.

He brushes his lips against my neck, to my breast and he takes my nipple in his mouth. Even though he is ramping up sensations again, the languid feeling that spanking gave me, stays with me.

I needed the stress release that spanking brought. I needed to let go of control for a moment, and it's been a while since I allowed myself to be vulnerable.

I curl my fingers and press them against his shoulders, needing to do something with the sensations he is firing through my body.

I moan, as he flicks his tongue over and around my nipple.

Finally, he takes his mouth from my breast. "Give me another one, Mara."

Before I can say, "I can't," he kisses me, long and slowly, as he flicks my clit.

I want to give this man everything he asks for, and I feel the orgasm starting, a coil of nerves ready.

He moves from my lips to the hollow of my throat and kisses between my cleavage as his fingers are stroking me, ushering me to the orgasm he wants.

My hips lift toward his hand, and he presses a palm against me to keep me in place.

"No fair."

"So fair." His tone is cool and controlled, and the heat in his gaze makes me believe he means what he says.

My head clouds with a syrupy infusion.

He flicks my clit in a sure, sharp pressure, and I can't stop the coil of nerves springing into a surge of pleasure.

It's quick, fast and hard and leaves me catching my breath, toppling forward to clutch his strong shoulders.

"Good girl, that's what I want." He presses his lips against mine, kissing me as the aftershocks send sharp shivers through my body.

I kiss him back hungrily, wanting more of his touch.

"I want to see how these look on your pretty nipples," He stands, grabs an item off the table and comes back.

"Have you tried vibrating nipple clamps before?"

"No, Sir."

"May I?"

"Please." The whimper in my voice surprises me, but his smile of pleasure rewards me.

"Hold this one." He presses one of the clamps into my hand.

The clamp is softer than it looks and light.

Grasping my nipple, he fits the clamp on, and screws it in place.

The pressure feels good.

"How does that feel?"

"It's the right amount of snugness," I gasp at the slight pinch as I move slightly.

It doesn't pinch but my nipple feels clamped, and it doesn't feel like it's going to fall off.

Evan drops a kiss to my lips, takes the clamp from me, and fits it on my other nipple. "So pretty, Mara. Ready?"

I nod, and he reaches down to press the buttons on the top of the clamps.

Vibrations throb through my nipples. The sensation is surprising, powerful, and sends my pussy dripping with need.

"Oh! I like them." The words come out in a whisper.

"Good." Evan runs his hands through my hair, then lifts my chin and kisses me.

The vibrations are a steady rhythm, and I moan against his kiss.

He lets go, sinks to his knees. "I want to taste your pussy."

"Please," I squeak out.

He grins at me wolfishly, and like it's nothing, parts my thighs.

"Evan!" The first touch of his tongue against my clit has an intense wave of pleasure climbing my body, a flush is spraying across the top of my breasts.

He swirls his tongue around my clit as I lean forward, wanting more from him. He delivers, eating my pussy as if it's a desert.

Oh god, I've never experienced anything so good before, so pleasure-inducing that I don't realize I'm panting.

He grabs my hand, and holds it firmly in his.

I'm reduced to these short little pants, my toes are curling and before I can grasp what is happening, the orgasm breaks, rippling pleasure through me.

It's so forceful that tears spill along my cheeks.

He sucks my clit, and my hand lands on his head of their own accord. I want so much more of this man. I'm gasping for breath when he lifts his head.

His lips are glistening. "You taste delicious, Mara."

Oh, god. This is too much and exactly right but it's overwhelming me in the best possible way I know I'm on my way to shattering.

Every awful thing that has ever happened to me feels as if it's erased at this moment.

He raises me from the floor, wraps an arm around my shoulder, and kisses me.

I taste myself on his lips.

The vibrations on my nipples are suddenly sore and I break off the kiss.

"Off." The words are stuck in my throat. I'm so infused with pleasure and bliss it's hard to form a sentence.

"Please get the clamps off me."

"Of course," Evan presses the buttons, bringing them to a stop, and removes the clamps.

"Thank you, Sir." Evan sets the clamps on the table, then leans over me, dropping a kiss on my lips. I run my hands along his chest, tugging at his shirt.

He laughs. "Is there something you want?"

"To see you."

"I can oblige that request." He grins, his brown eyes gleaming.

He stands, slowly unbuttons his shirt.

My mouth goes dry as he takes off his shirt, tossing it on a chair.

His arms are muscular and strong, his abs are visible and I want to lick him. I slide from the chaise to the floor.

"I thought it was my turn to be on my knees."

"Did you?"

I hear the smile in his voice, the faint whirl of his belt coming off.

"Yes, Sir," I smile, feeling so relaxed here on my knees, in front of this man. Playing before has never felt so easy, so good.

"Then I must reward such a choice." He pets my head. I feel him lean away from me, taking something off the table.

He steps out of his slacks, removes his boxers and his cock is free. It's hard, glistening with pre-cum,

I reach for it, and he holds a palm up.

"One second, eager girl," he takes my hand, and presses a bullet vibe into my palm.

"Set that on your clit." I hold it in place.

"Good girl." He palms his cock. It's thick at the head, tapering in a slight curve. "Take my cock into your mouth, Mara, and suck as you orgasm."

Shivers run down my spine at the heated command. "Yes, Sir,"

He holds his cock to my mouth as my lips slide around him. With my other hand, I flick on the vibe, nestling it into position.

"I want to see what you look like orgasming while sucking my cock."

His words send a shiver down my spine.

I fumble with the vibe, I'm so wet it's hard to hold it in but I get it after a moment, my fingers coated with my juices.

I take my time, lavishing my tongue along his length.

He twirls a strand of my hair around his finger, pulling gently.

"More, Mara."

I take the full length of him into my mouth, swallowing, matching the rhythm from the vibrations in the vibe.

Oh, it's so delicious. It's an experience I've never had and I feel like I am going to be torn from my body, shattered at any moment.

"You look so pretty right now, Mara, following my directions." The warmth in his tone wraps me in praise and I close my eyes as I swallow on his cock.

I rock forward, my pleasure mounting. I don't know if I can keep his cock in my mouth.

He laughs, gently, and his hand steadies my neck, keeping my mouth on his cock. Never have I been with such an intuitive man.

I swallow as the pleasure rises, and his cock coats my mouth with his salty taste.

I feel his pre-cum on my tongue and suck.

"Good girl, Mara, let me have it."

His words are all I need. I suck the head of his cock, my body buzzes with bliss and I am lost in it that the rising wave takes me by surprise.

The orgasm is so strong, it makes me gasp, sputtering around his cock. It slips from my mouth, and I sit back on my heels.

"Sorry, sorry."

"No need to be sorry, Mara. you did exactly as I said." Evan covers my hand with his, flicking the vibe off.

He kisses me until my lips feel bruised, brushes his lips against my forehead.

I let out a long exhale, feeling so satisfied.

"I want to know how your pussy feels around my cock. Should we move to the bed?"

The way this man looks at me has only ever happened to me in my dreams.

"Yes." I definitely want to be in his bed.

"Good." He helps me to my feet.

The bed is covered with a white duvet and burgundy pillows.

Evan gently guides me to the end and pushes me against it, so I'm falling down.

"Now who's eager?"

"I am," he flashes me a grin.

From the nightstand drawer, he takes out a condom. Holding my glaze, he slides it over his cock.

"Where was I?"

"Right about there," I giggle, as he settles himself between my legs.

"Evan!" I shriek as he kisses my collarbone, brushing his mouth along my mouth

Every pass of his lips sets off a new tingle. My body is on fire with want and need by the time his mouth touches the soft rolls on my stomach.

"Evan, you don't have to touch me there." I lift myself up, sliding back on the bed, reaching for him.

"I want to touch you everywhere."

Oh god, he rubs his face against my stomach, grabs my hips, kisses the inside of my thighs.

I can't believe this is happening. Against the pleasurable sensations, a tiny bit of doubt is in the back of my mind that this isn't real.

"Stop thinking, Mara," Evan demands, then kisses me.

His kiss works, because all I feel is his mouth against mine, insistent and in control. I moan against his mouth.

"Spread those thighs for me, Mara,"

"Yes, Sir." I feel like I'm going to cry as his hot gaze travels down the length of my body, to my pussy.

"Still wet and gleaming." He drags a finger over my clit then brings it to his mouth, his cheeks hollowing with how hard he sucks.

"Delicious."

"Evan, oh god." I turn my head from him, lost in so much emotion I forget to breathe for a moment.

"Mara, stay with me. I've got you,"

I feel his body sink against mine, as he settles between my legs. "Do you trust me?"

6 EVAN

Her eyes dart everywhere except my face. I lay a gentle kiss against the hollow of her throat, and slide my hands down to her hips.

"Yes." Her voice wobbles.

"What colour are you, Mara?" I wonder if she'll tell me the truth.

I know I need to give her reassurance but I'm not sure what exactly set her off to this emotional state.

Maybe it's everything between us. I've never been with a woman where it's been so intense, so all consuming.

"Green, Sir."

"Glad to hear it." I smile, dropping a kiss on her forehead.

Her hands glide up my back, pressing me to her.

I kiss her, loving how her mouth and tongue feels against mine.

Sitting back, I stroke my hard cock, and line myself up just right.

"You're so beautiful," I say as I sink into her heat.

Her pussy is like magma as I slowly slip in, inch by inch.

"Yes, Evan!" Her cries curl into my heart, bringing forth a part of me I've closed off for a long time.

This woman brings forth my protector.

I want to treasure her for more than one night.

I thrust in long, slow strokes, drinking in how shiny her eyes are, the slight sweat breaking across her brow.

Her legs come up and I reach back, supporting them, loving how she gives me more space, allowing me to go even deeper.

"You've made me the happiest man in the entire city tonight, Mara," I tell her, gripping her legs.

"Harder," she says cheekily.

I laugh, and give her what she wants, drilling into her with one long thrust. And another. Two more, with her gaspy breaths urging me on.

"Oh god! Yes."

And I am lost, thrusting in her repeatedly, so hard that the bed hits the wall.

I press myself to her, my chest to her soft breasts, and lose myself in this spiral of pleasure.

I'm breathing hard, as I grip her ass, wanting more leverage, wanting to be even deeper into the heat that's enveloping my cock.

One more thrust, hard and fast, and at her cry, I tilt my hips and sink into her softness, into her blazing heat, again.

Nothing has ever felt better.

"I'm going to come!" Her voice is high, filled with desperation.

I move so her legs are over my shoulders and gyrate against her, rocking into her steadily, not wanting to ever leave this moment.

Sweat breaks out across my back and my shoulders and I am consumed with red hot need for this woman.

"Come with me, Mara!" I shout.

Her pussy clenches around my cock, a tight vice that rackets my pleasure.

Electricity hums from my spine, rolling over me.

"Yes, oh god, Evan!" Her legs drop from my shoulders.

My balls are so heavy and tight my orgasm breaks in the next instant and my release comes hard and fast.

"That was...oh, Evan." Her eyes widen as I kiss her, in open mouth kisses, covering as much of her as I can.

I gently ease out of her pussy.

"Give me one quick moment, pretty girl," I drop a kiss against her brow.

She nods, tears in her eyes.

In the bathroom, I clean myself up, and wash my hands.

On my way back to her, I grab two bottles of water from the fridge. I uncap the bottle and hand it to her.

"Here, Mara."

"Thank you." She takes the bottle from me and drinks.

"I loved spending this night with you. How are you feeling?" I brush a hand through her hair.

"Good. I need the bathroom." She glances away.

I squeeze her shoulder, feeling a tad hurt that she's not meeting eye contact. "Mara, are you all right?"

"Yeah. Bathroom?"

"Right through there," I gesture.

She gets up, strides to the bathroom and closes the door behind her.

I stretch out, satisfaction humming through my body.

I didn't expect the night to end with this sexy woman beside me, but I'm glad it went that way.

When I hear the door open, I sit up, remembering Mara's request for aftercare.

I stand, going to my closet and coming back out with a fluffy blanket.

"Can I drape this around your shoulders?""

Yes." She rubs her arms, looking lost.

"Mara, how are you feeling?"

"I'm okay," she says, but her eyes don't meet mine.

"Here, come sit." I guide her to a loveseat and sit down next to her.

I sling my arm over her and nuzzle her neck. "You were a very good girl for me."

"I liked it, everything we did."

"Good." I take her hand from her lap and hold it in mine, it's cool.

"I just feel...weird."

"Weird, how?"

"I don't know." She bites her lip and shakes her head. "I've tried to explain it to partners before."

"It's all right." I gently stroke her jaw.

"Do you want to talk about anything we did?"

She shakes her head. "I liked playing with you. I liked the spanking. My ass is sore, but not too much."

"Good."

"This was really nice." Her voice trembles.

"Mara, can you tell me what's wrong?"

She ducks her head, and grabs my hand. "Can you just hold me like this for a while?"

I want to soothe her, I want to carry her back to the bed and kiss her until she's asleep.

"Yes, I can do that," I tighten my arm around her shoulders, and she puts her head on my shoulder.

I brush my lips across her forehead and remember what she said she needed.

"Mara, you're a confident, beautiful woman who deserves to have all sex and all the play you want. You're not dirty."

She whimpers, her ocean eyes fill with tears. "Thanks, Evan."

I want to tell her that I want to see her again, that I want to take her to breakfast and ask her how she's spending Christmas, but I wait and give her space.

Ten minutes later, she takes the blanket off, and sits up.

"Are you ready to sleep now?"

"I don't think so...my mind is still racing."

"Want to watch a movie?"

She moves to the edge of the couch.

"Yes."

"Let me get us a snack. You can pick the movie."

She grins. "You might regret that. I like romcoms."

I laugh. "'Tis the season for them, right?"

"Right." I drop a kiss on her lips, take her hand and we stroll to the kitchen. "The remotes for the TV are on the shelf to the left," I tell her.

"Got it." Mara smiles.

Whistling, I assemble a plate of cheese, nuts and grapes.

"I think I figured it out," Mara grins, gesturing at the TV.

"Oh, that's an old one," I grin as the credits for *Serendipity* roll by.

"My mom's favourite." I put the tray on the table, pat the couch. Mara settles next to me.

From behind me, I grab a throw blanket and spread it out between us.

Mara leans her head against my chest, and this is the only way I want to spend my nights.

We watch the movie in comfort, laughing and snacking, and when it stops, Mara yawns.

"Now I could sleep," she says. "Good. Can I take you to breakfast tomorrow?"

She blushes. "Yes, I would like to have breakfast with you."

"Good," I press a light kiss against her brow. "Let me tuck you in, pretty girl."

She glances away, but takes my hand and I walk her back to the bedroom.

Mara helps me turn down the bed, a pensive look on her face.

"Are you okay?"

"Yes, just tired. It's late."

"Get into bed." I come around to the side she's standing on, fluffing her pillow.

"Thanks," she grins shyly. She gets into bed. I pull the blankets up to her chin, kiss her lips.

She giggles.

I climb in next to her, turn on my side, and reach for her.

Mara turns, so her back is against me, and I softly glide my hands from her arms to her hips.

"Good night, Evan."

"Night, Mara."

She turns over, and I spoon against her, humming with the pleasure of this evening's experiences.

***

Before I even open my eyes, I know Mara's gone.

It's the absence of her scent.

The space is empty next to me, the place where she lay in my arms cold.

My phone buzzes from somewhere.

It's my brothers.

I need to check in with them but I can't get up for a moment, my mind whirling trying to figure out what I did wrong to make Mara leave without saying goodbye.

Whatever it is, I want to make it right and filled with that intent, I stroll across the room.

There's a note on the bathroom door.

Evan, thank you for last night. I'm sorry I have to go. It isn't anything you did or said...it's just me. - Mara

I realize I didn't even get her cell number but I know where she works.

Pushing down a tight ball of emotion, I step into the shower.

The moments from our time together last night flash through my mind. I don't know what I did wrong.

If Mara was being honest with me, she felt comfortable and enjoyed everything that we did.

If she wasn't being honest with me...

I shake away the thought, turn off the shower and get out.

My phone rings, the ringtone tells me it's Noel calling.

I answer it with a harsh, "What?" and grip Mara's note in my hand.

Never have I felt such an instant attraction to a woman and never has a woman made me feel so protective.

As I listen to my brother Noel, my eyes land on the flogger that I didn't get to use on Mara.

Somehow, I have to convince Mara we need a second night.

7 EVAN

FEBRUARY 9TH

"Can we take down the doors to create one giant room?" Nevie Cartwright runs a palm along the wooden door to the private dining room, her sparkling long acrylic nails glimmer in the light. I suppress a shudder, at the clickety click sound as she taps them against the door.

My cheeks ache with how hard I smile. "Anything for you, Nevie."

I mean it and jot down a quick note on my iPad to ask Steff, my designer, about the doors being removed for the night to make it look intentional.

Nevie walks ahead of me, through the private dining space into the main restaurant area of Sinful Bites.

Chandeliers hang with their gentle cascade of crystal, now dark with only the house lights on above us. The dark wood floors gleam, so does every place setting on the glass top tables.

The restaurant is done in rich blood hues and divided into grids by three long communal tables, each with seating for eight. Small groupings of glass top tables fill in the space.

"We should move these long tables. I don't need them. Someone will feel left out, better to keep it to the four seatings. Can we move these oblong tables?" Nevie tapped one of the oblong glass tables, with the nail of her index finger.

"Of course," I say, wondering how I'm going to find matching tables to join the custom made rectangles.

There were very few people that I would cater this much to or for, but Nevie Cartwright, wife and submissive of Griffin Cartwright, is one of them.

The Cartwrights are fetish/kink celebrities, owning the private BDSM club, Shivers.

Each year they host an infamous yacht party and have written numerous books on kink and sex ed.

I'm rich, but I'm not yacht-rich.

Sinful Bites has a waiting list going into next year. We are an experience catered to the kinky minded and I make no apology that eating in this restaurant which sits on the fortieth floor of the luxurious Hugo Hotel, will run you six hundred dollars a plate.

"Good. This is going to be a night to remember, Evan. Chef sent me the latest menu, but I want to reiterate that there is to be no egg dishes and absolutely no seafood. Griffin hates seafood."

"I have it noted on the event details and on the menus." I had also covered it during the last meeting for this event, which is going to be the anniversary party of the year. "I promise, no eggs and no seafood."

"Great, the last thing I want this night to resemble is a church potluck." Nevie shudders, tossing her golden blonde braid over her shoulder.

"I can't think of anything worse."

"You're a star, Evan. The only other thing I want to go over is decor. I must say, the place looked a little sparse last time Griffin and I came to dine. Have you thought of adding some floral touches?" Nevie has a smirk on her face and I wonder how she heard that I fired my florist.

"I'm between florists right now." Flowers aren't my thing and I haven't been in a hurry to replace Kyle and Sabrina Wilson.

"An establishment like this really needs a floral team on their payroll. I'm happy to send you who we use."

"I have it covered, Nevie. Thanks for the offer."

Nevie turns on her heels and tilts her head. "Do you know that I turned Griffin down twice before finally agreeing to go to dinner with him? Sometimes a woman likes a little pursuit?"

I slide my hands into my pockets but can't help but level a glare at her.

I didn't think she and Griffin were there that night, but maybe they'd come early.

She shrugs, smiling.

"And sometimes it can come off as a creepy stalker guy."

Nevie tilts her head back and laughs, her model worthy grin shining. "Nobody can accuse you of being creepy, Evan."

"I think my ex-wife would disagree with you." I smile, but there is a sour taste in my mouth.

"Don't let your past stop you. Now remind me of how many guests I'm allowed to have?"

I shake my head in mock desperation. "Even for you, Nevie, the place only holds eighty people seated."

"Then it's a good thing many of us won't be spending the evening on a chair but on the floor."

"Still counts." I smile, but make my tone firm.

"You can't blame an old girl for trying." Nevie flashes me that smile again.

"I'm going to do everything I can to make sure you have a memorable thirty-fifth anniversary party."

"I can't wait, Evan."

"Nevie, are you done giving Mr. Brennon a hard time?" A booming voice calls out before we even see him.

Griffin Cartwright strides through the room, grinning at his wife.

"Making sure it's perfect for you, my love," Nevie says.

Her face lights up with a real smile as Griffin throws his arms around her and they kiss deeply.

I turn my gaze away, shuffling down a wave of jealousy so unexpected it almost literally knocks me off my feet.

What is it like to have that kind of love? My attempt at marriage didn't last. I was too young and too inexperienced.

Now my thirty-fifth birthday is a couple weeks away and I haven't found love yet.

An image of a woman with the most fantastic breasts and delightful laugh flashes through my mind.

Mara.

She gave me one night, but I wanted more.

Maybe Nevie is right and I need to pursue her again.

Though I had tried since the morning after, when I woke up and she wasn't beside me.

I tried her place of work and I sent a message to her Instagram account.

Both were busts.

If Mara wanted to hear from me, she'd reach out.

It's not like she doesn't know I live in the Hugo Hotel.

"Evan doesn't have a date for our party," Nevie says, with an exaggerated pout.

"I'm sure our friend can handle his own love life. Right Evan?" Griffin slaps me on the back.

"I hear you can't be good at everything." I smile ruefully. "I'm good at being a restaurateur, but bad at relationships. How's that for a new tagline?"

"Awful, but then you know that." Griffin shakes his head. "Come to the club sometime, pick up a willing submissive and have a great time."

When I was younger, there would have been nothing more appealing to me than doing exactly that.

Now, Sinful Bites takes up most of my nights and there's only one woman I'm interested in.

"Keep trying, Evan. A little bribery never hurts." Nevie raises a shoulder.

"Are you causing trouble?" Griffin threads his hand through her braid, leaning her over his arm.

"Always my love." Nevie grins at him.

Griffin laughs and they lock lips again.

"Hi Evan, sorry to be running late. Traffic," Steff Goldstein rushes through the doors, with a smile.

Her long brown hair trails behind her. She nearly trips over her long skirt.

"Hi Steff, thanks for coming."

Steff, whose interiors have been featured in restaurants from Amsterdam to Zimbabwe, sets her briefcase down on top of a table toppling the glassware.

Nevie rushes over to help keep the glasses from falling but I wave her off and set them upright.

"Sorry, Evan," Steff says.

"Don't worry about it."

Steff is clumsy and scatterbrained but always willing to try new things and easy to work with.

"I got it, you don't have to do that," Steff says to Nevie, taking a fork from her.

I snatch the fork from Steff to walk it to the kitchen.

"Time for us to get going. Call me, Evan, we need to catch up properly."

"Sounds good." I shake Griffin's hand.

"Remember what I said about not giving up," Nevie says with a wave. "And no doors!"

I wave bye to them, as Griffin slings his arm around Nevie's shoulders and ushers her out of the space.

"They're a lot," Steff says.

"But refreshing," I say, still holding the fork.

"So I got pictures of seating to consider, but I have a couple in my warehouse I want to bring over to try in the space. Do you have any bookings on Wednesday?"

"Yeah, we have the Bear Daddies group for their monthly meeting."

I stare at the ceiling, surprised by the swell of emotion.

This month we are full for Valentine's Day parties and it's a reminder that I don't have anyone to be mine.

But thinking of the Bear Daddies has me gritting my teeth.

The last time they were here was the same night that Mara's bosses treated her and their other employees to the Sinful Bites experience.

The Wilsons stuck us with the three thousand dollar bar tab and they aren't welcome back.

We open from Thursday to Sunday and take private bookings on Wednesdays for dinner. Special occasions like the Cartwright's anniversary were on a case-by-case basis.

In any other restaurant, this would be a poor model.

For us, it has only furthered our aura of exclusivity.

"I think these grey love seats could work if we swap out the chairs, or at least some of the chairs that line the middle of the room. Is this what you were thinking of?" Steff hands me a glossy picture of a tufted couch with a curve.

I wasn't thinking of new chairs. I was thinking that the table was an obstacle to putting my arms around Mara and I didn't want to be separated from her by a glass table or a hardback chair. The chair might have been perfect for bondage but I wanted to cuddle.

"I don't want to replace all the chairs. Would I lose seating?"

Steff shrugs and her traveller mug of coffee slips out of her hand, spilling onto the floor.

"Sorry Evan! I'll go get a mop."

"I'll get it, don't worry about it,"

"If you're booked Wednesday, then let me call my guys to see if they can bring one of the loveseats over right now to try. Is that okay?"

"That works. I'll be right back."

Steff nods, her cell to her ear.

I disappear into the gleaming kitchen.

My front of house manager, Dawn Keats, is sitting at the table with my head chef, Blake Crane, going over the bookings for this week.

"Is that woman gone?" Blake asks.

"Nevie? Yes, and she's great."

Blake snorts, his tattooed arms gleaming under his black shirt. "She has emailed me sixteen times about the eggs. I get it, no eggs!"

"She wants everything to be right, just like any other guest." I smile. He glares at me, and I laugh.

"I came for a mop. Steff is here," I say, heading into the supply closet.

"I got it, Evan." Chantel appears from the pantry and takes the mop out of my hands.

"Thanks."

"I like Steff, I wonder how many cats she's up to now." Dawn sweeps by me.

I grab myself a cup of coffee from the machine and take a seat beside Dawn.

"How's it looking?"

"Fine. We had a cancellation for Thursday, so I'm about to make someone's day." Dawn pulls up the waiting list.

I kind of hate Nevie's suggestion of trying again but I know that's my ego talking. I usually have women throw themselves at me. But there isn't anything I won't do for Mara.

"Hold off on that. How many seats is the cancellation for?"

"Two. Why?" She narrows her gaze at me.

I flash her a smile. "Those might be comps. I'll let you know."

"Evan, I want to get this set today."

Dawn is highly efficient and leaps ahead of me.

She hates it when I mess with her organization, but what's the point of being an owner if you can't take advantage now and then?

"I know. It'll be fine." I stand. Dawn glares at me. Blake laughs.

I dial Wilson's Superb Floral Designs and hold my breath, counting the rings in my head as I make my way out of the kitchen.

Steff is measuring the middle row and Chantel is helping her.

I take a seat on one of the spanking benches

"Hello? Hold on a moment!" A high-pitched voice answers me.

"Who is speaking?" I ask.

"Um, it's Jenny. I don't know what's going on either, okay? Our suppliers stopped sending deliveries, no I don't know where the owners are and I can't help you. Bye!"

"Wait! You're the person I wanted to speak to."

"Who's this?"

"Evan Brennon, owner of Sinful Bites."

"Mr. Brennon, I'm sorry, but we can't do the floral designs for your restaurant. I only came in today to get my stuff. I don't know what happened to Kyle and Sabrina. Ever since Christmas, they haven't been in that much and last week they stopped coming in at all."

"That sounds tough." I try to be empathetic, but I don't care that the Wilsons' business is failing. "But I'm not calling about that."

"What are you calling about, then?"

"I want to know where Mara is."

Something clunks down on a table or something. There's a cracking noise. "Mara quit."

My chest hums with pride. Good girl.

"Do you know where she's working now?"

"No, I don't, Mr. Brennon." Jenny's tone changed from level to panicky.

"I have a table open this Thursday. It's yours if you want it."

"No offence, Mr. Brennon, but I can't afford it."

"It's comped, Jenny. I'd really appreciate knowing if Mara is okay. I want to get in touch with her and talk to her."

"Mara got a break." Jenny's tone is harsh. "Wendy Svennson asked Mara to design her open house party."

"The hockey commentator?"

"Yes." The jealousy in Jenny's voice is unmistakable. "I don't know where Mara is going to get the team or the space to store all that stuff."

"What stuff?"

"You know, like frames and sculptures, some of them I worked on. But when Wendy heard the Wilsons took off, she sent a van over to get all her stuff delivered to Mara's today."

My heart thuds in my chest. "Do you have the address?"

"This isn't a joke? You're actually going to give me a table for Thursday night?"

"Yes, consider yourself a cupid's helper," I say.

Jenny snorts. "Okay, I'll text you the address. What time on Thursday?"

"Seven. I hope you have fun."

"Thanks. Good luck with Mara. I don't know what happened, but ever since we went to Sinful Bites, she's changed."

"How did she change?" I'm concerned that something's happened to Mara.

"When we asked her if she wanted to work late, she snapped at us and said no and then she told the Wilsons she quit, just like that. She was in the middle of a project, too. It's not easy to get jobs that aren't working in a florist shop, you know? But Mara just walked out the door."

"Sounds like she had enough," I say mildly.

"Yeah, I wish I had walked out."

"It's not too late, Jenny. Thanks for the help. Don't forget to text me."

"I won't." Jenny hangs up on me.

There's the sound of something heavy knocking into the door and I look up to see two burly guys carrying a love seat.

Steff walks around it, while they are holding it in the air.

"Evan, what do you think?"

Coming over to the front, I nod. "It looks great."

The curve of the sofa beckons to something elegant and smooth, and it's going to fit in fine. "They can set it down."

"Oh right, sorry! Set it down and then we'll move the tables, see how it looks."

My cell phone chimes with an address in Maple Ridge.

I know the traffic is going to be hell, but I'm determined to go see Mara and find out why she left me that night.

8 MARA

"**M**ara, watch out!"

I catch a lamp before it falls to the garage floor, setting it against an old trunk.

"Thanks, Alex."

This is the farthest thing from the sleek, professional design studio I spent the last eight years working in, but it's all mine.

I brush a drop of rain off my jacket and shove my hands in my pockets.

I'm smiling like a cartoon character despite the rain hitting me from the open door and I don't care.

"Guys, the delivery driver called, and he's half an hour out! Any questions about the designs?" I say to the three people huddled around an old milk crate.

Marc Mitchell ran his hand over his scruffy beard. "No, it's perfectly laid out, Mara. Wendy Svennson wants you to come and deck the place out for her open house party. Four rooms, the requested colour theme is purple and silver."

"These are large pieces," Suki Winters says, flipping her sleek, long black hair off her shoulders. "Are you sure we have enough hands to get it done?"

I swiped on the design to the material list. "We can handle it. The arch for the front entrance is the largest. It's going to take nine hours. The other three pieces aren't that big."

"No, it's painful, all this intricate detail about butterflies blooming." Alex O'Riley taps a silver nail on my sketch. "But it's awesome, Mara."

"Thanks," I say, grinning.

The last six weeks were a whirlwind after quitting my job at Wilson's Superb Floral Designs—known floral designers to the stars—and I struck out on my own.

It's not how I imagined it, but at least I was free from self-centred bosses with big egos.

"Thanks for coming in to help me unload."

"You have no idea what's coming in?" Marc asks.

"Wendy said it was pieces she bought and handpicked the structures and some other odds and ends she thought I could use."

"Clients are so unpredictable," Suki says.

"We're here anytime you need us, Mara," Alex says.

"Thanks guys," I hear a truck roaring on the drive and step back out into the rain.

The driver of the truck wheeled down the window. "Hey! Mara Cotter?"

"That's me," I say, scrawling my name on the clipboard.

"Perfect. We'll back up to the garage and make it easy."

"That's a bigger truck than I thought," Alex says, coming up behind me.

"I know." My stomach is flip flopping because I don't know if I'll have room to put all this stuff in the garage.

They park the truck, then the guy with the driver gets out and opens the back of the truck.

I peer in and my stomach twists in a knot.

There are pieces of metal, an oversized birdcage, bolts of fabric, broken pieces of something, but the truck is so stacked I can't see everything.

"Come on Mara, we'll get this done in no time," Marc says.

"I know it's not glamorous," I say, grabbing for a cylinder metal tube.

"Are you kidding? This beats making another birthday bouquet," Suki grins at me.

I shake my head, but I'm swimming in the warm and fuzzies.

When I called my friends from college, I wasn't sure they'd return my calls, nevermind show up for a few days of work here and there. I could only pay them peanuts, but they were happy to do it.

Working for the Wilsons was a dream, but it came at a high price.

I worked long hours and lost contact with my friends, swept up in the strong personalities of Kyle and Sabrina.

They changed my life forever, but when they took me out to dinner and humiliated me, I knew I couldn't keep working for them.

My cheeks heat at the memory of Sinful Bites.

What was the worst night turned into one of the best nights of my life and the memory hasn't been far from my mind since.

"Whoa, I got it." Marc takes a twisted wire sculpture out of my hands.

"Thanks."

The only reason I was able to quit my job was because I moved in with my mom and stepdad.

Both of them are supportive and happy to have me home, but come on, moving back home at thirty-two wasn't on my vision board.

Working efficiently, we have the truck emptied in half an hour.

The garage is so stuffed, I can't get the door to close.

"Call us when it's time to start working," Marc says, dropping a kiss on my cheek.

"Thanks."

"You're welcome." Suki squeezes my arm. "Just remember us when you're the next floral designer to the stars."

"She better or I'll post drunken pictures of her." Alex winks at me.

"There are no drunken photos!" I protest, laughing.

"That's what you say!" Marc calls, holding the car door open for Alex.

They wave and I notice Arthur, my stepbrother, drive-up.

He steps out of the car, as three trucks with a trailer drive up behind him to the house.

"What's all this?" I ask.

Bryan runs his hands through his wavy hair. "Hi Mara. Didn't you get my emails?"

"Sorry, I didn't."

My personal email is for store discounts and I barely touch it.

I only have one client right now, and Wendy has given everyone my cell number.

Arthur shuffles, looking uncomfortable. "I told you about the surprise renovation? The guys are going to set up today."

I spot one truck for counters, one for floors.

"Surprise renovation?"

Arthur blushes, pushes his glasses on his nose. "You know how dad and your mom are away on a cruise for a month?"

"Yeah, Bryan's Valentine's Day gift to her. It's sweet."

Bryan adores my mom, and this cruise was on her bucket list.

"You know how they've always talked about someday taking out that wall between the living room and kitchen? Miranda and I thought they needed a push and wanted to seize the time they're gone. You can come stay with us if you want."

My mind whirrs, trying to take in this information. My mother is going to hate having people go through her stuff and moving things about, but she's going to love Miranda and Arthur for doing it.

"I would have asked you to chip in, but Miranda said that was silly because you just lost your job—"

"I quit my job to go out on my own."

"Yes, and you're living here to avoid what happened in the past."

I swallow past the lump in my throat. My financial past isn't great, even if it's not my fault.

"I mean, you probably don't have the money to throw in for a renovation."

I laugh at how miserable Arthur looks.

I really lucked out when my mom married Arthur and I gained this awkward, sweet bonus brother.

He's ten years older than me and has his own optometrist practice and three noisy but adorable kids. His wife, Miranda, is just as sweet.

"It's okay! I'll make sure there is a flower arrangement on the counter when mom and Bryan get home. So it's going to be noisy for me for the next month. I can live with it."

Arthur scratches his beard and looks down at his boots. "Mara, you can't be in the house while this work is going on. If you had read the email, I offered you our guest room."

I bit my lip, glancing upwards at the stormy sky.

Cold rain drops fall on my cheeks and I swipe them off.

Arthur and Miranda's house is chaotic with the three kids and I don't know how I could get any work done.

Also, if memory serves, they have a small bed in the guest room and it's not the most comfortable match for my fat body.

Both of us turn, hearing another vehicle drive up.

A sleek black Audi parks next to Arthur's car.

My mouth goes completely dry as I catch sight of Evan Brennon behind the wheel.

My heart beats wildly as he steps out of the car, like he's stepping out of a cologne ad.

He's all sleek in his black sports jacket, with a checkered shirt underneath.

His dark wavy hair is perfectly styled, despite the rain.

His pools of obsidian rake me over with such heat, I can feel it from here.

"Hi Mara."

His voice caresses my name.

I shove my hair behind my ear, wondering why the hell he is here.

As much as I've tried to push it away, that night swims through my mind, behind my eyelids each morning.

He's the reason my night went from worst to best. He and I shared one hot night together.

Then I ran out the next morning.

"Hi Evan. What are you doing here?" I squeak the words out past the lump in my throat.

His gaze swings from me to Arthur, and I quickly step between them. "This is Arthur, my stepbrother."

Evan immediately relaxes, throwing out his hand. "Evan Brennon."

"Nice to meet you," Arthur says, returning the handshake.

"I came here to see you," Evan says, his attention back to me.

Arthur shoves his hands in his pockets, looking uncomfortable. "Mara, I got to get back to work. I'm sorry to spring the news on you."

"What news?" Evan asks.

Heat climbs up my neck. "Arthur and his wife are renovating my mom and stepdad's kitchen while they are on a cruise. I have been staying there."

"You can stay with us," Arthur says.

For a brief moment, I consider it, but I know it won't be a good fit.

The old pang of wishing I had a father, who was somewhat responsible, tugs on my heart.

"You can stay with me," Evan says. "At the hotel."

"Are you visiting?" Arthur asks, his glasses sliding down his face.

"No, he owns a restaurant in a hotel. In the Hugo Hotel."

I've never seen Arthur blush so furiously.

"Oh." My stepbrother stares at the ground.

"Come try it out sometime," Evan says, smiling.

"No, I don't...from what I've read...Mara are you okay? I really have to get back. If you decide to stay with us, call Miranda, okay?"

"I'll figure something out, Arthur." I reassure him.

"She can stay with me," Evan says again.

I'm furiously blushing.

I can't stay with Evan. The one night we shared together was amazing and everything I wanted. He was tender and caring and so intense I thought I'd combust from how hot his tongue was on mine, his every touch setting me on fire, followed only by orgasms that made me leave my body. But the next morning, I ran out.

"Take care Mara." Arthur gets in his car and drives away, leaving me alone with Evan.

"Mara?" Evan steps close to me as Arthur drives away.

"Yes?" I step back.

He grips my arm, lightly. My skin feels hot and clammy, even in the cool rain.

"Stay with me."

"I can't stay with you." I cross my arms over my chest.

"Why can't you?" Evan steps even closer to me.

I back up, because I'm a chicken like that. My back hits the garage door.

"Evan, I have work."

"You can stay with me and work." He leans forward, a breath away from my lips.

"My storage is here."' I pat the garage door awkwardly.

"I want to hire you for Sinful Bites."

"I don't believe you," I spit out.

He cocks an eyebrow and takes another step. "Are you calling me a liar?"

My head swims with heat, with intensity. I remember when he asked me exactly that, in that tone the first night we met.

"Evan, thanks, but I need to find somewhere to stay. I'm busy."

"You don't look busy to me," Evan says, sliding both hands on my arms.

"You don't know my schedule."

"Tell me why, Mara. Why did you run out the next morning? Why won't you come and stay with me?"

Oh god, I want the ground below me to open up.

"I don't...because I can't. I don't like the sex stuff, the restaurant."

I bite my lip because that is a lie and by the huge grin on his face, he knows it.

"You lie again, my sweet girl."

My cheeks are flaming. "Evan...I appreciate the effort, but I can't."

He takes a step back, shoves his hands in his pockets. "I will pay triple whatever your client is paying you if you come and stay with me for five days."

My thoughts tumble together, remembering that night how slick my fingers were with my own juice, as Evan pressed a vibrator into them and told me to hold it there.

"You've lost your mind. You can't buy me."

His eyes darken, his lips press together tightly. "Now you're making me want to throw you over my knee and spank you, Mara."

"You couldn't lift me." I manage to step aside, out of his gaze and shove my hands into my pockets.

He takes a step forward. "Tell me to go, otherwise I'm throwing you over my shoulder."

My face is flushed. "You wouldn't!"

Evan puts his shoulder to it, but the door won't budge. "What on earth do you have in there?"

"Stuff I need for my work." My voice is hoarse and husky.

"I haven't heard you say 'go.'"

My throat is so dry. "I don't know...I can't stay with you." But my heart is fluttering because that night we spent together? He made me feel adored. So I can't tell him to go, even though this is a terrible idea.

He steps close to me, lifts my chin, his touch firm. "I'm going to escort you inside where you'll pack a bag for five days and I'll spend the next week showering you with affection, convincing you what we had was good and we need to continue," his touch is burning hot, despite the rain. His hand rests on my shoulder, his gaze staring at me.

The world seems to stop for a moment as I'm flooded with the memories of the one night we spent together.

I'm remembering how treasured he made me feel. I swallow past the lump in my throat.

I know I should say no to him because it could never work between us, but I've been so lonely after I left my job and it's hard to deny what he's offering me.

But I need to put some emotional distance between what he wants.

"Triple my fee?" I bit my lip.

Evan showcases his impressive dimples as he strokes my hair.

The rain peters off to a stop.

"You have my word."

My heart is in my throat.

I want to say yes.

Looking into his dark eyes, his pleased smile, I'm going to say 'yes'. This is the wildest, most out there moment I've ever had.

"Yes."

"Good girl."

My heart flutters at the praise. Evan laces his fingers through mine.

"Let's go get that bag packed." He takes a step forward, his hands coming around my hips, and it suddenly occurs to me what he's about to do.

"Evan! I believe you!" I'm laughing so hard I can barely breathe and I'm trying to twist out of his grasp.

"Are you sure?"

"Yes! Don't lift me."

Being with Evan is so easy. This flirting between us is fun.

"I need to remind you that I am a man of my word."

"I know you are."

"Is that why you left so suddenly?"

"No."

The sorrowful look on his face makes me want to reach out and tell him it wasn't his fault. I ran out of that apartment the morning after because I couldn't deal.

"Whatever the reason, I have five days to show you that you don't ever have to bolt on me again, Mara."

His tone softens as he says my name.

"Evan, I'm trying to work here."

His mouth quirks. "Really?"

"Yes," I say it defensively but he's smiling huge and I don't know why.

"Give me five days, Mara."

"Evan, this is wild...what if I hate you at the end of five days?" I shake my head, not able to look at him.

"If you do, then I will find you somewhere to live and somewhere for you to work. Actually, I'm going to find you somewhere to work as soon as I can. It's a painful commute here to the city and you need to be where people can find you and if you put one more thing in your garage, the whole thing is going to fall down."

"Nothing is wrong with here."

"I didn't say there was, but location matters, Mara. Let's get you packed because I can't wait to spank you."

"Why would you spank me?" I ask.

Evan spins me to face him. "I need it out of my system because I haven't stopped thinking of spanking your ass since that morning I woke up and you weren't next to me. Spanking you is how we're going to seal this deal."

My thoughts whirl in a cluster. I need somewhere to stay. Having somewhere to work would be a relief, especially if it was in the city. Also, if Evan is serious about hiring me for Sinful Bites, I'd be dumb to turn that down. And I'm lying to myself if I keep insisting I don't want the spanking the man is offering.

"That's a tall order for one spanking."

"Also?" Evan raises his eyebrow. "I know how much you like it."

I'm blushing so hard, I can barely swallow. "Yeah."

He touches my cheek. "Good girl."

Before I can reply, he's looped his arm in mine and is walking me around the shed, stopping at an old concrete bench. My pulse races and I'm damn wet because his touch on my hand is electric. I let out an undignified shriek of laughter because the man is serious about that spanking.

"You mean now?"

"Oh yes, right now."

"How did you know there was a bench?"

Evan's dark eyes meet mine and my tummy lurches. "I didn't. I was only going for privacy. Are you ready, Mara?"

He sits down and pats his lap.

I clench and unclench my fists.

Stuff like this doesn't happen to a woman like me and even though I'm thinking this can't be happening, I'm walking towards him.

He tugs me over his lap and I'm staring at his shiny loafers, my heart thudding out of my chest.

9 EVAN

I don't know why she ran out on me after that one incredible night together, but right now, having her warm body over my lap, it doesn't matter.

She turns her head to look at me, ocean eyes bright and glassy, and I just want to rip her jacket off and touch every part of her skin.

"I'm so proud of you for quitting your job," I say against her ear.

She purrs under me and I cup my hand against her back.

"Thank you?"

The question is clear in her voice.

From our first night together, when Mara had a hard time believing that I found her attractive, I know that taking compliments isn't something that comes easily to her.

I want to change that for her.

"It takes guts to do something new."

"If my stepdad and mom didn't let me stay here, I probably wouldn't have," Mara mumbles.

"It's okay to take people up on their offer of help."

"Maybe," Mara says.

I bring my hand down hard against her leggings-covered behind. She gasps.

And then the skies open up, blasting us with rain.

I get her to her feet quickly, and laughing, we run to the car.

Pulling the door open, I get her in and run around to the driver's side.

I'm soaking wet, my shoes are squishing in the mud.

"Saved by the rain." Mara grins.

I'm hoping this car will power through the mud and smile, thinking of how my dad would tell me this is why I'm better off with a truck.

"A temporary reprieve." I squeeze her thigh. The house sits on a gentle slope, with the shed off to the side of the road, among some pine trees. I wouldn't have noticed it, if it wasn't for her step-brother's car.

I drive the car up the gentle slope and park at the end of the driveway. Trucks are parked on the grass at the side of the old farmhouse, close to the door.

"So many construction vehicles." Mara observes.

"You didn't know about this?"

The corner of Mara's mouth turns up in the most adorable way. "My stepbrother is kind of a non-confrontal guy. He sent me an email, but I didn't read it. I've been busy finishing the designs for my client and getting a team together."

I watch two guys carry tool boxes inside. "Your mom didn't mention it?"

"She and my stepdad are on a month-long cruise and it's a surprise for them. My mom always said she wanted the kitchen done."

"It's a generous gift, even if it inconveniences you."

"Yeah."

"I'm quite happy about it." I tug her close to me and nuzzle her ear.

"Because you're mine for the next five days."

"Glad that my inconvenience could benefit someone." Mara unsnaps her seatbelt and opens her door.

I get out of the car and jog up to the door with her. We enter a wide hallway that leads past a living room, right to the kitchen.Guys are measuring walls, others are stacking packed boxes in the living room.

"You didn't notice any of the packing?"

Mara blushes. "I did notice my sister-in-law was packing up some dinnerware when she was here the night before last, but I thought my mom asked her to do something. I swear, it didn't look like this when I came down this morning."

Mara opens a hallway closet and passes me a fluffy red towel.

"Thanks."

"Help you?" A man with a scruffy beard stopped us.

"Just here to get a bag and then I'm out of your hair."

"Good." he nods.

I take note of the construction company's name, keeping them in mind.

These guys are efficient and who knows when I might need a reno team.

Mara rushes past me to the staircase.

"I'll be five minutes."

"Take your time." I sit on the stairs, taking out my phone.

It rings in my palm. "Hey Theo. What's happening?"

"You know I'm trying to buy this business?"

"Yeah."

Theo, my quiet younger brother, found a restaurant in the middle of nowhere.

I suspect he's fallen for the woman who works there.

Noel, our oldest brother, has been looking into buying it at Theo's request.

"The town doesn't care if this building sits empty after having the restaurant in it for years. They're afraid of being overrun by cupcake shops and cafes so they are only approving unique businesses."

I can't help but grin.

Four guys carrying lumber walk in, another two with plastic sheeting.

This is going to be one hell of an involved renovation.

"The Brennon Consortium owns one kinky resort in the middle of nowhere and a fetish restaurant. Why not another fetish café or a B&B?"

"Noel said the same thing," Theo says. "But you know...I don't like being out with my tastes."

"Think about it," I tell him. "Are you in the city?"

"I'm finishing a job in Victoria. It's taking longer than I thought," Theo grumbles.

I smile, suspecting that he just wants to be back in the middle of nowhere.

"It often does," I hear Mara on the stairs and I stand. "Talk to you later, little bro."

"Later."

I slip my phone in my pocket and take the rolling suitcase from Mara.

"I can take it," she protests.

"Yep, I know you can," I tell her as I walk it down.

She's carrying a crossbody bag over her shoulder and her handbag.

"Thanks," she says at the last stair. "I'm all set."

She brushes past me and almost runs right into a guy carrying extension cords. "Sorry!"

"No problem." The man smiles.

"I'll be out of your way for the next five days."

"Five days? Miss, did anyone tell you how long we are scheduled for?"

The colour drains out of Mara's face.

I grip her arm. "It looks like a massive undertaking."

"Yeah. Floors are being done, the wall between the living room and the kitchen is going to be taken out and then we have a kitchen install to do."

"That's...wow. Okay." Mara shakes her head.

"This has been planned for weeks..." The guy starts.

"Of course it has," I say smoothly. "We'll let you get to your work."

"Yeah, no, of course. Sorry, I should really check my email more often."

I take Mara's arm and walk her out the door.

"I need to check that email," Mara says.

"Okay." I open the passenger door for her, grinning like a loon.

"Evan, why are you happy about this? This is the worst possible timing. I was just getting on my feet with my new business and now I need somewhere new to live and somewhere for my work."

She blinks away tears. I brush away a tear with my thumb. "It's going to be okay, Mara. You have somewhere to stay. We'll find you a workspace."

"You make it sound so easy."

"It is." I brush my lips against her cheek.

Mara shakes her head, sending her curls bouncing. "What if you hadn't come along?"

I slide into the driver's seat and roll down the long driveway out onto the highway, contemplating how to answer Mara. The subject of money is touchy for a lot of people.

I don't know if it's that or if she needs reassurance that I am not some kind of knight rescuing her.

"I'm an opportunistic kind of guy, especially when it comes to something I want. I came here to talk to you. It's my good fortune that you're out of a home because I know what I want. I want you, Mara." I take her hand in mind. "What would you have done if I hadn't shown up?"

She glances at her phone. "I guess I would have stayed at Arthur's place. Or I would have asked a friend if I could crash there."

"See? I'm not your knight."

Mara laughs, a whole body shaking spirited sound. It's the sound I fell in love with that first night I met her. I squeeze her knee, my cheeks aching from the grin on my face.

"You fit the role of knight very well." She flashes me a sly smile.

"I do?" I sweep my hand up her thigh.

"Yes. You have a sleek horse." She pats the dashboard of the car. "And as I recall, a very nice sword."

The comment is so surprising. I know I am blushing. And I'm not the kind of guy who blushes.

"I thought you forgot all about my sword."

"Nope. It might have scared me a little," her tone is wistful.

I squeeze her thigh. "I'll be more gentle with it next time, milady."

Mara shakes her head. "Maybe not a knight who rescues me, but one who came and took me back to the kingdom because I escaped."

"A princess who likes role-play?" My pulse races.

"In the right circumstances." Mara ducks her face, her curls curtain it.

"Milady does surprise. I'm dragging you back to the kingdom and I'm going to convince you that's where you belong. After I punish you for leaving."

"Well...if you do a very good job of convincing me, I might have to reward the knight," her voice is thick with lust.

The blood zips to my cock. It twitches in my slacks.

I run my hand along her leggings, wishing I could feel her skin but I fumble and slide my hand around the curve of her stomach, to under her waistband.

The smile on her face and her catch of breath urges my fingers lower.

My foot is a tad heavy on the gas, as I finally see the Hugo Hotel towering next to the harbour.

"No rope, no degrading words, no anal...am I forgetting anything?" I nudge her legs open with a squeeze and finger her through the soft fabric of her panties.

"Those are the main ones...I want this..." Mara leans forward.

"Good. My princess should get what she wants."

"Even if I was a bad girl that ran away?" The arousal in her voice is so delicious.

"Especially then. I'm going to make you regret that." I work my fingers along her folds through her panties.

"Evan!" She slaps my thigh. "You're going to make me come!"

Fortunately, I have great reflexes and I get the car parked underground in my reserved space without an issue.

"That's my intention. I love seeing how worked up you are." I lean over and snake my hand through her soft curls.

"I know you don't like being scratched, but I need to tell you I feel like scratching the roof of your car."

"The repair cost might be worth it. I like to see you wrestle for control." I press my thumb against her clit, wondering if I can bring her over the crest, undecided if I want her to explode right here or make her wait.

"Please, Sir Evan!" Mara's blue eyes blaze with need, her head lolls back against the seat.

Beautiful and I can't deny her.

I finger her soft folds, circling her clit. "Come for me, princess."

Her pussy clenches hard on my fingers and she lets out the sweetest cry. Her body shakes as she moans, her eyes closed. "So beautiful, Mara," I wipe my hand on her leggings. She blinks open those blue eyes and shakes her head. "I can't believe…you showed up," Mara pants out.

"Lots of upside in it for you, princess." I lean over and kiss her forehead, running a hand through her hair. "Let me escort you to the tower and convince you never to leave again."

Mara exhales, her cheeks flushed, but the smile around her mouth delights me.

I get out of the car, whistling as if I am not going to explode in my pants, open her door, then pop the trunk and grab her bags.

She reaches for them.

"You would deny me my chivalric duty?" I say it softly, but with a touch of command in my voice.

She lets out a giggle.

"What is so funny?" "Are you for real? Who says words like *chivalric*?" I flash her a grin. "I am for real, my princess," I bow slightly.

"I am not going to turn down chivalrous acts by you, Sir Evan."

"Good girl." I toss her bags over my shoulder, and depress the handle of her rolling suitcase.

"The purse matches your suit."

"Thank you, dear princess. To the left," I instruct.

Mara walks close to me, and it makes my heart soar.

I don't know if it's because of the little role play or because of the reassurance that I'm not rescuing her out of something she can't handle, but Mara being relaxed like this makes me feel damn good.

We reach the elevators and after the doors close, I use my key to get to the private floor.

"The impressive transportation continues," Mara murmurs, gripping the back of the padded car.

"You're too easily impressed, princess."

Her adorable lips twitch, looking so kissable. I am having a tough time containing myself.

"I didn't say you're impressive, Sir Evan."

I raise an eyebrow at her and the sassy princess covers her mouth as she laughs.

"I'll have to work harder." I crowd her space, and lift her chin. "You're worthy of it, princess."

The elevator opens to the vast hallway.

"What pretty alliums." Mara rushes to the vase on the pedestal table, and the cluster of dark purple flowers.

I don't take care of the decor. That's left to Julian's capable staff, but her admiration of it makes me smile, even if flowers aren't my thing.

I set the bags down, swipe my key to unlock the door.

The lights come on as soon as I step in, automatically adjusting to the amount of grey daylight the huge windows are letting in.

"It did seem like a movie set," Mara mumbles behind me.

The tone changes in her voice, pulls at my heartstrings.

Did she leave because this was too overwhelming?

I set Mara's bag down, take off my shoes and throw them on the shoe rack.

"I'm delighted to have you, princess."

I don't care about why she ran out on me the morning after our one-night stand.

All that matters is this beautiful woman is here, inside my apartment, and I plan to have my way with her.

I wait until her shoes are off, and then I take her bags, storing them away and hanging her handbag on a hook by the door. I take off my blazer, and then take her coat.

"There," I say, reaching for her.

She doesn't pull away, a small smile on her lips. I pull her close to me, lean down and kiss her plush lips, lightly. Her arms come around me, pressing me closer to her, and she kisses me back, tugging on my lower lip. She tastes so delicious. I devour her lips, my cock hard.

I press myself against her, kiss her once more firmly. "I'm so hard for you, princess. I'm going to have to skip hospitality because all I want to do is take you to bed and ravish you."

Her cheeks turn bright red. "I'm ready."

"Come with me, princess. It's time for your punishment."

"Yes Sir Evan," her voice husky with desire.

I wrap an arm around her and as soon as our feet touch hallway, the floor lighting turns on.

"I didn't have to drag you kicking and screaming through the halls, princess. I'll reward you for your compliance." I push her against the bed, my hand snaking through her mess of curls. My lips touch hers, then her arms are around me, pressing me to her.

Laughing, we tumble onto the bed, Mara falling on me.

Gently, I squeeze her ass.

She moans low in her throat as I knead her flesh, and continues that sweet sound as I kiss her neck, her mouth before she shuffles off me.

"I don't want to crush you."

Her big blue eyes are woeful, her mouth is nice and pink from our kissing.

"Mara," I try to put a gentle warning in my tone, but it comes out like a growl.

This woman makes me growl.

I cup her face, pushing her wild curls out of the way and kiss her, throwing my leg around her waist.

She gives in, kissing me back and moves with me.

My skin is buzzing with how good this feels, as if I am a horny teenager who can't get enough of this girl.

In one smooth move, I'm under her, my hands on her hips.

"I'm a grown man. You're not going to crush me."

Her blue pools turn bright, then she kisses me ferociously.

Her hand grabs mine playfully holding it to the bed.

She nips my lips, then kisses my throat, her soft mouth on my collarbone.

I am so hard, I am going to burst through my pants.

"Oh no you don't, princess. I'm the one in charge here." I reach for her hips and lift her away from my body.

She laughs, but I have her hands in mine and I'm back on top, staring into her bright blue eyes, her beautiful curvy body below me.

"This is where I want you, princess."

10 MARA

My pulse races, excitement sizzles through me as the heat in his eyes blazes into me.

My mouth goes dry.

I want this.

There's a smoking hot man inches from my face, who has said over and over that he wants me.

But wanting it doesn't stop my thoughts from scurrying, pulling me in different directions.

This is too fast.

What kind of woman has sex with a man in the middle of the afternoon?

What if this doesn't work?

Or worse, what if he does think I'm only using him for his money?

And past hurts buried deep in my emotional well bubble up to the surface.

What if, after I get to know Evan, he complains about my weight?

He's reassured me that he finds me attractive and he has never made a comment that makes me feel bad, but experiences tell me that only lasts for so long.

"Stop thinking, Mara."

His soft lips touch mine, slowly, as if he's trying to coax my thoughts to stillness. His tongue dances with mine and my thoughts do come to a stop.

I'm lost in the feel of his devouring kiss, then his lips are skimming my jaw, dipping to my collarbone.

He moves above me, pressing his hips against mine. "I'm so hard for you, Mara."

His sultry voice makes me blush.

I thread my fingers in his silky strands, needing to feel his hair through my fingers.

His hands glide down to my hips, he shoves down the waistband of my leggings, pulling me towards him.

"I'm desperate to taste you. I've thought about you every night since the one we shared together."

Goosebumps break out across my skin from the coolness of having my leggings off of me or his hands on my thighs.

Shoving my panties off, I lay back, still with my shirt on, which strikes me as funny.

"What's making you giggle?" Evan grabs my fingertips as he presses his thumbs along my inner thighs.

"I still have my top on. You're fully dressed."

"I didn't want to rush things but I'm impatient." Evan grins that wolfish smile at me, and my heart skips a beat.

He drops a kiss on my lips, stands and then unbuckles his pants. "Better?"

My mouth goes dry at the sight of his carved muscular thighs and legs. He's just as strong as I remembered.

"Getting there."

He cocks an eyebrow at me, and I giggle.

He takes off his shirt, revealing his wall of muscles. He struts to me. "Now, better?"

He runs his hand up my leg, sending little shivers through my body. Wrapping an arm around me, he pulls me close.

"Yes, so much better." My hands brush over his hard pecs.

"Mara, sit on my face." His hot breath on my neck is delicious, sending little shivers along my skin.

But then his words sink in.

I move away from him. "You can't be serious."

A knot of anxiety breaks forms in my stomach.

I'll crush him. My inner voice whispers.

"I'm always serious. I thought you knew that about me." Evan twirls a stray strand of hair along his finger and it looks so innocent.

I'm blushing furiously, grabbing the bed sheets in one hand. "No, you don't want me to do that. Is this some kind of... I don't know. Evan, look at us."

"I don't have a mirror in here." Evan pulls me against him. I feel his firm muscles against my plumpness. "But I'm going to fix that. Because I want to see us together, Mara, so I can see exactly how my every move affects you."

"Evan, this is too fast."

"We've already played, we've already had sex. What's too fast?" His hand slides down my back and I relax at his touch.

His voice is calm and even.

I squeeze my eyes shut tight. "I didn't expect my day to end like this."

"Neither did I. But I'm glad it did." He kisses me, taking my bottom lip gently between his teeth and I give in, kissing him back.

"You did agree to five days," Evan murmurs.

"I agreed to stay with you for five days," I counter. "We didn't cover sex stuff." With my leggings off, my pussy throbbing with need and Evan all disheveled, it's a ridiculous thing to say.

He smirks as if he knows it, but he's indulging me. "I thought we did in the car, but let's go over it again." He drapes an arm around my shoulders and pulls me close. "Over the next five days, I propose there is a lot of sex stuff. I want to see you shatter in orgasmic bliss. I love how your eyes roll upward and your neck strains when you're about to climax, as if you're bearing yourself to me, all vulnerable and needy."

"That doesn't sound like a turn on."

"It very much is, princess." Evan takes my hand and places it against his cock.

His cock is steel hard under my fingers.

The pure adoration he has for me wraps me in a cocoon of warmth.

I want to please him and give him what he's asking for.

"If I sit on your face, I'll suffocate you."

Evan takes my chin in his hand. "No you won't. I'm a grown man. I've considered the 'risks' as it were."

Evan is way more experienced than I am when it comes to BDSM, but neither of us is new to playing or to the lifestyle.

Except, this is one thing that I have never done.

"I had one long-term relationship. We dated for the first two years of college. He said it was too bad I was so heavy because he could finally make me orgasm if I sat on his face."

I bite my lip and look away, even though Evan is still holding my hand.

"Mara?"

"Yeah?"

"You dated the guy for *two years* and he couldn't make you orgasm in that time?" Evan raises his eyebrows to his hairline, his voice incredulous.

"Yes. I wasn't exclusive with him, but yeah."

That was before I started working for Sabrina and Kevin and discovered kink.

But I always knew I needed something more during sex and I blamed myself for not having fulfilling experiences with my partners.

And even though I've done a lot of work on myself and love my body for the size it is, I blamed a lot of those unsatisfactory experiences on my weight.

"I want you to sit on my face so I can pleasure every inch of your soaking wet pussy. And I need to see these impressive breasts." Evan slides his hands under my shirt to my breasts, lifts them in his hands.

They spill out of his palms.

Gently, he massages my nipples through my shirt.

A swirl of pleasure so intense it makes me gasp, bursts from me.

He's taking my shirt off in the next instant, and I'm helping him get my blue bra off.

I toss it across the room.

"Present them for me," Evan says, a note of curiosity in his voice.

Oh yes. I can meet this request of his.

I cup my hands under my breasts.

"Squeeze them together for me." Evan has a hand on my thigh.

I do, a shiver of pleasure breaking out across my spine.

His voice is light but commanding, his tone clearly says that he expects to be obeyed.

"Beautiful." Evan pinches my nipples between his thumb and forefinger.

I close my eyes against the pleasure, as he gently places his hands where mine were and squeezes my breasts, tugs my nipples.

"Now princess, sit on my face." Evan gives my breasts another squeeze, then moves against the headboard.

Maintaining eye contact with me, he throws a pillow out of the way and lies down.

"Are you sure you want to do this?"

"Be a good girl and let me eat your pussy."

With my heart galloping in my chest, I crawl over to him, sliding my hands up his strong legs.

"I'm waiting, Mara."

"Okay."

I feel all kinds of awkward and unsure as I grab the headboard for support and slowly lower myself on Evan's face.

His stubble tickles the sensitive skin on my inner thighs and I giggle.

"Lower." His hands cup my ass cheeks, bringing me down to his face.

Oh god. This can't be happening.

I try to push away the anxiety, to relax, but I'm too freaked out by cutting off his air supply.

"Stop it." Evan gives my ass a quick slap.

Before I can say anything, his lips are working my pussy, sucking my labia lips.

"Oh, Evan."

His tongue is swirling around my clit, furiously.

Every swipe of his tongue makes me wet.

And wetter, as he holds my hips, presses me down against his face, I can feel his nose against my seam.

His mouth is hot over my pussy. His tongue works in a rolling way, covering every inch.

The pleasure climbs with every suck.

My heart is racing, sweat is breaking out on my brow.

Behind my closed eyelids, a pleasured frenzy breaks out from the cluster of nerves.

"More, please!" I pant out.

He's taking me almost to the edge. I can feel it, my body tightening in anticipation.

I feel so wet. And full. I'm warm and freaking out. "Evan, I think I might pee on you."

His tongue swipes deep into my pussy, flicking and lapping, and I don't care about the weird sensation. The fullness sort of eases, and it turns to pleasure, so bright and hot.

It feels good as I gush out liquid, exploding on his face.

Using the headboard, I try to lift myself off, but his firm hands keep me in place.

His tongue is laving my sensitive clit making my heart thud in rhythm to his licks. My pulse is racing, setting off a new climax. I'm shaking with the force of it as I explode again. It feels as if my soul wants out of my body, in some kind of pleasure bender.

Tears are rolling down my face.

Gently, Evan lifts me up.

I stare down at his dark eyes and I see warmth there and trust.

I know I can trust this man and that makes me want to run out on him again.

"Beautiful, Mara. Have you ever squirted before?" His face is shiny with my juices.

He has me in his arms, pressing my head against his shoulder.

He throws a blanket over us and nuzzles my neck.

That explains the fullness, the immense sense of pleasure.

"Don't think so."

"I'm glad to be your first, then." He laces my hand through his.

Being in his arms is something I didn't think would ever happen again. I nuzzle against him and kiss his mouth, tasting myself.

"Thanks for the orgasm."

"You're very welcome, princess."

"Let me show you how grateful I am." I smile.

Evan grins. "Be my guest."

I toss the blanket off, buzzing with post-orgasmic bliss.

I try to be gentle because he's mentioned that he doesn't like scratching and I don't want to accidentally catch him with my nail.

His cock is long, thick and as impressive as I remember.

I palm it from root to shaft, loving the moan of pleasure that emits from his mouth. The tip is already dripping with pre cum.

"That's what you do to me, princess." Evan swipes his finger through the liquid and holds it to my lips.

I open my mouth immediately and he paints my tongue with his cum.

"Keep open for me," he murmurs.

I do, and he caresses his finger along my tongue, fucking me.

My hand is around his cock, tugging in one long pull.

He takes his finger out of my mouth, then cups my nape and pushes me to his cock.

Greedily, I set my mouth over his tip and taking my time, swirl my tongue around his slit, then the head of his cock.

I like how his leg twitches, and I reach up, cupping his balls with my hand.

"Princess, you have no idea what you do to me." He pushes my head down and I take in as much of his length as I can.

His taste is so intoxicating, it makes me feel on the edge of another orgasm.

Our glances meet as I swallow on his hard length.

He's so close, I can feel his body vibrate.

I want him to come apart, just like he wanted me to shatter.

I can't give this man much, but I can give him a really good blow job.

Relaxing my mouth, I swallow past the bump in my throat. Catching on to what I am doing, he tilts towards me, giving me a better angle.

His cock pulses in my throat, it's so thick it takes up all the space.

It feels so good. I lick, swallow and feel giddy as his eyes roll up to the back of his head.

I suck on him, slowly taking my time and then I amp up my pace, milking his length so hard my tongue tingles.

"Mara!" Evan cries out my name as his hot cum shoots down my throat in one satisfying long burst. I swallow, reaching for him. He takes my hand, runs his thumb along my index finger. I'm so pleased that I have given him pleasure, my body hums in satisfaction.

His cock is wet in my hand as I hold it to lick up the rest of his cum.

"Good girl." His voice is husky.

His eyes are glassy as he reaches for me. His mouth slams against mine and he kissing me hotly.

Evan nuzzles my neck and wraps me in his arms and I feel safe.

But can this last between us, or is this another...fling?

Not a night this time, but a week?

I try to push my anxieties away because nothing feels better than being cuddled by this man.

11 EVAN

FEBRUARY 10TH

"You cook?" I come up behind Mara, rubbing her shoulders.

"I mean, I'm not a chef, but I can make breakfast."

I kiss her, and laughing, she nudges me away. "Hey! Hot pan."

"Not as hot as you are, princess." I nibble her ear.

Mara laughs. "Do you drink coffee in the morning?"

I grin at her redirection and pour myself a cup. "I won't be snarky and say, 'well, if you hadn't run off on me that first night together, you would know the answer to that.'"

A dimple appears in Mara's cheek. "I knew you weren't that snarky."

I lean against the counter, drinking my coffee, watching Mara cook eggs and feel like I'm the luckiest bastard alive.

"Do you cook?" Mara hands me a plate.

"Yeah. Mom taught us all how to cook and do laundry because

she didn't want our partners to do it. My Dad can, he's just so scatterbrained it's safer if he's not in the kitchen, at least unsupervised."

Mara passes me a plate. "I like your mom."

"What about your parents?"

Mara shrugs a shoulder. "My mom's idea of cooking is a frozen pizza. My stepdad loves to barbecue."

"What about your dad?" I sit the plate down on the island and bring our coffee mugs over.

Her face closes. "I don't have much contact with my dad. I had the best sleep last night."

"Me too."

After falling asleep in each other's arms, we woke up around midnight and raided the fridge for a snack. And then we had sex.

Slow, wonderful, sleepy sex.

Her head on my chest felt right.

Mara's alarm clock went off at a time I didn't know existed.

"These eggs are good," I say, taking another bite.

"Added a little sharp cheddar. Foods you don't like?"

My eyes feast on her as she takes a seat next to me.

"Ketchup chips and spinach. I need coffee or I won't function in the morning. You?"

"Agreed, coffee is a must. Ketchup chips are gross. I don't mind spinach. Cauliflower is fine if it's raw. I'll have the occasional glass of wine or drink when I'm out. I'm more of an early bird than a night owl."

"How early do florists start?" I pop a piece of bacon into my mouth.

"Depends if you are working in a shop or doing something silly, like being a freelance floral designer." Mara shrugs.

"It's not silly. But what's the difference between florists and what your former bosses did, what you do?"

Mara takes a sip of coffee, smiling. "A floral designer is an artist who uses flowers and plants to create one of a kind pieces for events. Unlike your florist shop, we won't re-create a design once it's been used. It's creating one of a kind of art pieces for a special event. I have a portfolio, but I don't have a catalogue of bouquets you can order."

I know she has a profile from looking her up online. She's a talented artist.

"I think I get it. You got a degree in this?"

She shakes her head, sending her curls flying. "No, I have a degree in horticulture and a degree in design."

"I know your former employers did a lot of restaurants and corporate places. Are you doing that?"

"That was what kept them going day-to-day. I'll take what work I can get at this point."

Her tone is so wistful. I want to take out my contact list and get her work and I will, after I convince her to let me help her in that way.

Her phone buzzes on the table and she glances at me. "Is it okay if I take this?"

"Yes, go ahead."

There's a part of me that likes that she asked but wonders why she did. Did she ask to be polite or to ask my permission?

I clean the table, get up to rinse the dishes and try not to overhear.

"Of course I'll come and help," Mara says. "I have to figure out how to get over to you and then I'll be there."

She stands from the table, bringing over her coffee mug. "That was my friend Alex. She's down two staff members and they have a nighttime wedding."

"I have a meeting this morning. I was thinking we could have lunch together, but dinner's fine."

Mara tucks a strand of hair over her ear. "This is silly because I don't have a car. Instead of being whisked away in your carriage, I should have taken mine."

"Hey, impulse is the best spice." I lean down to kiss her. Her arms are folded across her chest.

"Take my car." I rummage through a drawer in a small desk in the kitchen that I never use. "And here is a key to the apartment. I'm not keeping you locked away in the castle, Mara. Though I might want to."

I press the keycard into her hand and nuzzle her neck.

"I can't take your car."

"Why are you going to crash it?" I gently run a finger along her cheek.

She laughs, the high and light sound that's featured in my dreams since the night I met her.

"Evan, you can't give me your super expensive car to drive."

"Yes I can." I take her hand and kiss it. "This is what being mine means, and you agreed for the next five days."

"That you force me to drive an ultra expensive car?"

"This is me taking care of you. I get to show you that I want more of what we had...have." I crash my lips against hers, kissing her hungrily.

Her body softens against mine, a little sigh escaping her pouty mouth. "No other expectations?"

"What expectations did you want there to be?" I put a bit of a bite in my tone, thinking back to how she asked to take the phone call.

"I don't know. It just seems one sided."

"I'm a Dominant, but I am not huge on formality. Is that something you want?"

Mara shakes her head. "I've never really explored it before."

"I need to be dominant in the bedroom and, to an extent, outside. I need my partner to let me take care of them. Can you give me that?" I brush my hand through her hair.

"It feels...like I'm giving up control."

I kiss her mouth, hard. "Think of it as participation. You're not just responding passively, Mara. If I said, 'please text me when you arrive at your friend's shop and let me know when you're leaving,' how does that feel to you?"

She brushes a hand along my arm. "Like you're looking out for me."

I kiss her forehead, cup her hand with my jaw. "Then let me look out for you. Please text me when you arrive. And as often as you want during the day."

"Okay. What are you doing today, after your meeting? Is that okay to ask?" She flushes.

"Of course. I'm seeing Steff Goldstein, my designer, in the afternoon. We have this anniversary party next month and I want to go over details with her. Then I have a staff meeting. We have three private group bookings for this evening. I like to be there to greet the guests. It makes them feel exclusive."

Her face turns scarlet.

"What is it?" I crowd her space, staring into her blue eyes.

I'm pretty sure her reaction is because I dropped Steff's name.

"Nothing. You do like looking after people," Mara murmurs.

I hadn't thought of looking after the restaurant or the guests as looking after people like I would romantically, but I guess it isn't a stretch.

"Especially you. How long do you need to get ready? I'll walk you to the car."

"Five minutes."

"Good." I lean down and kiss those lips.

It's not like I don't know this is a little...wild.

But I'm thirty-five. I'm tired of one-night stands and commitments that don't work out.

I'm tired of people being after me only for my money and I am tired of head games.

One night with Mara was all I needed to know that I wanted her to be mine forever.

I'm determined to do whatever is necessary over these days to convince her of that.

Mara touches my forearm, pressing down on me. She stands on her toes, kissing me back.

The sweet taste of her is so good, this is what I have missed. A woman who gives me what I want.

Her hand turns, her nail catches my skin and I jerk away immediately.

"What? Evan, are you all right?"

"It's fine," I murmur.

I feel stupid because her nail caught the top of my wrist, but that little scratch floods me with anxiety. Her nails are beautifully manicured, not even fake nails and yet, I still reacted as if she tore skin off of me.

"Evan, I'm so sorry. I didn't mean to catch you." Mara's light touch on my waist brings me back to the moment.

"I know." I kiss her quickly. "Go get ready."

She gives me a puzzled look but brushes by me, her fingertips touching mine in reassurance.

You're okay, I tell myself. I know I'm going to have to tell Mara about my monster of an ex—Hannah—but it's not a conversation I look forward to having.

But if I want more than five days with Mara, and I do, then I need to air the dirty laundry.

From the same drawer, I found the key, I take out some ointment and squirt it on the scratch.

Mara didn't even draw blood but I hate the feeling of a nail on my skin and putting the ointment on makes me feel better, emotionally.

"I'm ready."

"Let's go, princess." I smile, even though I still feel jittery and with my hand on the small of her back, I lead us out into the hallway, to the elevators.

In the elevator, I press the button and a short ride later, the doors open to the main lobby of the Hugo Hotel.

It's a typical weekday morning. The patrons of the hotel are with men in suits, women in dresses and everything in between, including a man walking six yapping puppies out the door.

There's a parrot on an elderly man's shoulder that's squawking loudly.

Nina, the head receptionist, waves at me as I catch her eye.

"You live in a hotel," Mara stops and shakes her head.

"I thought you knew that." Her bewilderment makes me grin like a fool.

She glances at me sharply. "I mean, I did, yes, but it's a little much to take in, you know?"

"You get used to it," I tell her, guiding her past a crowd of women holding tennis rackets.

Outside, there is a little sunshine and a slight chill in the February air, but Mara relaxes, grabs my hand as I walk her to the car.

"Evan, are you sure you want me to drive this?"

"I'd rather drive you myself but I need to take this meeting." It's with a wine rep from the valley.

"I don't want you to miss your meeting." Mara squares her shoulders.

"It's just a car."

Okay, the words hurt a little as I said that about my Audi A4 Prestige.

Mara cocks her head to the side. "Do you let your brothers drive it?"

"Noel and Theo have." I slide my hands in my pockets. "Hunter...no. We try to keep him away from things with power."

She laughs. "Younger brother, right?"

"Yeah."

Hunter is a bit of a maverick and there was that one time when we were growing up that he crashed my first ever car.

"You have to tell me more about them."

"I will. I can't wait for you to meet them." I open the door for her.

She drops her hand out of mine and I tense, sure she is going to tell me that this is all too soon and we should take a breather.

Instead, she drops a light kiss on my lips. "I'd like to meet them."

I grin huge enough to split my face.

She climbs in the car and buckles up.

"There you go. Adjust the seat as needed."

I wait until Mara has the mirrors just right.

"This seat is comfy."

"It looks good on you." I gently close the door and give her a wave.

Mara sits for a moment, staring straight through the windshield, then she puts the car in drive and expertly rolls out of the parking lot.

I want to clap for her and cheer her on, and I'm smiling as I hold the door open for an old woman using a walker.

My phone rings as I walk through the doors of Sinful Bites and I grimace, seeing the number on the screen.

The-devil's ears must have been ringing.

"Hannah," I say with as much displeasure as I can muster.

I can't wait to wrap my arms around Mara tonight and ease the sting of this unpleasant conversation.

It's never good when my ex-wife calls me.

Hannah knows damn well she's supposed to go through my attorney.

I remind her of that and close the phone, eager to get through these meetings so I can have another night with my princess.

12 MARA

I love seeing people happy and that's one of the reasons why I wanted to be a florist. Before I knew that floral design—making art with flowers for special occasions—was a thing, I had planned to have my own florist shop one day.

Helping Alex out today was exactly the kind of distraction I needed to stop myself from coming up with reasons of why I shouldn't spend the days I had agreed to with this handsome guy who let me drive his luxury car.

But he's not just a guy, he's Evan.

My Evan.

My Sir Evan.

All throughout the day, I could only think of how his eyes darkened with need as he kissed me, or how he felt against my body. I caught myself blushing while finishing an arrangement for a tenth anniversary.

But the look on his face, when I grazed his skin with my nail, the look of pain, of hollowness, is one that flashed through my mind, too.

I wanted to ease whatever had put that look on his face.

This quick romance might be wild and out there, but it doesn't make how I feel about Evan any less true or real.

And it's not like I had a line of available, attractive men who wanted to date me. No, I had Ryder the wannabe Dom. It's not the first time I have heard the, "lose weight and I'll play with you" line and though I love my curvy body, in the back of my mind, I wonder when Evan is going to deflate the happiness I feel with him by commenting on my weight.

So far, he hasn't. He said that he's attracted to me and loves my boobs.

I grin now, stuck in traffic behind an old work van that is coughing in front of me.

The bouquet of gardenias that I brought with me in the backseat gives the car a pleasant smell mixed with leather. It's kind of yummy.

My phone chirps on the dash, but I ignore it.

I can see the impressive Hugo Hotel and I switch lanes to get into the hotel parking lot.

Evan had texted me earlier this afternoon, asking about dinner plans and I hadn't had a chance to respond, though I did send him a text saying I was leaving.

As fun as it was to help Alex and be back in a florist shop, my feet are aching and I'm definitely going to skip the heels tonight. I park the car, double check that I'm in between the lines, grab my phone, purse and the bouquet and find my way into the lobby.

My phone buzzes with a text.

Finishing up a meeting at the restaurant in the dining room, come up when you're here.

I press the button for the elevator in the lush lobby, feeling like an imposter. I hit the floor for Sinful Bites and it gives me a kind of thrill to be here again. I know I tried to tell Evan I didn't like it and I couldn't pull off that lie because the truth is, this place is dripping with luxury. I can't believe I'm here.

The elevator shoots up to the restaurant floor without any interruption and the doors whiz open.

I don't know what time the restaurant opens for service, but staff are setting the tables.

It's an impressive space; dark panelled walls, elegant lighting, and beautiful loveseats break up the rows of chairs.

I'm blushing as I walk through to the dining room, the pair of closed bamboo doors an elegant addition to the room instead of being out of place.

The night I was here with my former bosses, Evan told me that he had to change the seating because he wanted to wrap his arms around me and the arms on the chairs didn't let him do that, though they were great for bondage and I blush, as I notice beautiful curved two seater sofas.I tap on the door before opening.

"Come in."

Evan is sitting with his back to me, a coffee mug to his left, a stack of papers spread out on the table. My heart does that fluttery thing it does when I see him and I can't wait to cup his smooth-shaven face in my palms.

I need to apologize for accidentally scratching him again.

He shrugged it off as not being a big deal, but I haven't been able to stop seeing that flash of pain across his face all day.

He glances over his shoulder at me with his phone pressed to his ear, his face lights up with a smile. I can swallow my doubts at this moment, because the way he's looking at me, making that little beckoning motion with his hand, leaves no doubt that he likes the sight of what just walked in his door.

"She's going to wait until her new business is up and running and then come after me for everything she can. She's a bitch, Noel, you know that."

My throat closes up for a moment but Evan rises from his chair and his eyes go to the bouquet I'm holding. He frowns.

"I know you set me up with the best lawyers money can buy, but I wish you were back in the game to take this one." Evan takes the flowers from my arms and puts them on a seat."Okay, thanks, Noel."

"That wasn't about me?" I can't hold back the wobble in my voice.

"No my beautiful princess, it wasn't." Evan leans down to kiss me but stops, raises his eyebrows to someone at my back.

"Thirty minutes to service, Mr. Brennon."

"Thanks, Dawn." Evan stands, still holding my hand. "Did you want to have dinner, here?"

"Honestly, I'm a little beat. I didn't plan on working in retail the full day. You still haven't asked me about your car."

His mouth quirks. "I trust that it's fine, Mara. Are you fine?"

I glance down as he takes a step towards me and brushes his hands along my shoulders.

"My feet are sore. I'm a little tired, but I'm okay. I'm not sure if I want to hang out at the restaurant tonight."

It feels intrusive. If Evan had gone with me to work today, it might have been fun for the first hour or so, but I'd feel like I had to do things differently.

Maybe he has more confidence than I do, but I don't want to be in the way.

"Not going to run out the door?" He leans close, wraps one of my stray curls around his finger.

"I agreed to these five days." I'm blushing because I feel awful about running out on Evan that night.

"Perfect."

He slants his lips across mine, bringing me to his chest. "Then I will get through this booking. Do you need me to take you to the apartment?"

"I can find my way."

"Good. Can you do me a favour, pretty girl?" He tilts his head.

"Of course."

"It's a nice bouquet, but I don't like the scent."

My stomach rolls. I recalled that Evan had said he didn't want flowers that smelled for the restaurant and I remember the calls he used to have with the Wilsons on low scent flowers.

"Sorry."

"No, you didn't know, Mara. It's a nice gesture."

"A lot of people are scent sensitive." I smile, trying to cover up my unease.

"I can't wait to spend time with you later. I'll be down as soon as I can."

"No problem." I clutch the bouquet. Evan opens the dining room doors for me and follows me out.

In the entrance way of the restaurant, two big beefy security guys are standing around.

"Your guests are on the way up, sir," the bigger one of them says.

"Thank you." Evan touches the elevator button for me. "I'll see you soon, Mara."

He brushes his lips against mine as the doors close.

Instead of stopping on the floor of Evan's apartment, I take the elevator down to the lobby, the doors opening to a bustling evening scene.

I step through and walk around the lobby, passing a waterfall and turning left past the gym, the business centre and the hotel's café.

Sitting in a seating area, is an older woman with grey hair, reading a Kindle.

"Here, these are for you." I extended the bouquet to her.

She looks up, a flush on her face of surprise. "Oh, thank you! Where did these come from?" She inhales and closes her eyes.

"A secret admirer," I grin.

The woman chuckles. "That can't be true but I'm going to pretend it is!"

I give her a wave and make my way back up to the apartment.

I have friends, but nobody I'd want to explain this one night stand turned into a fling to. Not that I'm embarrassed...I frown. Maybe it is because I'm embarrassed and I don't want to be talked out of it.

I think of calling my mom but she'd only tell me to feel and shut off my brain because that's been her advice with pretty much everything from the time I wanted to try to skateboard, to when I discovered that floral design was an actual thing and changed my career ideas.

Mom would be delighted with this whirlwind romance.

But is it a romance if we don't spend loads of time getting to know each other?

Or is it better this way, a taste of what having Evan in my life would be like?

He's caring and kind and a great partner when it comes to kink and sex, but he hasn't told me about his ex-wife and what if there is something there that I can't handle?

Glancing around the apartment, with its high-end fixtures and huge gallery windows, it's spotless. There's a basket of bath bombs and body oils and loofahs on the counter and a note that says to help myself to whatever I find in the apartment.

It makes me grin silly, and I kick off my shoes, finally, and groan as my soles hit the floor.

In the fridge, I find ingredients for a stir fry. I take out a pan, set it on the stove and I start to work. I'm humming as I'm adding the veggies to the pan.

Making Evan breakfast this morning was nice.

A little bit of domestic life that I haven't ever had.

Also, this is totally my choice to be alone right now.

Evan gave me the option of spending the night at Sinful Bites.

But as I continue to make dinner, I realize that this is pleasant. I have no worries at the moment and I'm eager to see Evan but I like that I'm here, cooking in this fancy kitchen.

I needed time to decompress from the day and sort out my tangled emotions.

I don't know where I thought I'd be at thirty-two, but this isn't it. Okay, maybe I thought I would own a house and have a husband. Maybe I thought I would have my business established. So being in this apartment, in the Hugo Hotel, waiting on the smoking hot restaurant owner to get home, is definitely not where I thought I'd be but it's not bad.

****

I'm lounging on the super over stuffed couch, watching an animal documentary, when I hear the click of the door open.

My pulse races and I grin. Reaching for the remote, I flick off the TV.

I stand, watching as he takes off his shoes. He grins at me.

"Hi princess."

"Hey." I try to be casual, but I want to run to him like a puppy.

His suit jacket is over his arm. He puts it on a chair by the kitchen island and then he sets a box on the counter with a bottle of wine.

"You weren't waiting for me?" He grins like he's pleased by the idea of me waiting for him.

"Yes, I was...it didn't feel right going to bed without you."

Evan reaches for my arm, tugs me against him and kisses me, long and lingering.

I melt under the touch of his lips, my insides jumping around in excitement.

"I like that you were waiting for me, princess."

"Good."

"Now I get to reward you." The grin he gives me is so electrifying, the hairs on my arms stand up.

"Yeah?"

"Yes, sit down on the couch." He holds up a bottle, passes it to me.

It's a bottle of sandalwood massage oil.

I take it with me and sit down on the couch.

He returns a moment later with a fluffy white hand towel.

"What's this for?" I ask, holding the pretty green bottle to the light.

Evan's fingertips brushes mine as he takes it from me. "For your feet. Which one hurts the most?"

"Evan! You can't touch my feet."

He gives me a look that has my insides quenching with anticipation and a bite of fear.

"I can't? Is it a hard limit?" Evan's dark chocolate eyes study me, watching my face closely.

He sits next to me on the couch.

"No...it's just..."

"If I don't touch your feet princess, how will I know if the glass slipper fits?" He gives me that wde dimpled grin.

I laugh, because nobody has ever called me a Cinderella before. "You don't need to know my feet."

"I want to know everything about you, Mara. Come on, set your foot right here." He puts the towel on the top of his leg and pats it.

Not believing that this is happening, I stretch my leg out to him.

"This is selfish of me." Evan smiles, dripping oil into his palms.

"How is it selfish of you?"

His thumbs stroke down each toe and I can't talk. The warmth of his touch combined with the pressure is so good.

"I like taking care of my partners. I always have. Knowing that you got to work safely today gave me a buzz all day. I couldn't stop smiling tonight thinking of you here, waiting for me. Doing this for you?" He moves to the ball of my foot and presses down with equal pressure on either side. It makes me moan in pleasure. "Yeah, princess, it fires me up." His cocky grin makes me blush.

"But that's not selfish."

"It depends on how you look at it. It's getting my needs met and maybe you're not used to being taken care of or you think I question your independence or ability." He works his thumbs back up to my big toe. "But I don't. I wouldn't be attracted to you if you weren't—"

"Willing to submit?" I swallow back a moan of pleasure.

"Driven. I don't want a partner who can't do things for themselves or doesn't have ambition. I guess I want someone who lets me be the Dominant I want to be. But I also want a partner. I have a feeling if I asked you to help seat guests in the restaurant, you would jump in."

"You're right, I wouldn't mind helping. I think I'd be a horrible waitress, though. So you want a partner and a submissive?"

"A woman who can submit in the bedroom, yes. But I didn't know this." Evan presses down on my foot in some kind of wizardly way and the soreness melts.

"Know what?" I murmur.

"That a Dominant could be a protector or a Dom who likes to give their partners pleasure is still a Dom." Evan swallows.

He gently sets my foot down, then motions for the other one.

I lean back against the warmth of the couch, lost in his massage.

I want to ask him what he means, but I bite my tongue.

His couch is comfy enough for my large body, and this moment feels so blissful.

He moves his thumbs up and down the length of my foot, before working on each and every toe, easing every bit of tension out of my foot.

"Would you like a glass of wine?" Evan asks, moments later.

"Yes please."

He gives my shoulder a squeeze and gently slides my foot off of his thigh to the couch.

He putters around the kitchen, pouring the wine into glasses.

"Need any help?"

"Sit there and look pretty."

My cheeks grow instantly hot.

He passes me a glass of wine, sits it down on the sleek teak coffee table and brings back a box and one fork.

"Something delicious is in that box." Because it's a fancy box from his exclusive restaurant.

"My chef hasn't failed me yet." Evan grins. "Dark chocolate mousse cake. Open."

The first time I met him, Evan fed me. I don't hesitate and open my mouth.

"Good girl," he praises as he feeds me a bite of cake.

It's the lightest, fluffiest, ooziest cake that's ever touched my mouth.

"When my ex-wife asked me to do things, like take out the trash or mow her lawn, I didn't think anything of it. I was happy to help. When she asked me to help her carry her groceries or pick up her dry cleaning, again I was happy to help. And even in the bedroom, when she demanded I pleasure her, I thought that was who I was." Evan glances at me, then quickly away.

"Evan, you don't have to tell me." I place a hand on his arm. The woeful expression on his face tugs at my heartstrings.

"I want you to be honest and open with me, Mara. I need you to know." He wraps an arm around me.

"Okay." I squeeze his arm.

"As time went on, Hannah's demands got more insistent and because that's who I thought I was...I gave in to them all. I moved out and stayed at her place, even though my parents and Noel told me it wasn't a good idea. A month later, and to be clear, this was a lie, she's telling me she's pregnant and we're walking down the aisle together."

"Oh, Evan." My heart shatters for him.

He runs a hand through his hair, looks away from me for a moment, and I know he's blinking back tears.

I slide off the couch and wrap my arms around his waist.

He exhales and we stay like that for a long moment, I press my cheek to his knee and he plays with my hair.

"We got married super young because of that," his tone is hollow.

I glance at him, remembering what he told me that night I first met him.

"This is the same person who didn't want you to do kinky things to her?" I can't believe this woman and I'm not usually a violent person, but I hope lots of bad days rain down on her head.

Evan nods. "Yeah. it was okay for her to step on me and scratch me until I bled and call me names but when I realized I didn't want to be sexually submissive, that there was another way that called to me, and I wanted to give her a spanking, she freaked out."

"That's so twisted that she couldn't understand that."

"She was young too, but that's when she said I'd never be successful if people found out I was kinky. So she's not a Domme. She is a controlling narcissist."

"I'm so sorry this woman crossed your path."

"She's been a thorn in my side ever since, even though we are legally divorced. She goes through periods of leaving me alone, but then she'll get an idea in her head for a new business, and then she'll start a campaign of harassing me."

"She sounds awful."

"Not my favourite person." He touches my cheek with his knuckles.

"How did you find out that you were...not a submissive?"

"It was a process. My older brother Noel helped. My mom was the one who started to question Hannah's whole story about being pregnant and then my parents got involved. I resented the hell out of them for meddling."

I squeeze his fingers lightly. "It sounds like an awful time."

"It's the past now, mostly. See, I told you I'm not a catch." He leans over me and cuts a piece of cake with the fork and holds it to my lips.

I open my mouth, and take the cake into my mouth.

"You did tell me that you're terrible." My hands slide in between his legs. "But I kind of like you."

His grin is so over the top and ridiculous. I laugh.

"You need to know what you're getting into, Mara. I don't want you to run out the door."

Those words should have made me afraid and in a far-off corner of my mind, they do.

But with the chocolate cake coating my taste buds, the scent of the wine on his lips as he leans down to kiss me, the passion in his touch make the fear disappear for the moment.

I want this man as much as he's made it plain that he wants me.

"Since I'm already down here." I giggle, reaching for his belt buckle.

"Are you comfortable?"

I shift, so that my knees are a little further apart. "I'm okay, why?"

"Because I want to fuck that pretty mouth." Evan takes a pillow from the couch and shoves it under my knees.

"That's better," I murmur.

"Good." His hand on my nape feels so strong it sends hot shivers through my body.

His pants are off, and his cock is free.

"I love your cock." I slide my hand along his length, following the slight curve to his balls. I cup his sac gently in my hands.

"And I love watching you suck it, princess." He guides my head to it, but I'm already opening my mouth.

His musky taste dances on my taste buds. I suck just the head. He moans above me as my tongue dips along his slit. "Good girl, princess."

His sultry tone has me flooding between my legs. I take more of him into my mouth, swallowing on his length, still playing with his balls.

"Mara, you're driving me wild."

His admission drives me further on, and I lick his salty underside.

I want to see him lose control and I double my efforts.

Evan laughs. "Not so fast, princess."

13 EVAN

Wrapping my fist in her hair, I tug, directing her to a slower pace.

The lava of her mouth on my cock feels so amazing, I could stay here forever.

I want this to last, but I changed my mind. I don't want to come inside her mouth; I want to feel her pussy clench on my cock as I bring her to orgasm.

I can't stop taking in every move she makes, from how she shifts on the pillow to how her fingertips gently press into my thighs. With her, I feel like I'm experiencing something new and wonderful.

Something rare.

And it isn't because she gave me the most fantastic blow job, with her jaw all relaxed, her lips sealed around my cock, her throat working in a steady rhythm.

No, it's because when I shared with her about my ex, she didn't flinch.

I hadn't dated in so long because of the wounds of my past. I had

Char as my regular play partner, but I had convinced myself long-term commitment wasn't going to happen for me.

Until I saw Mara that night.

She brought out my protector because the people she was with were treating her badly, but how she handled it melted my heart like a heatwave in February.

I groan, low and gravelly, as her warm, lush tongue hits the underside of my cock.

I tug on her hair, bringing her up.

"Come here."

She gives me one more long suck and then lifts her gaze to meet mine, licking her lips.

"I could let you suck my cock all night long, but I need to be inside your pussy, princess."

"Yes, Sir,"

I stand, extending a hand to help her up, and then I take her chin in mine and kiss her, devouring her mouth. Her taste is so addicting. I keep kissing her, tugging at her bottom lip, twirling her tongue with mine.

My balls are ready to burst.

I break off the kiss, slide my hands under her shirt, Mara reaches for mine and laughing, we get each other's shirts off and she's standing before me, her abundant breasts encased in a lacy burgundy bra.

"So pretty." I kiss her as I lift up one of her breasts and gently press her nipple. "So delicious."

She emits the softest little moan of pleasure.

A shiver runs up my spine as her hands trail over my pecs, down my back, where she squeezes my ass.

"Not bad yourself, Sir." Her eyes are bright with arousal. My cock is so damn hard I could drill for oil.

"I need you now, princess." I bring her to the couch, and guide her so her breasts hang over the curve of the arm.

"I'll be back one quick second." I rub my thumb across her lip and then I dart into the kitchen, finding a condom in the junk drawer.

In record time, I glove up.

"Are you comfortable?" I slide my hand along her panty covered ass, kneading her luscious ass cheek.

"I could stay here for a long time."

"Good. Are you ready for me, princess?" I roll down her panties, sliding them off of her legs.

"I think so, Sir."

I hear the grin in her voice and drag a finger through her slit.

"Oh yeah, you are," I say, examining my glistening finger. "See?"

I bring it to her face.

"Yes." Her voice is thick and husky

"Taste for me, princess." I hold my finger to her lips.

She blushes furiously as her eyes meet mine, but like the good girl she is, she opens her mouth and her lips close around my finger.

"Good girl." I love seeing her shudder as she swallows, her cheeks flush red.

I pull my finger out of her mouth and wipe it on my leg.

Settling behind her on the couch, I slide my hands along her sides, over her hips.

"I love this view of your ass, though I think I like it even better when it's nice and pink from my hand. I still owe you a spanking, don't I?"

She glances over her shoulder, her eyes dark with desire. "Yes, Sir, I believe you do."

"I can't wait to cash in on that spanking, but I don't think I'm going to last much longer."

"I can't wait for you to put your cock in me, Sir."

That's all the green light I need. I settle behind Mara on the couch, holding her hips.

I drag my palm along her spine, to her neck. "Put your head down, princess."

She does, with a little sigh.

Thank god this couch is wide enough for me to settle behind her.

I grit my teeth as I enter her sweet pussy.

Her hotness coats my gloved cock and I rock, titling her hips to get a deeper angle.

That's it, because I don't want to go anywhere.

With the first long thrust, she sighs.

On the second thrust, I bring her hips back to me and she lets out a mewling noise that has my spine tingling fiercely.

"Damn princess, I'm so hard for you." I slid even deeper.

Mara gasps, clutching the couch rest. I need to make that mewling sound a ringtone.

"Yes, I love your curves," I slide my hands over her ass, to her wide hips, along the softness of her stomach. She is plump, her flesh malleable and alluring.

I dimple my fingers into her ass.

Right now she is all mine. I rock in her, keeping up my rhythm, loving the view of her ass, her head down; she's all willing for me.

I slam into her, her pussy grips me and I groan, lost in the rhythm. Both of us are panting. Her legs tense under me. Sweat is breaking out on my brow. A line of fire is licking up my spine

She gasps as I slam into her so hard the couch squeaks under me.

But I don't care.

There is only how absolutely hot and tight she feels, as her pussy clenches around my cock and the pleasure that's nipping at me, that I can't hold back.

I pick up the pace even more, heat searing my skin with the need I have for her.

"Mara!" I yell out her name as I explode inside her.

I release into the condom, making circles on her back, as I catch my breath.

Under me, she's all pretty, a flush across her back. I lean down and lift her hair, kissing her nape.

"You made me lose control, princess."

"Good." Mara smiles slyly, the dimples showing in her cheek.

I go for her mouth and miss, catching her nose.

Mara laughs.

I dislodge from her warmth. "I'll get you back, princess."

"That sounds like fun." Mara grins.

I dispose of the condom, wash my hands and come back to her.

"Room change, come on." I guide her from the couch, but I can't help palming her breasts, slanting my lips hard against hers.

She laughs, grabbing me around the waist. "I can't walk like this!"

"We can try," I say, and then I bump into the armchair.

Mara laughs so hard her face turns red. She's adorable, I kiss her forehead.

I want to bottle the sound of her laughter and use it to chase all of my demons away.

"Wrong, Sir."

"I did mention pay back, right?" I grin, pulling her close to me. I drape an arm around her shoulders and this is how we walk into the bedroom.

When I first moved into this apartment, I thought all of it was over the top, like the floor motion lighting but now I've never been more grateful for it as the soft white light comes on as we step to the bedroom.

"Get up here," I tell her, patting the bed.

She climbs on and I have to kiss her. So I take her chin between my thumb and index finger and lift her mouth to mine. I kiss her with all the admiration I feel for her. I kiss her so hard I know my lips are going to bruise before I let her go.

"Going to grab something."

"One day you're going to have to show me the toy box."

"But then I won't be able to surprise you," I call from my walk-in closet.

From the drawer, I take out a new toy, giving it a quick wipe with a toy cleaner.

I set it aside and pull out another drawer and take out a Wartenburg wheel.

I like to collect toys.

Grabbing what I need, I turn to see Mara posed on the bed, with her knees under her, like a goddess, her curly hair messed up, the flush still on her face, all naked and all mine.

"Have you ever played with a Wartenburg wheel?" Keeping the wheel part against my palm, I drag the handle slowly along her collarbone, up along the slides of her neck.

She grabs my arm, exhaling softly. "I'm game."

"I can't wait to find all your ticklish spots." I grasp the handle of the wheel, and then drag the wheel on the underside of her right breast, turning it sideways.

"Oh! That feels...oh!" Mara lifts her neck, the way she does when she's about to climax.

Taking full advantage, I lean in and drop a row of kisses along her soft skin, as I roll the wheel around her breast, dragging it, pressing it deeper against her areola.

"Oh! Sir!"

"Yes, Mara?"

"I like this." Her legs part as if she needs somewhere for the sensations to go.

I alternate with the wheel, rolling it along the top of her breasts, then turning it on its side, watching as it makes little scratches against her skin.

Using the wheel with my right hand, I squeeze her breast with my left and skim my mouth against her lips.

Her soft moans of pleasure echo in the room and I'm already half hard again. But this is about her pleasure. Switching to the other breast, I drag the wheel from her nipple to the top of her full breast, then around the underside.

Mara shifts on the bed, her legs falling closed.

"So beautiful princess." I squeeze her other breast and, watching her face closely, I press the wheel against the side of her ribs, watching as her face changes from intense concentration to mirth. Her whole body flutters as I roll the wheel close to her hip.

"Sir! Oh my god!" Mara giggles, her face bright and red.

I keep the steady pressure on her breast and the wheel, moving it lower, then higher, until coming back to that spot that set her off into a fit of giggles.

Tears are rolling down her face and I lick them away, lifting the Wartenberg wheel from her skin.

"The point of that is to tickle?" Mara gasps.

"Among other things. You can use it for sensation play too, pop it in warm water or in cold water. I'm told the scratches feel scratchy."

Mara wipes her eyes that are full of curiosity. "It doesn't...you don't like being scratched, but doing it to a partner doesn't bother you?"

I place the wheel on the nightstand, grab the rose clit sucker and the lube. "I'm using it as sensation play not to try to scare you."

I swallow over the lump in my throat. I don't think I had ever said that to anyone before.

Noel got a sense of how bad things were with my ex and my play partner Char knows enough to know what is going on if I had to stop.

But I never came out and admitted how intentionally cruel Hannah was intent on being.

"Evan...I would never hurt you." Mara places her hand on my chest.

I take it and bring it to my mouth, kissing the back of her hand. "I know, princess. Now lay back for me and spread those legs."

She scurries against the headboard and obeys.

"I need to put my face in this needy pussy." Before she can react, I drop the vibe and the lube on the bed, settle between her thighs and lick her folds.

Her salty taste is bliss and I lick her mercilessly until she's grabbing at my hair.

"Sir! Oh Sir!"

I feel her thigh close against my cheek and I push it away, gently taking her clit between my teeth.

"Evan!" Mara's startled cry makes my heart pound in pure lust.

I withdraw from her, kissing her lips.

"I want three orgasms from you, princess before we say goodnight."

"Yes, Sir."

Her eyes are glassy with need.

I kiss her while flipping the lid of the lube open.

I take the lube and squirt it on the rose shaped clit stimulator.

"Do you have one of these?"

"I have vibes, not that one." She draws a sharp breath, as I spread open her labia and position the soft silicone toy over her clit. I jab the button of the device and because they are right there and I can't help it, I suck her nipple into my mouth.

She grabs me with all her might as the device starts pulsing air against her sensitive bud.

"Sir! Yes!" Her skin is rosy and pink, her eyes glowing with arousal.

"Does it feel good, princess?" I change the setting on the toy to the second highest, and switch nipples. Her hardened tip tastes sweet and I take my time, circling it with long swipes of my tongue.

I feel her tense under me, as I slide the vibe to another setting. I lift it off her clit for a moment, pressing it against her inner thighs.

She moans, in relief or protest, I'm not sure. I hold it there as I flick her clit hard with my finger.

"Oh Sir! This is so much," she twists against me.

I lift my mouth off her nipple and watch her face.

She grabs me, pulling me as close to her as she can, while emitting a string of high keening noises. I press the toy as firmly as I can against her and move to the very last setting.

Her head flings back, her curls spilling against me.

"I am going to come!"

"That's exactly what I want you to do." Her head tilts back, giving me access to her neck. I lick her entire soft column as she moans, her mouth opens, her face relaxes as the orgasm rips through her.

She nuzzles her face against me and my nostrils fill with the scent of her shampoo and her arousal, perfuming the air, heavy and thick.

I turn the toy off and nuzzle her.

"Good girl, princess. Give me another one."

"I can't," she pants out.

"Yes you can," I nibble her bottom lip.

She opens her mouth, deepening the kiss.

I love her softness, how post-orgasm she is all relaxed, her skin is glowing.

Breaking off the kiss, I shift. "Stay right there."

"Yes, Sir."

I reach for the lube and reapply it, making sure to cover it all..

"I like what this thing does to you. What does it feel like?" I slide in between her legs.

"It feels good, like a fluttery sucking sensation," she sweeps her hands over my shoulders.

"Yeah? I like to suck, too," I lean down, the scent of her pussy is intoxicating and I lick her, slowly and gently.

Her legs try to close, and I push them firmly apart.

I press my lips over her clit and suck, feeling it harden in my mouth.

Her leg trembles against my cheek. She whimpers and moans, as I work my tongue, wanting to get even more delicious noises out of her.

But I want to give her another orgasm with the little rose, so I lift my head from between her legs, place the toy against her swollen clit and flick it to the medium setting.

"This feels too intense! Sir!"

"Mara, give me a colour." "Green. So damn green, Sir."I chuckle, drawing a circle on her inner thigh.

"That's my beautiful princess. Give it to me." I stretch out beside her, putting more pressure on the device.

"Stop! I can't," Mara gasps. She twists from side to side, but it wasn't a safeword, so I keep going, switching the vibe to a gentler setting.

Her neck is bared again and I love that.

"I have never seen anything as beautiful, as stunning as you are right now, princess. I want one more orgasm before I cuddle you to sleep."

"Sir...I...yes, Sir! I'm coming."

Her whole body ripples with the intensity of the orgasm, her toes curl and she reaches for me, grabbing me to her.

My head ends up on her breast. I drop gentle kisses on her nipple, as she pants against me. "Good girl."

The sheen of sweat on her brow, her glassy eyes, so damn beautiful.

"You're so addictive, princess. I want one more."

She shakes her head, but a small smile curves around her lips. "Don't think I can."

"Want to bet?"

I toss the vibe to the side and drop a trail of kisses along her stomach.

Her legs open at my touch and I kneel between her thighs, bringing her legs over my shoulders.

She's all soft, and open and it makes me feel all warm and gooey, as if I'm wrapped in a pleasure bubble.

Her clit glistens.

I sweep my tongue through her wetness, it's so damn good I feel like I can come apart from the pure taste.

I take my time, tracing her folds with my tongue, nibbling on her labia.

Mara's fingers entwine with mine. Her breathing has moved from gaspy and panting to slower. I put my whole mouth over her clit, forming a tight seal, and I suck.

Mara's body vibrates, twists away from me. I clamp a hand down on her thigh, sucking her clit into my mouth as hard as I can.

I want this orgasm from her, and I know she'll give it to me. She's a good girl.

"It's so much! Your tongue feels too good." I lift my face from her, to see her blues glassy. "Nothing is too good for you, princess," I settle back between her thighs.

Give her the licking-lapping treatment. I suck gently on her clit and then ramp up the rhythm.

She grabs for me, her hand on my head, her fingertips swipes an eyebrow and I don't care.

I keep up the sucking pressure, loving her tangy smell.

"Sir!" It's a half scream, a guttural moan.

I suck through her aftershocks for a solid minute before wrapping her in my arms.

"Oh...that was a lot."

"Told you I could make you come again."

Mara laughs. "Yes you did."

I press her head against my shoulder.

Her body is heaving, she's shivering slightly.

"Good girl, princess." I bring a blanket around us, and I nuzzle her neck.

"Thank you Sir." The way her eyes meet mine, I know this woman is mine.

"You're a good girl, a very good girl. You're not dirty," I reassure her, remembering her aftercare request.

"I feel...good," Mara snuggles against me and she's asleep a moment later.

I watch her sleep, determined to make her laugh every day and give her so many orgasms she shatters every night.

I push away the thought that I only have three more days to do that and fall asleep holding her in my arms.

14 MARA

FEBRUARY, 11TH

I'm staring at Evan sleeping, thinking how perfect waking up next to him is, just like this when his dark eyes open and that sultry smile of his greets me. "Good morning princess."

"I'm a little wrung out from all those orgasms."

"Yeah?" He raises an eyebrow.

I cup his cheek in my palm, liking the feel of his stubble. "Yeah.."

He leans forward, kisses me deeply and my phone rings. And keeps rinigng.

"You can get that," Evan runs a hand through my curls.

"I'd rather stay here," I mutter but it rings again. I reach for it, feeling how languid my body feels. The things this man can do to my body leaves me breathless.

But my phone flashes my dad's number. It's like a bucket of cold water, an unwelcome intrusion to this bliss.

"It's nothing," I reach for Evan and he kisses me, soothing anxieties he doesn't know about, the unwelcome intrusion is easier to ignore.

He moves over me, his legs somehow straddling my body perfectly, not making me feel awkward or like my body size is too much.

"You can get that."

He groans, eases himself off of me.

I kiss his check, as he answers the call and go to shower, pushing thoughts of my dad firmly way.

As I came out of the shower, Evan kisses me, while his phone is pressed to his ear as he took his turn to get cleaned up.

I'm toasting a bagel when Evan comes out of the shower, looking his usual perfect self in a light grey suit and a dark silver shirt.

"I like that dress on you. It hugs your boobs nicely."

The dark green dress was a gift from my mom and I had stashed in the back of my closet. It was a size twenty-four but this particular outfit hangs loose on me. The flowy skirt tapers down from under my bust, kind of baby-dollish and I like it.

"Thanks."

"It's perfect for our errand."

"What errand?" I was distracted when Evan mentioned it, thinking about my dad.

I had managed to get through Christmas without talking to him, but he always showed up around this time of year.

"To buy more furniture," Evan takes my bagel off the plate and wraps it in a paper towel.

"Hey! What about coffee?"

"We'll get some on the way."

"Fine," I grumble. But he raises his eyebrow at me. "It's worth it princess, let's go."

We get coffee from the hotel café and then we are in his car. Evan chats to me about his parents. His mom and dad have been married for decades and it sounds lovely, the kind of upbringing I wished for even though he called it fun chaos.

At some point I hadn't meant to, but my thoughts drifted, thinking about my dad and I lost track of what Evan is saying.

"Mara, everything okay?" Evan asks me now, a firm hand on my shoulder.

"I like waking up next to you, too," I say, with an effort pulling my thoughts from the jumbled emotions of the past to this moment.

"I can't wait to repeat it." Evan grins, his eyes sparkling. "Here we are."

I can't tell where we are, because we're in a plaza with several stores, the doorways facing the parking lot.

I go to reach for my door handle.

"Wait, Mara." That Dom tone does something to me, makes me all fluttery and hot. I take my hand off the door handle, drinking in the sight of Evan straightening his jacket.

He comes around and opens my door.

"My princess."

"Thank you, Sir Evan." I accept his hand and he closes the passenger door, beeping the car locked.

"I love hearing 'Sir' from your lips," Evan murmurs in my ear. The timber of his voice makes me shiver. The press of his hand to the small of my back feels almost familiar.

It makes me feel kind of panicky for a moment, like I shouldn't be here with this hot guy. I don't deserve to be in this relationship and I need to bolt.

"Mara, come with me," his cool tone bats away those fears as he leads me to the second doorway.

"Winsome Lighting and Decor," I read from the sign.

"This is the place to get a mirror." The bell chimes as Evan opens the door.

I step into a room of white walls with gold specks, soft beige carpet under my flats.

The room is huge, with mirrors hanging on the wall, lighting fixtures hanging from the ceiling, and tables and chairs in elegant arrangements throughout the space.

I stop at one display that has a green theme. A green oversized armchair, a green and grey coffee table and a light that looks like a huge mushroom.

"Something you like?" Evan asks.

"The light that looks like a mushroom is...interesting." I trace the lid of the green and gold light. The glass is smooth.

He gives me a smirk, turning from me as a woman with short brown hair approaches him.

"Mr. Brennon , how nice to see you," she says.

"Hi Rita, you're looking well."

"Please don't touch the top, there's a switch on the bottom of the stand," Rita reaches in front of me, knocking my hand out of the way.

I'm blushing stupidly, feeling very small. Evan reaches out, running his finger along the rim of the top of the fixture. I know he's trying to make me feel better and that makes me smile.

"It's so inviting to touch, isn't it? I don't know if I like how that cord comes out."

Rita straightens the light on the table. "People touch it all the time," she murmurs. "Should I show you the mirrors?"

"Yes." Evan's hand is comforting on the small of my back.

I cover my mouth, stifling a giggle as Rita leads us through the shop, stepping off the beige carpet.

Her black heels click on a tile floor. She opens a door to a long narrow room. "Here is where we keep our larger mirrors. We have many designs, as you can see. There are some concave mirrors in the back."

The door chime rings out and Rita glances behind us.

"We need a few minutes here, Rita. Thank you for your help," Evan says.

"Take your time." Rita presses her lips together in a smile and scurries off to the front of the store.

Evan takes my hand, pulling me further into the room.

It's way too elegant a space to have a fun house effect, but there are mirrors everywhere and to keep from catching sight of myself, I focus on Evan.

"Please don't buy that mushroom lamp."

Evan laughs, closing the door.

The room suddenly feels hot.

"I think it's hideous, though if you really want it, I'll get it."

"No I don't. Why are you buying a mirror?"

He strides over to me, the heat in his eyes making my panties instantly wet.

"I told you, I want to see you from every angle. Should we go with a mirror wall or something framed?" Evan spins me to his back, and I have no choice but to see myself in the oval mirror that's in front of me.

I see the back of me by the mirrors that are hanging in a sequenced row and want to run out of the room.

"Evan, you can't buy things just because..."

"Because you give me good ideas? I certainly can." He wraps his arms around me, nuzzling my neck, then his mouth slants across mine.

His dark head is against my frizzy curly one, his sleek body against my plump one. I'm dizzy as he keeps kissing me, his tongue twirling with mine.

"Evan, what are you doing?" I gasp against him as he lifts up my dress, cups my breasts.

"Choosing a mirror. Do you like that one?"

"Which one?"

He grinds against me, like he's leading us in a slow dance, and my throat goes dry.

We're in public. He shouldn't be touching me like this...he squeezes my breasts through my bra.

"Look up, Mara."

Reluctantly, I raise my eyes to the large rectangular mirror in a black frame.

My breath stops as I watch Evan lean against me, kissing my neck, squeezing my breasts. We look in sync together.

I'm a big girl, there's no denying that, but with his lean muscular body over mine, I feel...small. Not in a bad way.

And it's not how I feel...it's how Evan makes me feel.

As if he could and would protect me, that he's strong enough to handle me.

"Very pretty." Evan unsnaps my bra, letting it hang down under my dress, then he's expertly sliding down my leggings and panties.

"Evan, what are you doing now?" I giggle nervously as his hot breath is against my neck.

"Testing out the mirrors." His amusement eases my worries. I kiss him back, but then he captures my mouth, firmly taking control of my lips.

I gasp in pleasure as his thumb lays against my clit.

"So pretty. Come for me, princess."

My heart races.

In this room full of mirrors, this man wants me to shatter for him.

I squeeze my eyes closed, not sure if I can do this. My body tenses.

But Evan slides a foot between my feet, tugs on my lower lip. "Open your eyes and look at me. Look at us. I want you to watch how pretty you are when you come for me." His soft but commanding tone has me meeting his eyes. He takes my chin and positions me, so that I'm looking in the mirror.

My face is all red and splotchy, my eyeliner is smudged, my dress is all bunched up, my leggings are rolled down to my knees, with my panties above them.

"You are so sexy, princess." His palm presses between my breasts.

All I can do is let him support my weight as I sag against his strong body.

My heart thuds in my chest, I feel like the world is spinning.His hand moves up, collaring my throat. Nothing has ever made me feel as cherished as I do in this moment.

"Now come for me." He curls his fingers in the perfect angle, hitting my G-spot so hard, I'm shaking. "Look at us," he orders, his breath hot against my ear.

He circles my clit. My sensitive bud of nerves leap awake as I stare at us in the mirror.

The look of pleasure on his face, the cocky smile, knowing he is pleased by what he sees, ratchets up my arousal.

A noise from outside of the room snaps my head towards the door.

"I won't let anything happen to you. The door is locked. Give me your orgasm, now princess."

My head comes back against his chest, his fingers curling, hitting my G-spot and I can't hold back the pleasure but my eyes are open because I want to do what he says, and seeing how he's kissing right behind my ear, his eye, his biceps tightening, breaks open the dam that was holding the orgasm back.

I scream and immediately his hand moves from my neck to my mouth, muffling my sounds.

Tears are rolling down my cheeks, my body is heaving with the release.

"Good girl." Evan pushes me back. My thighs hit something solid. Glancing at the mirror, I see it's a stand.

"Evan I'm going to..."

"Sit here, look pretty and watch me fuck you," he says, pressing a finger to my lips.

His dark eyes drill into me as he snaps off his belt buckle and slides his pants down. He throws his suit jacket over a chair.

"This is wild."

"That's exactly how you make me feel, princess." His lips are on mine again. He lifts my legs, positioning them right below his hips.

A sound is outside the door. My heart beats so fast.

"I got you, princess. Tell me what you see in the mirror as I fuck you."

"Your back." I'm feeling totally frazzled, completely out of my depth.

"Yeah? What about my back?" He drops hot kisses on my collarbone, moves my dress off to expose my shoulder, then his hands are on either side of me.

"I like how your muscles ripple as your lips glide me over."

"I love the taste of your skin." His lips skim along my breast, his mouth closes around my nipple.

I moan, my fingers in his soft wavy hair.

Catching sight of us in the mirror, I gasp. I can see my thighs spread wide, with Evan standing between them.

His ass is all hard muscled and his body moves like liquid grace over me.

He lifts off my breast, his hands glide to my hips.

"Hold on princess, this is going to be fast and rough, keep those eyes open and on me."

His cock slides into my pussy in one sure stroke.

I'm going to come apart. All my nerves are on fire.

He enters so deep, tears spring to my eyes, but then he circles his hips. I watch those muscles rippling as he tilts his hips and pounds into me, so hard the stand beneath my ass shakes.

"Evan!" I don't care how loud I am. My eyes are glued to us in the mirror.

His shirt lifts every time he pistons inside of me, my dress all bunched together but my legs open, welcoming him.

I've never watched much porn, never seen how I look while someone is fucking me and it's hot.

The muscles on his legs tense as he thrusts into me hard. My face is pink but my lips are open, my eyes are glassy.

"Going to come in your hot pussy now, princess," he grits out.

I clutch his back, wanting to feel his strength as I watch those muscles work in the reflected surfaces across from me.

His cock thrusts again, once, twice, has me gasping for air.

His fluid motion has me vibrating, practically humming against him.

I see how his whole body tenses, all those muscles grow tense, his eyes close briefly before meeting mine again, as his hot seed spills into me. Evan's breathing heavily as he kisses me. I kiss him back, my head floaty.

"That was good," I say against his lips, giggling at the absurdity of this moment.

"Yeah. Now what mirror should we get?" He grins in that cocky way and I laugh.

He gives me a hand, getting off the stand, and I do up my bra.

Evan rolls up my panties. "I like knowing that my cum is inside of you, Mara."

The realization hits us both at the same time. I bark out a laugh and cover my mouth.

He stands there frozen, beautiful in this mirror room, his face drained of colour.

"Shit, I forgot the condom."

My tummy forms a knot and I'm not sure why. I'm on birth control.

Is it because we didn't talk about it beforehand? I don't know.

Or is it because I'm suddenly remembering he has a casual play partner?

"I haven't been with anyone other than you since the night I met you," Evan says.

"I'm still on birth control."

"Okay," he kisses my forehead. "Is there anything you need from me to feel better about this, or is this just a shitty thing that happened?"

I laugh. "I'm fine. It's fine. We're adults."

Also? I liked how his ungloved penis felt inside of me.

Evan gets his pants and suit jacket back on, somehow looking as put together as he did walking into this room, when I feel hot and frumpy.

"I haven't seen Char in almost a year. I think she's gotten serious with someone." His voice is wistful. I reach up to brush a piece of hair off his brow. "Did you want something more with her?"

"No, she was my rock after Hannah and our arrangement's been casual from the start. It's not that."

"What is it then?" I swallow, wondering if he regrets this, if this is all going too fast and too heavy for both of us.

"I want to fill you with my cum again and again. I want you Mara, even though I just had you."

A shuffling noise makes me jump, reaching out for his arm.

"You better buy the mirror," the words squeak out past the lump in my throat.

Evan laughs, wraps his arm around my waist, striding to the door, he opens it to find Rita standing there, with a frown on her face.

"Hi Rita, so I'm going to take that large mirror with the silver frame. Can you deliver it today?"

"Today? Of course Mr. Brennon ."

Evan strolls out of the room, holding my hand as if we didn't just have the hottest sex ever on a midday afternoon.

There are other people in the store and as Evan takes care of the payment, I break away and stare at the mushroom shaped lamp.

"Are you sure you don't want it?" Evan's mouth quirks.

"I don't need a hideous lamp to remember this by." I'm blushing as I say the words.

"Good, let's go see your new workspace, princess."

My brain grinds to a halt, but he's ushering me through the door and into his car before I can form an intelligent sentence.

"Evan you..." I let the words hang in the air at his look of steel.

"This was the agreement, Mara."

I swallow, but for once I'm not feeling panicked and like I want to run away. I'm eager to find out what he's planned.

15 EVAN

There's a part of me that is waiting for Mara to bolt and I hate that I have that expectation lodged in my brain.

I'm determined to do everything I can to make her feel safe, to show her how much I want her past these five days.

The renovation at her parents' place is going to take weeks. But even after it's all done? I don't want her to go anywhere.

I hum as I drive, eager to show Mara the space I've chosen for her.I know she's a talented artist. After meeting her that night, I looked her up online and saw her portfolio.

If I can play a small part in helping her be successful, then it pleases me to do so.

"How did you get to be the kind of guy who knows where to buy a mirror?"

The question makes me laugh. "Owning a restaurant brings all sorts of connections. I've bought things from Rita before. I went and got my business degree because I wanted to help my dad be successful. I didn't think it'd end up in me choosing decor."

"Did it help?" Mara lays her hand on my knee.

"It took years for one of dad's inventions to be successful but when it did, I was in high school. He and mom kind of drowned in the business side of things. By the time I was finishing up my business degree, mom had quit her job as a paralegal, dad had sold three more successful inventions and I realized I wanted to travel and picked up a minor in hospitality management."

"What was your favourite place to travel to?"

"I like lots of sunshine and warmth. I lived in Belize for a couple of years."

"What made you come home?"

"I was home visiting for my mom's birthday when a college friend invited me out and that's how I met Julian Hugo. We became friends."

Julian and I both, being the second eldest with fathers who loved us but were in their own worlds, had a surprising amount of stuff in common.

"What made you stay?"

"Sinful Bites. I took a risk and threw the idea to Julian. He loved it and here we are." I swallow, grateful for Julian's help because three years ago my brother lost his wife and if it wasn't for Julian saying yes to the idea of Sinful Bites and the formation of the Brennon Consortium, I wouldn't have been home for Noel.

"What's wrong?" Mara's warm hand on my leg.

"You never know how things are going to work out. Noel's first wife died suddenly three years ago. If I hadn't been brave and okay, a little, tiny bit drunk, and if Julian hadn't said yes to my kinky restaurant, I wouldn't have been here for him."

I swallow past the lump in my throat. "Noel met Holly this past Christmas, and he's going to get married this spring. They haven't set a date yet."

"That's good." Mara brushes her hand along my thigh.

"I'm happy for Noel." The last three years had been really hard, watching him get lost in his grief.

But it's also made me hyper aware of how much I don't want to waste time.

"Evan, where are we going?"

Glancing at my phone, I realized I got a little distracted as we passed the parking lot for Science World.

"I have to turn around." I had only been to Steff's warehouse once, last year, and my memory of it is foggy. "Something you should know about me is that I have a terrible sense of direction."

"Yeah? How did you get around Belize?"

"Luck, mostly."

"You may have a terrible sense of direction, but you seem to have a lot of luck, Evan."

I grin, not being able to deny it. "Tell me something you're really bad at."

"You don't want to hear me sing." Mara grins.

"Yes I do. I want to hear you sing badly."

Mara fidgets on the seat. "I'm allergic to cats, even though I want one very much."

"I'll only bring allergy friendly cats home." I squeeze her knee, as I turn around again, my memory slowly kicking in.

It's not like the industrial warehouses that you find downtown, but it's still a massive space, taking up a whole corner.

Across from it is a bakery, a café, and an art gallery.

"I could use a bite to eat. Want to grab something and take a walk?"

"Sure. There's an empty parking spot right over there." Mara points to a motorcycle zooming out of the space.

I park, use the PaybyPhone app to pay for the spot, and then open

Mara's door.

"Good girl," I tell her, dropping a kiss on her cheek because it's been a while since I touched her skin.

She blushes. "I'm hungry."

Inside the little café, we order sandwiches and coffee to go.

"We can eat and walk or sit down." I leave it up to Mara.

"Let's walk."

I sip my Americano and loop my arm through her's.

We walk in comfortable silence for a few moments. I'm wondering if I should walk her around Steff's building but then I see the park up ahead.

"I like the warmer winter weather."

"Me too. Though I like snow," Mara says.

"Ah! Here I thought we were friends," I tease.

She shakes her head, a playful smile shows off her dimples and she nuzzles in closer to me.

In the park, I guide us to an empty picnic table.

"Should we keep playing twenty questions?"

"Sure. What's your middle name?"

"The princess is quick. John, after my grandfather." I shrug. "What's yours?"

"Catharine after my grandma on my mom's side. Pineapple on your pizza?"

"Yes. Mushrooms?"

"No," Mara says, squinting her face.

We dig into our sandwiches, watching a woman play catch with her german shepherd.

"Is there any kink you want to try that you haven't?"

Her shocked expression is so adorable.

"I...what about you?"

I tilt my head to the side, giving her a sly grin. "More role play. Your turn."

Mara blushes, takes a sip of her coffee, throws her shoulders back and meets my gaze, unflinching. Damn, she is so beautiful.

"I went to a few play parties but didn't have great experiences. I kind of want to play in public."

Mara is friendly and outgoing. She has a way of putting people at ease even if she doesn't see herself as being that person, I do. It surprises me that she wants to try playing in public because I know she's self-conscious of her body and a little anxious in crowded settings.

"Even if I didn't have good experiences, I liked how I was part of something and it made what I was doing feel more acceptable because everyone else was doing it too."

"I get that." I rack my brain, thinking over tonight's bookings at Sinful Bites. "Anything else?"

She glances away and spins her coffee cup on the table.

"Mara, there's nothing you can say that will make me not like you. I like you a lot."

I like her so much I can't imagine her not being with me.

"I have always been interested in primal play, like being chased by a predator and then taken down and captured."

She gushes the words out, staring at the inside of her cup.

All the blood rushes to my cock, imagining chasing Mara through the woods. I don't think she'd easily give in, and I'd love to wrestle control from her. But that fantasy dissolves and I shudder. Because primal play often involves clawing... scratching.

It doesn't have to. The thing about kink is that it's customizable. The scars Hannah left run deep and I hate that.

She used to chase me around the bed, daring me to come and get her. If I refused, she'd tell me I wasn't man enough.

"Are you all right?" Mara reaches for my hand.

"Yeah. Thinking of my ex." I push away those bad memories because I've worked for the past decade to heal that damage.

"If you don't want to do primal, I understand. We don't have to." Mara squeezes my hand. The woman across from me is good, and she's honest.

"I'd love to capture you by taking you down, princess."

Mara smiles and the light in her eyes makes my wounds close

Mara has never lied to me. I know she ran out on me, but I trust her not to hurt me, to be honest with me.

"Tell me, why did you run out the morning after?" There the words are out on the table.

I've wanted to give her time. I didn't want to push her, but I feel that if we are going to go forward, we need to sort this out.

Mara stands. For a moment I'm frozen, thinking she's going to bolt on me, right here, but she comes to stand in front of me.

"I wish I had an actual reason. You're going to laugh at me."

"Mara, come here." I place my hands on her waist, and help her to sit on my lap. "Have I laughed at you so far?"

"No, Sir."

"That's right, and I won't. Tell me."

"The night I spent with you felt so good. It was the perfect play scene, and you were so caring afterwards. But when I woke up and looked around your apartment, it didn't feel real. Like, it didn't feel like something that fit me. I convinced myself that it was a one time thing, and you didn't want me after that night."

"Not true, I wanted you. I called you. I messaged you."

"I know, but being with you made me brave enough to quit on the Wilsons and I thought...I had to just go and do that, get on with things and I didn't know. I was overwhelmed. I'm sorry."

"I'm sorry you got overwhelmed and didn't feel like you could have told me. I'm so glad you took another chance."

"Your timing was perfect." Mara kisses me as if she wants me to know how serious she is and I tilt her head back for more access, deepening the kiss.

"I have to thank Arthur and your sister-in-law for the renovation."

Mara giggles. "Did you see his face when you mentioned Sinful Bites?"

"I did. It's not the first time I've had that reaction. I can't wait to show you your new workspace. Ready?"

"Let's do it." Mara slides off my lap.

Taking her hand in mine, we retrace our steps, laughing and talking about the dogs we pass.

Coming out of the park, we walk by the car and then to Steff's building.

"Here."

"What is this place?" Mara shields her eyes from the late afternoon sun.

It's a large white building, with glass doors. The front part of the building is in a dome shape and behind the dome is a large rectangular shape.

"You've got to see the inside." I press the buzz box on the door, hoping Mara doesn't put it together.

I want to surprise her.

The light on the box flashes green and I hold the door for her, leading her inside.

We find ourselves in a huge lobby, with a staircase in the middle of the space.

Steff is walking down the stairs, on huge platform boots, her long hair flowing down her back.

"Hi Evan!" Steff catches the lip of the stairs, then grabs for the staircase.

I come forward, taking her hands and kissing her on the cheek.

"Hi Steff. Those chairs are working out great in the space."

"I'm so pleased." Steff claps her hands together.

"All thanks to you. This is Mara Cotter. Mara, meet Steff Goldstein."

Mara's face is beet red.

"Hi...hi...I love your work. It's been featured lots of times on the socials I follow for design and decor ideas," Mara says to me and blushes.

"That's always nice to hear! Let me show you the space. We have a group of sound engineers who have taken over the top floor studio and this space is a bit too small for me, but I think it'll be perfect for what Evan has told me you'll need."

We follow Steff down the hallway and to an L-shape room.

"So obviously, this could be studio space and an office. There's enough room for a desk," Steff says, showing us the room.

Mara peers into the all white narrow space. It has two big windows that look out onto the street, a huge empty space that she can make her own.

"And if you come across the hall," Steff says, fumbling with a bunch of keys. "I need to get these locks switched over to electronic ones but this floor has been empty for so long, I haven't had a chance."

"You work out of here?" Mara asks.

"It's my main office, yes. I use the back of the building as storage for props and design pieces."

Steff finds the right key.

The space is about forty feet by forty feet, with ceilings that have to be at least twenty feet. There is a door that opens to a loading dock.

"Wow." Mara walks around the space.

She looks at me, glances away. "Yeah, it's a great space."

"The only downfall is that there'd be no retail at all. Evan said you weren't a florist, but a floral designer?"

"Yes," Mara says. "No day to day retail. I need a space to meet with clients and to work on sculptures."

"Receiving deliveries is no problem. This building actually has three loading docks and these doors open to one," Steff says.

"It's a very cool space," Mara's voice is wistful. She drags her hand against the wall, frowning.

"It's yours, Mara. If you want it," I say quietly.

I'm holding my breath. I want her to say yes to this gift because I want her to succeed.

And I want her to think that she deserves a little help, and doing this for her is making me deliciously happy.

There are tears in her ocean eyes as they swing to me. She studies me for a half moment, then runs over, throwing her arms around me.

"Yes, thank you!"

"I'm so happy to have another artist here!" Steff says, grinning.

"Tomorrow, we'll get all the stuff you had stored at your parents over here, okay?" I run a finger along her jaw.

"I can't believe this. Yes, that's perfect!" Mara says.

"I have a keycard for you for the front doors, and here...take this key for the office and the key to here," Steff says, handing them to Mara.

"Thank you!"

"I'll email you the codes and a final copy of the contract."

"Mara will sign it and return it to you," I say.

"I can't believe this."

"I remember what it felt like to have my first studio," Steff says. "Congratulations."

She gives Mara a hug.

"Thank you for your help, Steff."

"I'm happy to assist, Evan." Steff winks at me. "Take your time. I got to run to meet a client."

Steff gives us a wave and leaves us.

"Evan, you have no idea what this means to me. I don't even have words," Mara spins on her heel, taking in the space.

"You don't have to say anything. There is one thing I do want you to do."

"What's that?" Mara brushes her fingers against mine.

"Come to dinner at Sinful Bites tonight."

She frowns lightly.

"You give me this and all you want is dinner?"

"Oh no, princess." I twirl a piece of hair around my finger. "All I want is you."

Mara laughs. "Yes, I'll go to dinner with you."

"Good, because I'm finally going to spank this magnificent ass of yours."

"Oh, Sir. You're teasing."

"Not even a little bit. You're mine and I can't wait to show you off." I capture her lips, hard and fast, al the blood rushing to my cock as she kisses me back, hungrily. I can't get enough of this woman.

16 MARA

E van's kisses turn into open mouth hot hungry kisses, as if he wants to possess me.

I grab the lapels of his blazer, kissing him back.

His hand tangles in my hair, he breaks the kiss, and gazes at me with pleasure dancing in his dark eyes.

My stomach tumbles into knots. How can I possibly accept this from him?

My mom said she'd be willing to help with a space of my own, but she couldn't afford this kind of real estate.

Besides, I feel my family has helped enough.

I had talked about starting a new studio with my friends who are helping me with Wendy's event, but it's the kind of talk you do in a wishful way, and I knew it wasn't going to happen.

This is more than I ever expected.

The space is perfect.

But it's not fair for Evan to give this to me, even if I agreed to spend five days with him.

Evan slips his hand into mine, tugs me against him.

"Mara, if Julian hadn't given me space for my restaurant concept—which was only half-formed when I pitched it to him—Sinful Bites would never have happened. This is just an empty space, and it's easy for me to give it to you. It's up to you to make it into something."

His cool tone calms down my nerves, but now a silver of pressure winds through me. What if I fail and make him regret his faith in me?

"I know you'll make something beautiful here."

I can't do anything other than pull him down to kiss me.

He laughs against my mouth. "I'm pleased I made you happy, Mara."

Is it this easy? It's clear how happy he is, with the way his beautiful mouth smiles, the light in his eyes is bright and he laces his fingers with mine, walking us out of the space.

"I can't wait to have dinner with you."

I can't believe we've spent three whole days together and there is still more to come.

Maybe I can be scared and still want to be with him all the time.

But not because he just gave me a workspace to use.

"When I mentioned Steff was my designer, I noticed your face. I had called her to set up a meet and greet with you but then I thought of asking her if she knew of any studio space that would be fitting for your needs," Evan's hand is warm on the small of my back, as he walks me to the car.

"Her work is amazing! That space is more than I ever dreamed, Evan. I don't know how to thank you."

"I want to make all your dreams come true, Mara." His fingers brush mine as he closes the door. My insides jump around.

I think of how fast the romance was between my mom and stepdad and I know, these things could happen, this instant love thing. I never expected it to happen to me.

"Steff wondered if not having retail access was going to be a hindrance. I think I explained floral design wrong."

"No, not having street access is perfect. It'll keep people I don't want to find me away." I'm so wrapped up in happy bliss vibes that I don't realize what came out of my mouth until I feel Evan's steady, cool glare on me.

"Mara, what do you mean?"

"Dealing with the public can be hard, you know?" I sputter.

Evan's expression relaxes. "Yeah, I get that. If only we didn't need customers, eh?"

I join in his soft laughter, my stomach twisting in knots.

I don't mean to keep things from him, but if he found out what terrible decisions I made, what would he think? I don't know if I can face him.

"We have time before dinner. May I suggest a shower?"

"Yes, someone got me all sticky." My cheeks are so hot as I say it.

"Yeah?" He raises his eyebrow in that cocky way and I melt.

I'm blushing furiously as Evan parks in his spot at the hotel and he's ushering me into an elevator I hadn't seen before.

"Private?" I ask as he swipes his keycard.

"Yes, I can't trust myself in public with you." He pins me against the elevator, dropping a kiss on my neck.

I giggle. "Maybe I should stay away tonight so I don't distract you."

"Don't you dare. I want to paddle your ass in the restaurant. How does that sound, princess?"

I'm so wet, I want to hump myself against his leg.

"Yes Sir." The words come out whispered .

Evan snakes his hand in my hair, holds it there, even after the door opens, he walks me down the hall like this, one hand in my hair.

It's a firm but gentle touch and there's a teeny tiny part of me that wants to know what he'd do if I broke away.

He holds me as he gets the door open, and we take off our shoes. He takes off his jacket, I hold open my hand for it, and hang his up beside mine, still with his hand in my hair.

"It feels slightly restrictive with your hand on me like this."

"Do you like it?"

"Yes, Sir Evan."

"Good."

Not moving his hand an inch, he marches me down the hall, right into the bathroom.

"I need that voice activated shower."

I giggle as he opens the massive shower stall, turns the taps on and steps back.

"Now I have a restaurant to get to. This has to be quick."

"Just like the mirror shop."

"Quicker, princess. Get in." In one quick moment, he has my dress off, my leggings are down. If there was an award for being the quickest at undressing a woman, Evan Brennon would take first place.

I yelp as he tugs me into the shower, his sinewy muscles against my back.

The warm water flowing over my shoulders, along with the heat of his body pressed to me, is amazing.

He reaches for a bar of soap, scrubs himself.

"Not going to let me have fun?"

"Quickie," he grits out.

And that's the last thing either of us say for a long while.

His mouth is on mine as he presses me against the shower wall, his hands caressing my breasts, making me wet. Making me so damn needy, I could squeal.

"Forget the quickie. By the end of the night, I want you to beg me to take you, Mara. I want you to beg for my cock."

Ripples of pleasure shoot through me. The hot wave of fire in my body is so intense, I think I'm going to come right here, from his hands soaping me, from his mouth tracing my curves.

"It seems a waste of a quickie."

Evan grins and kisses my forehead. "It'll be worth it, princess."

I almost want to cry at the absence of his touch.

Way before I'm ready, he stops the shower, takes a towel and dries me off, from head to toe.

"I want to cuff your hands all throughout dinner." He squeezes my breasts in both hands as he says this, staring into my eyes.

I'm gone. Whatever doubts I have in the back of my head, the fear of what happens when he knows about the poor decisions I made, all of that evaporates.

This man makes me feel like I matter. Tonight, I want everything he is going to give me.

I want to show him that I can handle it.

"If you want me cuffed, then cuff me."

"You're going to take whatever I give you?" His breath in my ear sends a shiver across my body, my nipples beaded to hard aching points.

"Yes, Sir."

"Good girl."

Opening the bathroom door, he brushes by me, going into his closet to get dressed.

I open the closet in the hall he gave me to use, and sort through my clothes.

I don't have anything really fancy and my stomach knots, anxious about what to wear.

"This black sparkly dress." Evan plucks it out of my closet and puts it in my arms.

I stare at the dress, with its lacy sleeves, and a ribbon under the breast line.

It's super short. I packed it on a whim, but now I'm unsure.

"You're going to see all my curves in this dress."

"That's exactly what I want to see," Evan says. He takes one arm, then the other, pinning them behind my back. "And when I put those cuffs on, with your wrists at the small of your back like this, those beautiful breasts are going to be on display. Who are these breasts on display for?" He rolls a nipple between his fingers, making me gasp.

"You Sir." Shivers, hot and cold, roll through me.

He takes the other nipple between his fingers, and pulls both nipples up, until I stumble.

"Good girl. You have ten minutes to get ready. No bra, no panties."

My cheeks are so heated, my head spins, but the excitement that is coursing through me tingles my skin.

Quickly, I throw the dress on, smoothing out the skirt around my wide hips. I apply a soft shimmer to my eyes and a red stain to my lips.

I shove my feet into the low slingback heels and I'm ready.

"I can't wait to see those lips around my cock tonight." Evan slides his forearm under my breasts, lifting them up as if they are on a shelf.

He holds up a pair of thick cuffs, leather with velvet on the inside, and rubs them against my arm.

"Your hands please, princess."

I bring my hands to my front, and gently he takes my right arm, presses it into my back, cuffs it, then repeats the move with the other one.

My heart beats wildly against my ribs.

He kisses me, long and slow.

"Let's go," he takes my arm and we walk down the hall, into the elevator and up to Sinful Bites.

The security men greet him, and with his hand on the small of my back, we enter the restaurant.

I thought it would be empty when we got here, but no, service has started.

The restaurant is full, the waitstaff is circling, guests are talking, the din of laughter is heavy in the air.

I feel super self-conscious with my hands behind my back.

"Keep your head up, princess. You're so sexy and you're mine."

His words send an infusion of pleasure through my veins.

I lean into him as we walk through the place, Evan stopping to clasp hands and greet customers.

It feels like everyone is watching me but my body hums, my cheeks ache from smiling because the place is electric.

One man is feeding his sub, her head on his lap, the look in her eyes pure adoration.

Two women are eating off the legs of one man who is propped up on a table.

Over there is a woman with her hands tied behind her back, licking her plate.

It's a huge kink party with food and the place buzzes.

Evan escorts me to a table tucked in the corner at the back.

I have a pretty good vantage point from here, and I can see a woman sitting on a queening chair.

To her left is a spanking bench and a bondage table.

Those are empty, for now.

A server comes by, touching Evan's arm. "Mr. Brennon, Chef wanted to see you."

"Thanks Dawn. Are you okay here?"

"Yes." And I realize it's true. I'm still smiling hugely, delighted to be part of this scene.

"I'll have Dawn bring you a drink, with a straw." Evan chuckles, leans down for a quick kiss.

I settle against the chair, trying to soak up all the details, but it's almost impossible to catalogue.

Across the room, there are three tables.

One woman is tied to the chair with intricate ropes, while one man is dotting her breasts with some kind of sauce. Another man is licking it off of her.

At the second table, two men are staring intently at each other, their hands wrapped around each other's glass, entwined. A moment of pure intimacy that has my breath caught in my throat.

The table next to them, a woman in a corset with a long red braid down her back, is sitting as her partner feeds her forkfuls.

There is mingling across the room, a group that knows each other, and people trying bites off of each other's plates.

When I was here that first night I met Evan, it was close to Christmas and though the atmosphere was fun, it was nowhere as electrifying as it is tonight.

My senses are on overload trying to watch every interaction that is unfolding. It's like trying to touch air.

"Here you are." Dawn places a drink in front of me.

Something with lots of ice and a straw.

I lean forward, take a sip, the bubbles fizzle pleasantly on my tongue; I taste cranberry and lemon and whatever the drink is, it's pleasant.

The thing that kept me coming back to the lifestyle was freedom.

It was the dangled promise of people being what they wanted to be and consensually engaging in activities that brought them pleasure.

I kept coming, hoping to find one ounce of joy that the guests in this restaurant are experiencing tonight.

And after all my horrible hook-ups, I'm here as the owner's guest.

I'm waiting for him, my large breasts exaggerated in front of me, and my body doesn't feel too big.

I'm not trying to shrink into the space I am taking up.

I'm sitting here, looking pretty, accepting it, eagerly waiting for more.

"There's my princess." Evan appears beside me, setting down a plate.

The heated once over he gives me makes me throb. I shift, super aware that I am not wearing panties.

"This is an amazing place you have."

Across from us, the woman's face closes. Before she lets out a heavy pant and falls forward on the table, her partner catches her just before she falls.

"I'm rather fond of it," he says, taking the seat across from me. "But you know, princess, it's much better with you here. I've never had a guest here before."

"You're lying."

He fists my hair so quick I gasp. "Didn't you learn what happens when you call me a liar?"

"You spank me."

"Yes, I do. I'm so glad I brought my favourite paddle with me. Open."

He lifts a fork to my mouth.

I part my lips. He places the fork in my mouth.

"Chew."

I do, even though it's like I'm detached from my body.

"Swallow."

I'm zoned in on his every move and follow his command. I'm sure the bite of food he gives me is delicious but I can't taste it, my mouth is coated in need that food can't assuage.

"I love how tight your nipples are. Open."

I do. He feeds me another bite.

And another.

"Watching you swallow reminds me of how you look when I've made you come. All that tightly wound control, straining to break free, and when it does, it's so beautiful. You are so beautiful."

My insides are as liquid as the river between my legs. His eyes smoulder with heat as he leans forward.

The lights overhead, the reflection of the glass of the table; everything seems heightened.

The purple stripe on his shirt stands out against his black blazer.

For the first time, I notice a couple of grey hairs at his temples. He's a handsome man who makes me feel as if I'm his prized possession.

He feeds me slowly and smiles every time I chew and swallow.

"Drink."

I sip the rest of the drink, hyper aware of my beaded nipples, of the thin line of sweat on my brow.

This meal has been orgasmic and I've nearly come with every forkful.

Another server comes to our table and taps Evan on the shoulder. "Sorry, Mr. Brennon . Shane is at the bar and wants to see you."

Evan flashes me a smile and leans across the table, dropping a kiss on my lips. "I'm going to take care of this and make sure it's the last interruption of the night. When I come back for you, I'm all yours. What do you say, Mara?"

Desire swirls through my body. "I can't wait, Sir Evan."

He stands, grabs my hair, and kisses me. "Don't move, princess."

I'm buzzing with desire, as he winks and turns away.

17 EVAN

On my way back to Mara, every single guest wanted to talk to me.

I know it's because my reputation precedes me.

It's not every night that I'm in Sinful Bites for full service and guests want to take a selfie with me or shake my hand, or in the case of one gentleman, asked me if I wanted to lick the wine off of his submissive's chest.

Seeing Mara sitting there, knowing she is waiting for me, makes my cock twitch. My body hums with the knowledge that she is mine. I'm beginning to think that things, some of which I had kept wavy since my ex, are possible with her.

Maybe I can try and move out of my comfort zone because I don't think this woman will reject me. I know she won't judge me.

"Ready for the next part, princess?"

"Yes Sir Evan." Her hand feels so delicate in mine.

I catch the gazes of the diners as we pass them, as I guide her to the front of the restaurant where we have play equipment set up. Not a full dungeon but options for our guests to use.

Being in this restaurant, hearing the laughter of guests, watching their kinky interplays.

This is what I had dreamed about and no matter how many excellent services we've had since Sinful Bites has opened, I don't take it for granted.

But tonight, it feels different.

The cool mask I usually have on my face as the owner, the man happy to solve the problems for both my staff and guests, has slipped.

Instead, I feel nervous, like I don't want to screw this up in front of all these people.

As I make eye contact here and there, passing the tables on our way to the front of the room, I have my figurative fingers crossed behind my back that nobody stops me or interrupts me.

Under my cool touch, Mara's eyes are glassy, her breath is gasping, her eyes are zeroed in on me.

We almost make it before Mara stops, stumbling into me.

"Mara, what's wrong?"

Her face is pale, she's biting her lips

"Jenny's here."

In the passion of the last two days, I had forgotten about her former colleague.

"She told me where to find you and I comped them tonight in exchange. Should we stop to thank them?" I trace her jawline with my fingertips, wanting to bring her focus back to me.

"What will they think of me?"

Her voice is hoarse, far away and I get the sense that it's not this moment that's going through her mind, but something else.

"Princess, look at me." I gently squeeze her shoulder until her eyes meet mine. "You are mine. The only thing they or anyone else is going to think of you is damn. I wish that was me. You're my princess. I brought you back to the kingdom and I own this place. What am I going to do to you right now?"

"Spank me...paddle me." Her voice is feathery light, but her eyes start to get glassy again.

"That's right, and you're going to take it like a good girl, right?"

"Yes, Sir."

"That's my good girl." I devour her lips, slowly, until the tension eases from her body.

I lead her over to the spanking bench, grab my toy bag that I had set under it earlier.

"I'm so proud to be here with you tonight. To have everyone know that you're mine."

Her cheeks turn bright red. I take the key to the cuffs from my pocket and unlock them from being pinned at her back.

I rub her arms, but leave the cuffs on.

"How are your wrists feeling?"

"Fine, they're comfortable. I don't like not using my hands." Mara's mouth quirks to the side.

I place my hand on her back and help her get to the bench.

"I like taking control from you," I whisper against her ear.

Then I attach her right cuff to the anchor point at the side of the spanking bench and do the same on her left.

"You are so pretty." I brush my hand from her nape to her ass.

I'm intently watching Mara, but I'm aware of the gazes on us.

I can't wipe the grin off my face because I feel like the luckiest bastard in the world to have this willing woman waiting for me.

From my toy bag, I take out a round wooden paddle. I thump it against my palm, making sure Mara sees it.

It's going to give a nice thud and I can't wait to use it on her ass.

"Princess, kiss it for me."

Her blue eyes are darkened with desire as she presses her lips to the edge of the paddle.

"Please, Sir."

My balls are so tight and my heart is on the floor.

My steps are heavy as I take my place at the end of the spanking bench.

I lift up the skirt of her dress, exposing her beautiful round ass.

Her ass is bare, because she's a good girl and doesn't have any panties on. I trace her freckles, then I give her a few good hand spanks to warm her up.

She sighs, as my hand makes contact, letting out little oomphs of pleasure as I increase the intensity.

"Your ass is looking so pretty, all pink like this."

"Ow!" But she stays where she is, and I work on covering every inch of her skin. I rest my hand on her bum cheek, feeling the warmth in my palm, then I drag the paddle over her ass.

She gasps out as the cool wood touches her skin and I want more of her noises.

I draw my arm back and bring the paddle down on her ass in quick succession. The sound of wood meeting her ample flesh is making me even hungrier for her.

Her hips rise towards me, as if she's asking for more.

Damn. I'm so gone for this woman.

I bring the paddle down, loving how it dimples in her fleshy ass and alternate, right, left, right left. I'm lost in the rhythm of the wood striking her skin.

My cock is hard, I almost regret the no sex rule in Sinful Bites because all I want to do is feel her sweet pussy around my cock.

But I built up the anticipation of this scene for days and I owe it to my princess.

With every gasp she makes, I respond to laying the paddle on her flesh.

We're in an intricate give and receive dance. She makes the most alluring sounds. I bring down the paddle.

Everything around me fades, other than this beautiful woman who is laid out on this spanking bench.

Her fingers are curled around the edge of the table, her head is down, and her ass is mine to paint with this piece of wood.

Her ass is now a darker shade of pink and after the next "Ow" from her mouth, I set the paddle on the top of her generous curves, and drag my finger through her cleft.

She moans, and then I add another finger.

Her hips raise up, as if she's asking me to reach deeper.

"Good girl, taking this for me, letting me fuck you with my fingers. Are you going to come just like this?"

She shakes her head no, but her eyes close, her toes curl, and I withdraw my fingers, wiping them on her ass.

"You're going to have to wait, princess."

"Sir!"

It's abundantly clear it's meant as an expletive. I laugh and bring down the paddle.

The thud of the wood echoes in the space. I'm going heavier on her than I have before, and she's soaking it all up like a sponge.

Each time I bring down the paddle, she lets out a breath of air. Her ass almost glows from the shade of red. I bring it down again and she lets out a different tone, a sound of pleasure.

The pain is only ratcheting up her desire and I know that I need this woman.

I need to wake up beside her every morning and I want to fuck her every night.

My heart expands in my chest, I'm moronically blinking back tears and with a blaze of renewed determination, I bring the paddle down hard on her ass, two times on each of her ass cheeks, hard enough that it vibrates through the handle and I think I'm going to break it.

She lets out a panty whimper. Pride blooms in my chest with how well she's taken this.

"Good girl," I press a kiss to the nape of her neck, brushing my hand on her heated skin. "Very good girl. You took that so well." Her eyes are shiny with tears and I kiss her cheek, while massaging her back, gently.

"Thank you, Sir." Her voice is husky and thick.

I set the paddle on top of my toy bag, while keeping a hand on her and then I take my time, tracing the red skin.

She shudders under my touch, making delightful little sighs.

I stroke her hair, lean down and find her lips, I kiss her, greedily.

I can't get enough of the feel of her mouth against mine, her scent, her taste. She moans as our lips touch. I break off the kiss. "How do you feel?"

"Good. Very good, Sir." I chuckle and massage her arms, rubbing circulation back to her body.

Slowly, I uncuff her from the table but leave the cuffs on, and help sit her up.

"My sweet princess," I nuzzle her cheek against mine.

I breathe in her scent, wipe away a tear with the pad of my thumb. Mara grabs onto my arm, holding me against her.

"Good girl," I coo to her, over and over.

We stay like that, melded together, her soft curvy body against mine. I could listen to her contented sighs all night. It makes me feel so good, knowing that I brought her pleasure tonight.

"Can I get up please? My ass hurts."

I laugh. "Of course."

One of my thoughtful staff has placed water and a plate with what looks like prosciutto wrapped melon and raspberries and bread on the table right across from us.

She's shivering, so I take my blazer and settle it around her shoulders and guide her to the table.

Good girl.

Damn, I really wish this was a soft chair or a seat, but I sit her down and fed her a few bites.

"You did so well, princess. I'm so proud of you."

"I felt everyone watching me, and it made me nervous."

Her voice catches and her eyes are glassy, beautiful. "But then the crowd, hearing them talk and laugh and feeling their stares felt good. Like I was part of a show and I liked it."

She flashes me a smile so full of warmth and excitement my heart melts.

I kneel in front of her and wrap my arms around her waist.

Her fingers stroke my hair and we stay like this, locked in this warm flow of post scene bliss for several moments, enjoying each other in silence, but when I see Mara's lip tremble, I know I have to reassure her.

"You're a very good girl. You're not dirty. You are beautiful and mine."

She relaxes as I kiss her knees, dropping a kiss above her knees to the inside of her thighs.

She takes another sip of water and eats a piece of melon.

I am buzzing with a high I've never experienced before.

The need to possess this woman, to make her fully mine beyond this week is now a mission that's flowing in my blood

I created this place as revenge against my ex.

Was it only a way to prove that I am not a deranged, kinky bastard? Okay, but so what if I was? Then I'd find other like-minded people, and I'd give them a unique space to enjoy.

Somewhere they could come to celebrate occasions or a Thursday night.

I wrap an arm around Mara and pull her to my body and swallow over the lump in my throat. But life is short and I'm not going to hold back.

If it causes her to bolt, I will go and bring her back and do whatever it takes to convince her that I mean the words that are on the tip of my tongue when I see a pair of shoes walk towards us.

I stand, holding Mara's hand, smiling at Jenny.

"Hi. Before we left I just wanted to thank Mr Brennon. It was a special evening. Mara, you looked so beautiful tonight, during your scene. I couldn't look away."

"Thank you, Jenny." Mara blushes.

Jenny's companion, a tall guy with dark hair, comes and joins us, his hands on Jenny's shoulders.

"Mara, it's nice to see you. We've missed you."

Mara glances at him. "You too, Matt."

"And we also wanted to say, we're sorry if we ever said or did anything that made you feel uncomfortable." Jenny never breaks eye contact.

"Really sorry, Mara. you're a talented artist and we hope things are working out for you. Sabrina and Kyle were their own kind of force. It was hard not to be swept up in their mind hive."

"I know," Mara says. "Thanks for saying that."

Jenny shifts from foot to foot. "Are you still working on Wendy's event?"

"Yes. I have a new studio space. I'm going to try doing it on my own." She squeezes my hand. "With help."

I squeeze her hand back and lean down and kiss her.

"If you need any help, let us know," Jenny says. "I tried to clean up their mess but they aren't paying us, so we decided to stop doing that."

"Good call. I can't pay very much," Mara says. "But I'm determined to make it work."

"Hey, we'll take anything," Matt says.

"We're setting up the space tomorrow, if you're free to come unload."

"We'll be there," Jenny smiles.

"Okay," Mara says.

They say goodnight and leave, and I catch Dawn's eye from across the room and she makes a shooing gesture, waving me away.

"Come on, princess, let's get you home."

I love the feel of her hand in mine and I'm humming in the elevator. My brain is spinning with ideas to help Mara make her business successful.

"Have you ever thought of a business loan?"

I'm mentally kicking myself as her face transforms from post bliss to a cool mask. "That's not an option for me."

"I can help you look into it if you want. I can even buy you the business, bank roll your payroll."

I'm tossing out ideas, and I don't know what I'm about to say, but Mara pulls me down and kisses me and I stop talking, kissing her back, demanding that she open to deepen the kiss.

I break off as I take her to my door.

"You made me the proudest man in the whole city, the whole fucking world tonight, princess." I'm caging her against the wall, kissing her lips again, as hard as the beating of my heart.

She laughs against my lips. "I needed that scene, Sir. Thank you."

I pull her into the bedroom and we get our clothes off in record time and we're nuzzling each other under the blankets and I've never been so damn happy as I am right now.

No matter what, I'm going to make Mara mine, permanently.

18 MARA

FEBRUARY 12TH

I never thought I'd be spanked in front of a room full of people at a restaurant, but the memory makes me feel giddy. My ass is still sore in a good, satisfactory way.

The scene last night solidified something for me in my brain.

My trust in Evan reached another level and I believe he wants me, that he's attracted to me.

Before I left his bed this morning, he kissed me, then moved down, his strong body over mine, as he kissed every inch of my skin.

We showered together, his hands gently massaging my head and shoulders until his finger dipped between my legs.

"I love making you come. My good girl."

With the water hitting my shoulder, his chest pressed against mine, it didn't take much to rip an orgasm from my body. Out of the shower, Evan answered his phone, frowning.

I'm drying off, hearing him through the open bathroom door, using a tone that's detached and growly.

"She's insane if she thinks they're is any chance that's going to happen when we are in our third decade of being divorced. Fine, I'm free. I'll see you then."

He hangs up the phone, turning to find me, and the pain in his face is so raw I want to hug him. I step out of the washroom and wrap my arms around him.

"My ex is determined to be a constant in my life. I need to meet with my lawyer this morning. But I can take you to your mom's to meet the rental truck."

He's so eager, his tone so hopeful.

All of this hot and heavy between us and it's so good but I don't mind having some space.

"I am going to text Jenny and ask her to drive me to mom's. Then I'm meeting the team at the studio." I can't help the excitement in my voice.

This is light years away from where I thought I would be.

I can't wait to get into the studio and start setting it up and making it my own.

Evan insisted that I choose furnishings, storage units, workbenches and a computer system for the space. Somehow, I'm going to pay him back.

"Okay, but I insist on having a business lunch with you." The dimples in his cheek appear as he smirks. He is so sexy.

"Why?" I reach out for his hand.

"To talk about your business." He twirls a strand of my hair around his finger. "You're going to be a good investment, Ms. Cotter."

I giggle in his arms, but my stomach is in knots.

Nobody will think that I'm a good investment due to my past.

Evan brushes his lips across mine, gives me a slap on the ass.

"I have to go and take care of this unpleasantness. Have a good morning, princess."

"You too, Mr. Brennon ."

"I prefer Sir Evan from you," Evan snakes his hand at my nape and kisses me.

My whole being sighs against him and I know what we have is good and it could be great between us. I'm not in a hurry to run out of this apartment at the end of the week. I want to stay with him, I do. But doubt is a demanding monster in my brain, demanding to be fed. Evan's made my dream possible. I don't know what I can give him in return that matches that.

"See you, soon princess," Evan has his shoes on and is dressed in khakis and a button down green shirt that makes his eyes sparkle.

"Can't wait, Sir. Evan."

He closes the door with a little wave.

I get ready, throwing on a pair of yoga pants and a flowy dress-shirt I liked. The clothes are comfortable but it's a little dressier than what I'd wear lounging around. I know I'm going to get dirty moving stuff in, but I want to feel...like I'm in charge.

From the closet I'm using, I grab my sketchpad, my iPad and pack it all into a bag. I text Jenny and ask if she can pick me up and take me to mom's so I can meet the movers and grab my car. She texts back a thumbs up.Fifteen minutes later, I'm in Jenny's car and we're on our way.

"Thanks for texting me," Jenny says. "Matt is going to meet the others at the studio. You must be so excited, Mara!"

"I am. Nervous, but I can't believe this is real."

Jenny flashes me a grin. "You're so talented. You deserve this."

Jenny is pretty, with blonde hair, serious amber eyes, and a perfectly aligned smile.

She's great at sculptures and large builds and she's just one of these pleasant, upbeat people.

Though Sabrina and Kyle made comments about my weight, Jenny didn't say anything...negative, but I frown, seeing if I am excusing the off-handed comment about me not wanting anything sweet.

"I'm not on a diet," I blurt out the words and look out the window.

"Okay," Jenny says, a quizzical expression on her face.

"I like my body. I don't want any comments about my weight."

Jenny turns bright red, her shoulders hunch up to her neck.

"Mara, if I ever said anything that made you feel uncomfortable, I am really sorry. Like I said last night, Sabrina and Kyle were like this force that it was easy to get wrapped up in. They knew all these glamorous people, took us to the most exclusive places, did everything they could to create the illusion that being in their company, never mind working for them, was an exclusive privilege. But I think Kyle's gambling got out of hand."

Suddenly, the world tilts on me and I bite my cheek hard.

Because I can't believe I went and worked for someone with a gambling problem and didn't clue in to that fact.

Maybe it's because Kevin had the job, the client list, the pretty woman on his arm?

Maybe it was because his addiction was prettier than my father's?

I know that is it and I don't like it.

I know over the years I justified it to myself, as Kevin only likes to bet on the occasional sports team.

He doesn't do anything like online poker or horse races or go to casinos and lose constantly at the blackjack tables.

Shame, hot and real, threatens to overwhelm me and I can't believe that I spent almost a decade of my life working for someone who really was the prettier version of my father.

But isn't it true that we'll tolerate things if they are pretty?

We'll put up with bad behaviour from our boss because he looks like he could be on the cover of a magazine.

I am a skilled artist and I've spent hours honing my craft. I could have taken a job with someone else.

"I wish I had found a new job. That I was brave enough."

"But look at you now! You're starting a new business. That's brave."

"Only because Evan is helping me."

"There's nothing wrong with that, Mara." Jenny flashes me a smile, but I'm uncomfortable.

It feels like I haven't earned this. Like I'm like my father, who has a long track record of taking advantage of people.

It's easy to push these thoughts to the side though, because it's a busy few hours of emptying the shed.

Thank goodness I have Alex and Marc and Jenny.

I'm sweaty and gross by the time everything is loaded into the truck but it's done and I can't stop smiling.

"Thanks guys, I'll see you there in a few."

"Can't wait to see the space." Alex gives me a wave and I venture into the construction zone that is mom and Arthur's house.

The floor from the front door to the back is taped off, but I just need access to my room so I can grab more clothes.

After I'm done packing, I peek in the kitchen.

Mom is going to love this and freak out. I text Arthur, telling him again that I want to be here for the reveal. I feel a smidge of guilt that I haven't talked to mom and I am going to fix that tonight.

Once I'm driving, my brain can't turn off, because mom and Bryan, even though they knew each other for years in passing, they only dated a week before Bryan ended it with a proposal.

If my mom can have happiness, why can't I fully dive in with Evan? Why can't I fully trust that he means everything he says?

I don't know.

I want to and I don't think there's an actual reason that's preventing me.

At the studio, we work the rest of the morning, setting the space up.

"This is stunning, Mara," Jenny says.

I look at my friends. They all look as tired as I do, but they are smiling and happy and it feels good to have people who believe in me.

My phone rings, Wendy Sevenson's number flashes. I smile as I accept the call.

"Hi Wendy."

"Mara, happy I got you. I need something for this weekend. My sister went and got engaged! I'm throwing a party and need something spectacular."

Valentine's weekend isn't exactly a lull.

I want to be with Evan and I know Alex and Marc will be busy with work.

Nerves swirl through me. I bite my lip. "Great timing. I'm actually in my studio. What theme are you thinking of? I have to tell you, it's super short notice, though."

I talk to Wendy for a few minutes, getting all the details and the size of the pieces she wants, one arch frame, something "magical" and one tabletop sculpture.

"We got our first job, guys," I tell my friends as Jenny and I stride into the studio.

They let out whoops and cheers and I can't help but smile so hugely my face hurts. Jenny immediately calls the supplier and Marc and Alex huddle over my iPad as I start sketching out a rough design.

I am lost in my work, wondering about colours, waiting to hear back on what our supplier has, thinking of the flowers that I want, trying to figure out the pieces.

"Something magical, like a unicorn?" Alex says.

"I don't want to be that literal." I start thinking of a shooting star design and I'm almost done sketching it out when Evan calls me.

"Are you on your way?" His voice is deep and sexy and it makes my stomach clench.

I check the time and yikes. "Yes."

He chuckles. "Lost track of time, did you?"

"Maybe," I admit.

I gather my things and ask Alex to lock up and wave to my team as I stride out the doors.

***

My stomach flutters, walking through the doors of the Hugo Hotel.

The lobby is all dark wood and crystal chandeliers and golden touches.

Evan said he'd meet me in the café - figuring correctly I'd want coffee and we'd go from there. I smile at the barista I recognize and make my way to the counter and stop in my tracks.

I see Evan's back, his wavy dark hair hits the collar of his shirt and in front of him is a tall thin woman with gorgeous red hair is wearing a mini striped dress.

She's leaning down to him, touching his shoulder and I swallow hard on the bile.

This doesn't look like someone random.

Did he really mean everything he told me if he can flirt with someone so casually like this? I don't know what compels me, but I take a step forward, and I see Evan lean back. The woman purses her mouth, and leans forward, her long nail grazes his cheek. Evan startles, jerks forward, crosses his arms. The woman shakes her head at him and marches out of the café as if she owns the place.

Oh wow. I hurry across to him, because I realize who that woman must be.

"Hey, Sir," I place my hand on his shoulder as I lean down to kiss his cheek.

His eyes are bright, but the tension in his face is an expression I haven't seen before, and it makes me feel so mad that he's been hurt.

"How's the set-up coming, princess?" Evan takes my hand in his, but I don't want to be here with him in the middle of the café.

"Can we go to your apartment?" I ask.

"I wanted to take you out to lunch." His voice is hollow.

He looks like someone has come along and shaken up his world and for a man who is normally super confident and sure of himself, this slip of the mask is heartbreaking.

I want to claw the woman who did this to him.

"Lunch later." I softly press a kiss to his mouth.

He kisses me back, the tension leaving his body.

"Okay."

He places his hand on the small of my back, through the walk to the elevator. The doors open, two smiling women are each holding an arm of a tall, broad shouldered, very attractive man.

"Hey Evan!" The man dislodges himself from the women.

They stare at me and I return their stares unflinchingly.

"Hi Julian." Evan pulls me to his side. "Didn't think you were back until next week."

"Afraid I'm going to miss your birthday bash?" Julian raises an eyebrow and claps Evan on the back.

"No, you're a guest of honour. This is Mara Cotter."

"Pleased to meet you." Julian holds out his hand to me. His handshake is firm, his smile is warm.

"I'm still on vacation and going to enjoy it, right girls?" Julian waggles his eyebrows at the women.

They blush and laugh.

"I'll see you soon, birthday man!" Julian gives him a salute before taking the arms of the women. Evan and I step into the elevator.

"So that's Mr. Madden Hugo."

"In the flesh." Evan holds the door to the apartment open for me.

"Can't he ban your ex-wife from the hotel?"

Evan's toeing off his loafer and stares at me. "Noel says the exact same thing. I'm sorry you saw our encounter."

"Can I ask why you still meet with her?"

"I don't. She's supposed to go through my lawyer, but once or twice a year she does this and I know it shouldn't jostle my brain, but it does," he brushes a hand through his hair and looks so wrung out.

"I'm sorry," I open my arms, offering him a hug.

"It's okay. You got me out of there and brought me here for some space. Thank you." He steps into my arms, kisses me, exploring my mouth with his lips and tongue.

"Someone's feisty today," he says out the side of his mouth.

"Someone's happy," I tell him.

"Yeah?" He cocks an eyebrow at me adorably.

"Yeah." Our lips fuse together, hot and heavy, and I can't get enough of how he feels against me, of his touch, his tongue.

And now I have the absolute assurance that this thing between us isn't a one-sided thing. I don't know why seeing Evan with his ex merged the jigsaw pieces together for me, completing the picture that this man means everything he says he does, but it did. And I'm going to accept it because I want to be happy. With him.

He breaks off the kiss, and strokes my hair. "I'm glad you're here."

I lean back against him and his arms come around me, pressing me to his front. "I thought about what was between us...it benefited me more than you."

"Mara," Evan growls. "I've been looking for someone I can have fun with and take care of for a long time. I like being your Dom."

"I like being your submissive."

"Good girl." He fists my hair, brings my mouth to his. "You're my submissive. Mine and it doesn't benefit me more than you."

My heart gallops in my chest. "What's this about a birthday bash?" I feel giddy, like I'm bouncing out of my skin with happiness.

"I'm having a birthday party. One week after Valentine's Day." Evan nuzzles my neck.

"Oh really?"

"Yes, Mara."

"What do you want for your birthday?"

He pulls my head back, stares at me with such intensity and longing that there is no doubt how he feels about me.

"You."

19 EVAN

"Oh, Sir Evan."

The way her blue eyes darken, and she grabs my shirt, makes my heart thud so hard against my chest.

My cock strains painfully against my fly. She stands on her toes and kisses me and I kiss her back, slowly, savouring her taste. But I don't want to be gentle.

I want to devour her.

Fire rolls through my body with the need to claim this woman, to show her she is mine.

She sucks on my bottom lip. I let out a soft moan because that's so damn hot I'm going to explode in my pants.

Slanting my lips against hers, taking control of this kiss, I lift her, grabbing her ass in my hands.

Her startled shriek is precious. I hold her against the wall, blood roaring in my ears.

She laughs, dropping kisses on my neck, my nose, my chin.

I set her down, loop my arm in hers, kissing her, walking her backwards.

In the sitting area, where we had that first scene, that very first night we met, I stop.

I don't know what is in the air between us right now, but it is like a rolling tide and I am not going to stand in its way. I break the kiss.

"Damn, princess. It's sinful what you do to me."

Pushing her back on the settee, I run my hands down her thighs, taking off her yoga pants.

"I prefer you in dresses."

"Is that an order, Sir?"

I almost don't catch the smirk on her face because I'm too busy pulling my shirt off.

"Get that top off now."

She laughs and takes the thing off and I swallow as she kneels.

Our fingers touch as we both go for the fly on my pants, she pulls down my boxers.

I sigh, playing with her curls as her hot mouth moves against my thigh.

"Call it a request." I raise an eyebrow, a grin slowly spreads on my face.

She takes my cock in her warm palm, and then her mouth seals around my tip.

The sight of her on her knees, her curly hair like a cloud, her lips glittering from the gloss and her breasts naked, in a pure offering of submission, makes me so damn proud.

She may be the one on her knees, but she has me by the balls as much as she does by the heart.

"That's a good girl. Show me how much you like sucking my cock."

She cups my balls, massaging them, with even pressure. I'm going to burst, but I want to come inside her pussy.

Closing my eyes, I let out a low growl noise as her tongue flicks the underside of my cock in a long up and down stroke.

I am so hard for this woman.

"I want to fuck you until you scream, Mara." I ease out of her mouth.

She grabs my thighs, her blue eyes so dark. "Then what's taking you so long?"

"Sassy princess, I like it. Get on your back and spread your legs wide."

"Yes Sir." She runs laughing into the bedroom.

Her request for a takedown scene flirts through my mind, but I restrain myself.

Our week might be up, but I am going to make certain she isn't going anywhere.

And that kind of scene needs to be planned out in advance.

I stalk towards her. I love how her breasts spill out, how her heels are against her thighs. Waiting like the splendid goddess she is, ready for me to worship.

The bed sinks under my weight, and then I am braced over her, slanting my lips across hers, my hands tangling in her mess of curls.

I kiss her, a slow, passionate, worshipping kiss.

From the first moment I saw this woman, she made me feel lighter than I had in years.

Her laughter is sparkly, even musical. Even though I had no right to it, I needed to hear it again and soak it up, wanting to absorb some of that lightness she moves through the world with.

Being with her has released the tension I've had in my heart for years.

I kiss her neck, skimming my mouth along her skin, loving how her hips raise off the bed, the sweet moan that comes from her as I take her nipple in my mouth.

I tease it, flicking it hard with my tongue. I slurp that nipple, pressing it to the top of my mouth.

She shivers under me.

I suck, lavish the pointed peak, her gasps and moans urging me on.

Letting go of her wrists, I switch to the other nipple, sucking it, taking my time.

It's so juicy and sweet, I can't get enough of it and I swirl my tongue around every inch of it.

I slide my fingers in her hot pussy. Instantly I feel her juices coat my digits.

I finger fuck her in time to long pulls on her nipple.

She grabs my head, pushing me against her.

"Sir Evan! That's so good."

I didn't need any encouragement, but I laugh, enjoying the feeling of the vibration in my mouth.

Taking one more suck of her nipple, I lift my mouth from it and meet her gaze, her pussy clenching around my fingers.

"You are so wet for me, princess."

"Yes, Sir, I am so wet for you."

"What do you want me to do?" I still my fingers, feel her flutter.

"For you not to stop!" She reaches for me, her fingertips brush against my shoulder.

"Tell me what you want me to do, princess."

"I want you to put your cock in me and fuck me, Sir."

"All you have to do is ask, princess," I kiss behind her ear.

I remove my fingers, slip them into her mouth. She opens her mouth and sucks.

I'm going to combust.

My balls draw up so tight, I can barely breathe.

I roll my fingers across her tongue, fucking her mouth hard.

"Don't you dare come until I'm inside you." I shift to line up to her entrance and push deep with one long thrust. "How's the new mirror?"

I feel how her whole body shivers at the question.

"It's fine, Sir Evan."

"It's more than fine. I get to see every inch of your body. And you get to see exactly what I do to you."

Mara cries out, already her neck is flung back.

She's sexy as hell and she's mine.

I stay with her for a long, luscious moment, enjoying how her pussy grabs my cock.

Leaning forward, titling my hips, I kiss her neck. "Keep your eyes on me. I want you to watch me as I fuck you."

"Sir Evan!" Her fingers dig hard into my shoulders, but I don't care.

I thrust deep, fire licks up my spine.

She darts her eyes away from me, and I shift back, a little, drawing up.

"Princess. Look at me," I grit out.

Those blues darken. She grabs my forearms and digs the pads of her fingers into my arm. I'm sure I'm going to have bruises and I don't care.

This woman can mark me all she wants. I know she isn't going to break my trust.

She's not going to leave me.

And she's not out for my money.

Mara wants me for me.

And I hope to spend a lifetime wondering why, and enjoying every moment trying to figure it out. I'm going to spend every moment showing her I am worthy of her.

My lips brush against her forehead, her nose, her cheek, any part of her flesh that I can lavish, I do, eagerly.

I can barely hold back my orgasm. I thrust in her, so deep I almost see stars.

"I can't wait to fill you with my cum, princess, but I'm waiting for you. Or did you not feel me inside you?"

I laugh against her as her pussy grips my cock, taking me even further into her heated depths. I rock my hips against hers, her arms are around me, both of us are panting hard.

Her pussy quivers around my cock as I push even harder.

I pound into her so hard, the bed shakes. She gasps under me, her moans and cries punctuate the air, but it doesn't satiate my raw need. We are fire together, our mouths meeting, tasting each other, our bodies melding, I'm moving in quick tempo, wanting to feel every inch of her.

She pants against against my mouth. Grabbing her hips, I lift her to me and thrust harder, faster.

"Oh Evan!" she shrieks, her entire body starts to shake and her eyes close.

"Open those eyes and look at me as I come in you, princess."

She obeys, her gaze behind me to the mirror and I'm even hotter, thinking of what she is seeing. I slam into her once. The vibrations of our two hearts meeting roll through me. I can't hold back any more and I come so damn hard I am shaking with the effort.

But I don't want to leave this pussy, not yet.

I roll my hips, lifting her to me.

My tongue tangles with her and I know I love this woman.

She has my whole damn soul.

The words dance on my tongue again, but I don't want to tell her like this. I need her to believe them. I kiss her, her tongue against mine, perfect, like it belongs there and her seductive body against me. I kiss her neck, the V between her breasts, back up to her collarbone, delighting in how she shivers.

She kisses me back, slowly.

"That was good, Sir Evan."

I ease out of her, wrapping my arm around her waist, pulling her to me.

"Yeah, how good?"

"So good, I forgot everything. Even my own name."

"Mara," I emphasize each syllable. "My princess." I lace my fingers through hers, resting my chin on her shoulder. "We look so good together," I mumble.

She turns her head to me, as if she could duck the mirror but it shows us just as we are, on a king sized bed with rumpled sheets, our hair standing up everywhere, Mara's body all plump and rosy, mine still heaving with the effort.

"That was more than a quickie."

"And we skipped the lunch part." Not that I care.

"Food might be good."

"Nothing tastes as good as you."

She giggles, lightly slaps me. "That's a little cheesy."

"I like cheese."

She's full out belly laughing and it's the best sound.

Reluctantly, I get out of bed.

"I could call for something."

Mara sits up, splendidly naked, and turns to face me. "Are you going to live in this hotel forever?"

"It has its perks."

I run a hand through my hair, trying out this conversation in my head before I speak the words to her.

Living here was an easy solution, because I didn't have to commit anywhere.

"I'm open to not living in a hotel."

"I like to garden." Mara brushes her fingers along mine

"I hate flowers," I blurt out.

The expression on her face is...okay, it's comical and I can't help but laugh.

I kiss her forehead. "I mean, I hate the scent of flowers."

She blinks those pretty blues. "You're in bed with a florist."

My chest feels tight. I start to pace, needing to move.

"I know. Your love of flowers is so interesting."

"I get that not everyone chooses it as a profession, but most people aren't offended by them."

I turn my back to her, to gaze out the narrow window.

This woman deserves a home, with wide windows that let in as much light as possible and a huge garden.

"I'm going to give you whatever your heart desires." My voice breaks on the words.

Mara stands, wraps her arms around my waist. "Gardenia and lilacs and lilies of the valley."

I stiffen, though I'm not sure why, but I force myself to move my hands to cover hers. My pulse is beating rapidly.

"That's her synthetic awful perfume. I'm not sure what flower it's trying to resemble, but that's why you don't like the scent of flowers."

I swallow past a huge lump in my throat.

All I can do is nod.

I never told anyone my dislike of flowers is because of my ex.

Noel's first wife, my sweet sister-in-law, caught on that I didn't like the scents and would move flower arrangements out of my way, but I never told her why.

For years, I told people it's because I don't want the flowers to mingle with the scent of food in the restaurant.

"Promise me you won't bolt on me again."

I have no right to ask that of her, but I need to know.

And maybe that's what I was waiting for, to see if I can share the hard things with her today.

Her sticking around after seeing the interaction between Hannah and me helped, but I need more.

I feel like an asshole.

Mara hugs me, lays her head on my back. "I thought this scared me, whatever it is between us. I didn't see how I was doing anything for you."

"Mara, you're amazing and I love being with you." I spin her to face me.

She shakes her head. "I know, but I didn't want it to be one sided. I thought I needed to do something for you. But I can't give you a workspace or...anything."

"Your trust, your submission. Those things are priceless. Making money is easy for me." I rub my thumb along her bottom lip. "But this? Trusting someone? I never thought that was going to happen. Until I met you."

She slides her hands down to my waist, and I gasp as she sinks to her knees.

Gracefully, she stretches her palms out in front of her, until they cover my bare feet.

"I promise I won't bolt on you, Sir Evan."

20 MARA

My heart is beating so fast.

There is something freeing about being on my knees in front of his pain, offering myself like this. Making a promise that makes me feel so incredibly fragile and exposed.

But I know it's true.

I can't run out on Evan Brennon again and no matter what happens after this moment, I know there is nothing he can do that'll make me bolt.

I might need to find new coping strategies, but I can do that.

Because this strong, beautiful man needs me.

I see that now.

I bite my lip, wishing he'd say something, but I feel his gaze roam over every inch of my body and I'm all wet again.

My clit is throbbing for his touch.

"Thank you, beautiful girl." Evan falls to his knees in front of me, falls into a sort of cross-legged position and pulls me into the space, so my back is to his front. He slants his lips against mine and kisses me so tenderly, it almost makes me cry.

My belly rumbles with hunger.

Evan caresses my face. "Let's get lunch."

"That was the plan. I hope my investor isn't going to fire me."

"I think he can be persuaded to overlook one long lunch."

I love how dark his brown eyes are, how serious they are, how they're banked with heat, and that makes me feel wanted.

"I'm going to shower quickly," I say.

He helps me to my feet.

"Good idea." He nuzzles my neck.

I laugh and playfully swat him away. "Separate showers or this will turn into dinner."

"Fine. I guess I'll have to wait until tonight."

A shiver rolls down my back at the promise.

I brush his lips against mine. "Yes, you do."

"Go shower princess, before I change my mind." He slaps me gently on the behind.

I laugh, striding across the bedroom into the shower.

Even though I feel giddy and wanted and cherished, I push away the dark thought that is telling me Evan doesn't know everything about me.

And once he does...I push the thought away. I want to believe that he'll want me no matter what.

I furiously scrub my body, drowning out that thought, not letting myself feel remorse over the promise I gave him.

I'm not going to bolt.

And if he does, once he knows about my skeletons in the closet, well, that's on him.

But for the first time, I don't feel like my trust has been misplaced.

I know it's wild to think that we could have a relationship in such a short amount of time, but I can't keep pretending that what is between us doesn't exist.

I step out of the shower, dry off and from the closet, pick out a dark green dress with daises on it that hits my knee.

It's still cold out there, so I throw on a pair of leggings to complete my official look.

My phone rings and I reach for it. "Hi mom."

I turn at the choked laugh behind me, see Evan disappear into the shower.

"Hi Mara! I needed to hear your voice. We've been missing each other."

That's kind of on purpose on my part because I'm worried about spilling the secret to her.

"Yeah. How is the cruise?"

"It's amazing! Last night we saw this magician, and he was fabulous. How is everything there?"

"Good. I have new work." I don't know why I say it like that, but I forge on ahead. "I'm working somewhere new with Jenny."

"That's great! Do you have plans for the weekend?"

Valentine's Day.

I pace in the room, wondering how much to tell her.

She and I have always been close and while I don't want to hide anything from her, I'm not sure how to explain the fact that I'm in the private apartment of the city's most luxurious hotel with the owner of an acclaimed and infamous restaurant.

"Yes. I met someone."

That's the truth, at least.

"Mara! I'm so happy for you! So you're going out then?"

"Yeah. I mean, he might have to work, but...yes, I'm going out."

"I'm so happy for you! I don't want to bring you down, but I need to remind you to change the pin on your bank accounts, okay? One of my cards got flagged today. It might be because I'm out of the country or it might be—"

"My father," I sigh wearily.

The man never gives up, and that's not a good trait in an addict.

"Okay, I'll check."

"Good. I hope you have a wonderful Valentine's Day! Tell me all about it."

Obviously, I won't tell her everything, but I can't wait to share the vanilla highlights with her.

I love how happy she sounds.

"Give my love to Bryan."

"Of course! Bye!"

I set my phone down, sensing Evan behind me. He looks so sexy in that towel that I almost tell him to cancel whatever he has today so we can get back into bed.

Instead, I settle for running my hands down his tight pecs.

"That was my mom."

"Yeah? Did you tell her about me?"

"Not your name, not yet." I shrug.

"We'll have to have dinner with them when they get back," he kisses me. The smell of his soap tickles my nostrils.

"Tell me about your birthday bash."

Evan grins, drops the towel and strides over to his closet.

"It's just a little gathering my brothers have been planning for my thirty-fifth."

"What's little?" There is no way Evan is going to celebrate his birthday quietly.

"Friends from college, people I know in business, my brothers' friends, that sort of thing. You know, a party."

"Are your parents going to be there?" I tilt my head.

"No, you're going to meet them the weekend after."

"I am?"

He is so damn sexy as he pulls on a dress shirt. "You are." His lips graze my cheek.

"This is not the kind of party my parents want to be at."

"Okay, but now I'm worried."

"Don't be worried. Scared maybe." He grins and kisses me.

A high pitch tweet-tweet sound rings out.

"That's your doorbell?"

"Yep," Evan says, as he brushes by me to go get it.

I can't help but giggle.

"Trust me, it's better than the frogs Julian programmed when I first moved in." Evan has two paper bags in his hands. I take out plates and get utensils.

He sets the bags down on the counter, then grabs us water from the fridge.

We get busy unloading the cartons of Thai food he's ordered.

"My mom reminded me that it's Valentine's Day this weekend."

"It is? It slipped my mind." Evan waggles his eyebrows as he pierces a piece of chicken and holds it out to me.

My mouth opens, without any thought, and it scares me slightly how responsive I am to him.

But it's a good kind of scared and I go with it, my belly fluttering.

"What will the night look like at Sinful Bites?"

His shoulders tighten and he sighs. "You might be shocked to hear this, but it's a very busy night for the salacious restaurant. We are packed have a waiting list in the hundreds. I have a staff meeting tonight to go over final details, it's going to go late."

He grins wickedly at me. "But despite how packed it is, I love it. It's one hell of a party and I can't wait for you to see it. Each table gets whipped cream, strawberries, cherries, chocolate sauce, and champagne. It's a really good time."

"I can't wait. Wendy has asked me to design pieces for her sister's engagement party that's on Saturday."

"That's presumptuous of her to think you are free, isn't it?"

I shrug. "She knows I'm new and on my own. I did tell her it was short notice. I'm going to go into the studio early tomorrow and we're going to get the pieces done. All I have to do is deliver them to Wendy's."

"Good, I can't wait for you to spend Valentine's Day with me."

"It's a busy day for florists."

Alex, Marc and Suki can't give me any hours because they are working this weekend.

If I didn't have a new studio space, I would be doing that too.

The thought sends a slither of guilt through me. "Evan, we should talk about the studio."

"There's nothing to talk about. I expect you know how to run the business."

"Your confidence in me might be misplaced. I've never run a business before."

"You'll figure it out and I'm here to help, Mara. Do you need full-time staff?"

"Honestly, not until we are building the pieces. Ideally, I need an assistant, someone who can help me with the day-to-day stuff."

"Pick your assistant." Evan raises an eyebrow.

"You make this sound so easy."

"It is." Evan shrugs. "What's hard about it?"

"That you're financing it."

"Don't make me give you another spanking, Mara. I thought you were accepting this."

"I am." I take a nibble of food. "It's just in one swoop you made my dream come true."

"Good." Evan's dark eyes meet mine. "We'll have a sit down with Noel and someone from our business team. I'll get everything in writing for you."

My stomach forms a ball of knots. "I did write a business plan. Want to see it?"

Evan pushes away his plate. "Yes! Why didn't you tell me?"

"I don't know. I feel shy about it," I mumble.

But I bring up the plan on my phone and hand it to him.

I'm so strung tight as Evan taps a few keys, then picks up his iPad. "I sent it to myself. Cotter's Creations. I like it."

"It's dumb. I probably shouldn't go with it."

Especially if my mom got a ping on her card and it was to do with my dad.

"I needed to call it something at the time."

He puts up a hand to stop me and I feel like I'm waiting to be graded.

"This is the most concise plan I've seen in a long time. But you're going to need more money than you estimated. I don't think you're giving yourself enough credit, either."

"I wanted to be cautious."

Evan strides across the room, snakes his hand under my hair and kisses me, hard. "Be brave, Mara. With your boss's business falling apart, there is opportunity there. If you have that contact list, I would call everyone on it and tell them that you are up and running."

My cheeks flush because I hadn't thought of that.

"I'll have an initial document drawn up today stating that you own this business a hundred percent and I'm your investor. Any more questions?"

My stomach flutters. "You know...when I told you that rope was off the table?"

"Yeah?" Evan touches my shoulder.

"Can we...I mean, I want to try that with you."

"You're killing me, princess. If I didn't have to get back to work, I'd tie you up right now and give you so many orgasms you forget your name, but that's something for later. Anything else?"

"Were you serious about planning that primal scene?"

He leans in, his dark eyes piercing mine, and wraps a piece of hair around his finger and tugs. "Yes."

"Good. I want that."

"How am I supposed to get through my staff meeting?" he moans against my lips.

"I want to be surprised. And when it happens...I want anal."

"Damn princess," Evan presses against me. I feel his hard cock through his slacks and I cup his ass in my hands.

"You made me brave."

"I'm proud of you."

We kiss, hot and long, and I don't want to break away from him, but my phone buzzes and his rings out seconds later.

"Tonight, after the restaurant closes, be prepared for so many orgasms that your pussy is going to scream for mercy."

"Can't wait, Sir Evan."

"Good girl." He kisses me quickly once more and then pulls me up off the chair.

"Come on, we got to work. I guess."

"Because it makes us happy?"

"You make me happy, Mara."

My stomach is filled with happy, fluttering butterflies. "You make me happier."

"And tonight, I can't wait to make us both happy." Evan taps my behind, and I laugh.

I never thought that I would risk my heart or my trust again, but with Evan, it just feels right.

I have to silence the thoughts in my head that are telling me this is wrong.

I'm a consenting adult and I don't need anyone's permission. I roll those words in my head as Evan walks me to my car.

"See you tonight, princess."

"See you tonight."

But I can't shake the thought that if I trust him, then why didn't I tell him about my father? Is it only that I'd rather not talk about it, or is it because I think Evan will recoil?

I push the thoughts out of my head and go back to my work. I need to make my Sir proud.

21 EVAN

FEBRUARY 13TH

I plump up the pillows against the headboard.

Nerves make me feel jittery. I want this night to be special for Mara.

I can't take her out on Valentine's Day tomorrow, but I can show her how much I want her, how much she is meant to be mine tonight.

On a side table, coils of rope ready to go, next to a pair of safety scissors because you can never be too careful.

A new vibe is next to the pile, and I can't wait to use it on my princess.

I click on music, a soft jazz fills the space.

Perfect for the sultry, slow, seductive tone I want to create this evening.

Moving to the kitchen, careful not to step on the paper red hearts that I have strewn from the doorway to the bedroom, I set out two wine glasses, next to the uncorked bottle and check my reflection in the toaster

I know, big ass mirror in the bedroom, but I'm here and I feel as nervous as I did when I asked the older sister of the next-door neighbour out when I was fifteen.

That's only memorable because the door was slammed in my face and it was my first rejection.

I glance at my watch and pick up my phone

I know today has been busy for Mara, as it was just her and Jenny in the studio getting the pieces done and ready to be delivered tomorrow.

Mara's alarm had gone off earlier than usual.

I made her coffee while she showered and only managed a quick kiss before she dashed out the door. I'm starting to wonder if she got caught up or if the car of hers had something fail when I hear the soft beep of the door.

"You look beautiful." I kiss her cheek and take her bags.

Mara laughs, shakes her head and gestures to herself.

"I feel like I've been run over by a moose. There is nothing beautiful about this." She motions to her yoga pants and a torn oversized T-shirt.

"There is plenty beautiful. There's no moose in sight." I lean in, fisting her hair and kissing her, burning with need.

"I missed you."

"I missed you, too, Sir Evan."

She knows just what to say to make my dick hard, and she wraps her arms around my neck and pulls me down for another kiss.

"I'm all set up for you. Unless you want to skip the play tonight and watch a movie instead?" I run my knuckles along her jaw.

She looks down, noticing the floor.

"Hearts!" Mara grins and clutches my hand. "You did that for me?

Thank you."

"I know you're busy tomorrow during the day and you know tomorrow night is impossible for me to have free time, so I thought I'd show you some Valentine's Day tonight."

"Aww! Sir Evan!"

Her smile makes her eyes sparkle like blue diamonds.

My heart can't stop jumping around my chest.

Still holding hands, I led her into the kitchen and pull out a chair for her.

"I'm a little tired, but there's no way I want to skip play. I'm dying to find out what you have planned."

"All in good time." I pour the wine and clink her glass to mine.

"Cheers to you, Mara."

"Cheers to us," she counters and stifles a yawn.

I laugh, running my hand through her hair. "I don't care what we do as long as you're with me."

"No, I'm okay. I feel better being home. Let me go freshen-up."

"Good. The scene starts as soon as you are out of the bathroom. Forget the clothes."

I am grinning so wide my face hurts.

Home.

She said home and I don't think she noticed or maybe she didn't mean it in that way, but I don't care, that's the way I am taking it.

While Mara's in the bathroom, I double check that everything's in place and wait for her, standing in the doorway of the sitting room.

"Ready, Sir Evan."

"Good, princess. You requested rope?"

"I did." Her hand brushes along my chest and a shiver rolls through me.

"Have you had a bad experience with rope before?"

Mara's cheeks flush and she glances down, then up. "No. But you know, most pictures of women in rope are ones who are strong and thin and I don't begrudge them that...the couple of times I tried it, it didn't go well and I could never see myself that beautiful like the picture I had in my head. But you make me feel different."

"Yeah?" My lips are on hers, quick and fast. She's standing on her toes, kissing me with the same passion I feel.

She breaks off the kiss.

"Yeah. you make me feel beautiful."

"Mission accomplished. Let me escort you to the bed, princess," I loop my arm through hers, and she giggles as I walk her into the bedroom.

"Oh."

I'm looking in the mirror and I see the splotch of colour appear on her chest, the slow wide smile as she takes in the rope and the bed.

"This is soft." she runs her hand along the waterproof blanket I had ordered a few days ago.

"I want to make you squirt again." I cup her ass, squeezing hard enough to make her yelp.

"I don't know if that's possible," Mara laughs.

"Anything's possible."

"I like the colour of the ropes." She picks up the blue coil and the purple coil.

"Variety is good. Are you ready?"

"Yes, Sir."

"Up on the bed. I want you to lie on your back. That's it, good girl.

Picking up a length of blue rope, I start by wrapping it around her ankle, then pushing it as close as I can get it to her thigh.

"Is that comfortable?"

"It's fine, Sir."

I bend in, kissing above the rope.

I drag my tongue along her skin while holding her ankle.

She laughs.

I keep kissing up to her thigh, then follow with the rope, getting it nice and high on her thigh.

I take the rope up her leg, then wrap it again and once more so that it's secure.

"How are you feeling?"

"Good, Sir Evan. I like it," Mara touches my arm, makes my cock twitch.

From the top of her thighs, over the rope, I brush my lips over every bare inch of skin.

Then I move to the inside of her leg, making another wrap with the rope.

Pausing, I check that the tension on the rope is enough, that the rope isn't going to roll off her knee.

I work down her leg, making a series of hitches, and the end result is amazing. I eagerly pick up another coil and start working on her right leg.

I kiss the inside of her thighs. She giggles.

"If you don't stay still, I can't complete this tie."

My admonishment only makes her giggle more, so I pull tightly on the rope, working quickly to finish this tie, and when I reach her foot, I tickle it.

"Hey! Not fair! Oh my god, stop, Sir Evan!"

"Are you going to stop giggling when I tie you?" I drop a kiss to the top of her foot.

"No. Not at all."

"I guess you're going to have to pay the consequences then." I give her foot one more tickle.

"Okay! Okay! I'll be good next time."

"I'm going to hold you to that." I pat her foot, then move so that I am beside her on the bed, with another coil of rope in my hands.

"Mara, look at yourself in the mirror."

She glances at me. I give her a nod of encouragement.

"Oh."

"Tell me what you see."

"I see my huge body flopped on a bed. My legs are tied," her voice trembles, she glances away.

"You mean, you see your *gorgeous* body placed on the bed."

She swallows. "Evan...I know what I look like."

"Yes. I love your curves."

"Seeing myself in the mirror..."

"What, princess?'

She shakes her head. "'Huge' is the first word that came to my mind."

"Let me give you others," I cup her breast and squeeze it. "Spectacular. Stunning. Goddess."

Mara laughs. "You do make me feel like a goddess."

"And I'm going to worship you like one. Can you move your legs?"

"No. I'm immobilized." Mara gives me an exasperated look; I laugh, and my fingers dancing along her inner thighs.

"Yes. What else do you see?"

"My pussy," she spits the word out.

"Exactly. I have complete access to your pussy. But first, I'm going to do something about these breasts." I drag a rope across her boobs, trailing kisses as I continue to lay the rope.

She moans low in her throat.

I gently help her sit up, popping a pillow behind her back, and I start the chest harness by wrapping the rope under her breasts.

For extra support, I make another circuit.

Her breasts are now on spectacular display, the rope between them.

"It's pretty," Mara brushes her fingers on the rope, tracing to where it stops, above her hips.

"Yes, it lets me do this to your breasts." I sit beside her and draw her nipple into my mouth. I suck and lavish it until Mara is twisting from side to side.

I hook my hand under the rope, pulling gently.

"Sir Evan!"

"I love this so much." I draw a circle with my tongue on the top of her other breast, before sucking on her nipple, I flick my tongue along the tip, and then I dip my hand between her legs, lightly pinching her labia.

"Ah! Damn," Mara cries out, and I laugh.

I work my way down her body, kissing the soft rolls of her stomach, brushing my cheek along the top of her inner thighs until reaching her pussy.

It's already glistening.

My heart drums in anticipation. Bracing my hands lightly on her knees, I drag my tongue in her pussy, sucking her clit.

I can feel a tremor roll through her tied legs, and I keep going, amping up my pace.

Her pussy is so fragrant and her taste is so succulent. I don't want to stop.

But I want to stick to my plan.

I give her pussy one more long lap of my tongue before pulling out and grinning at her.

Her eyes are closed, her breasts are heaving and Mara in my bed like this is the most beautiful sight.

"You stopped."

"Only for a moment." I pick up the vibe and show it to her. "It's supposed to be silent, and it has lots of settings. Let's test it out."

I lube it, then set it against her pussy, starting off on the lowest setting.

"What does that feel like?"

"Kind of irritating. I need more."

"You want more?" I tilt my head.

"Yes! Please give me more, Sir Evan!"

"Well, since you asked so nicely," I press down on the highest setting and muffle a laugh as Mara throws her head back.

"Too much!"

I keep it going for a moment, sliding it in and out of her pussy, moving it higher and lower in her channel, before switching to a middle setting, a wave.

"Ah! That's so much better,"

I watch her toes, realizing her legs aren't going to be able to flex tied up like this.

Her head starts to roll back and I switch to the lowest setting.

"Mean!"

"Thank you!" I laugh.

Her blue eyes smoulder with heat and a dash of irritation, and it's so damn sexy.

I lean in and bite her inner thigh while thumbing the vibe to the highest setting.

Her screech bounces off the walls.

Tossing the vibe to the side, I cover her mouth with mine and kiss her until I am so hard I have to be in her or I'm the one who is going to squirt all over the blanket.

"Give me another when I am deep in you, princess."

"Yes Sir," Mara whispers.

I shove my pants off, settle between her legs, and looping my fingers through the ropes on her legs, I pull her even further apart.

"Oh!"

"Do you like that?"

"Yes!"

"Good."

With one thrust, I am so deep in her pussy, that I could come in her right the hell now, but I hold off, pulling on the ropes, in time to my thrusts.

Mara lets out a low rumble and I slow down, giving one slow thrust, moving my hips and dragging my cock through her pussy.

She whimpers.

And I do it again.

One more dive into her until I can't take it and I pound her so hard I can feel every inch of her hot pussy.

"Please, Sir Evan."

Like lightning, I come so fast and hard, the room spins in my vision.

"Mara," I exhale her name and stay right where I am, feeling her pussy quiver around my softening cock.

Knowing Mara didn't come, I settle between her legs, lean down and lick her hard clit, tasting myself on her.

I would eat anything covered with her juices.

Her fingertips reach for me, and I grab them as I flick her clit with my tongue. At her long mewl, I suction my mouth over that sweet spot.

She whimpers, moans, twists.

I keep it up, until my tongue feels raw.

Moving my mouth from her pussy, I kiss her stomach, her breasts, before coming to her lips.

"Good girl."

She kisses me long and hard, swallowing on my tongue, and I know that there is nothing I won't do for this woman.

"You made me a mess, again."

"I did? I don't think you squirted."

"We can work up to it," she grins.

"You bet, princess. I'm going to clean up. Your breasts look so good I don't want to take you out of this." I roll my palm against her nipples.

Mara yawns.

She glances at me and laughs, and I laugh too, and then we're giggling like crazy with each other.

I lay my head on her stomach, my fingers entwined with hers.

"I'm going to get you out of these ropes. We're going to clean up and watch that movie."

"That's perfect, Sir."

"You're perfect, my goddess." I kiss her and feel like I'm dreaming because I've never been as happy as I am right now with Mara.

22 MARA

FEBRUARY 14TH

"Mara, these are stunning, way beyond my expectations." Wendy Svennson beams at me.

I blush at the gushing praise and stand, brushing debris off my knees.

Thankfully, the mild weather has continued and I'm not installing a sculpture in the snow.

"Thank you. I hope they brighten your party."

"They're the conversation piece, for sure. Wow, I'm so glad I said yes to this party just to have these. This one is beautiful, but the forest on the dining room table is my favourite.

"Jenny worked on that one" I gesture to Jenny who is twisting a piece of wire on the point of the starburst.

"Mara is the one with the vision. I only executed it. I've never made a half moon out of flowers before, but it was fun," Jenny says. "I'd love as many pictures as you can send."

"Count on it!" Wendy says.

"Mara, your phone is going to be so busy, I hope you're prepared." Wendy touches my shoulder.

"I moved into the new studio just in time. I can't wait."

"Are you sure I can't persuade you to stay? Both of you?"

I bite my lip, not wanting to be rude, but I don't want to stay.

"What am I even thinking? Of course you don't want to stay! It's Valentine's Day. Go and enjoy. I will send you pictures."

"Thank you, Wendy. Have a great time tonight!"

Wendy rolls her eyes. "I know I should be happy but ugh, nevermind!" Wendy gives a wave and disappears into the house.

Jenny and I exchange a glance and laugh.

We start packing up the tools and I snap several pics of the brightly coloured starburst.

I know it might not be the first thing you think of when you hear "magic," but I needed to do something fast and simple.

The unicorn pieces that are inside, along with Jenny's tabletop sculpture, complete the theme.

Besides, Wendy approved the sketches, and she loves the end result. Keeping my client happy is what matters.

"That was so much fun. Wendy is so much shorter in real life," Jenny says. Picking up a toolbox and carrying it to my car.

"She surprised me the first time I met her in person." I smile, taking the toolbox from her and putting in the trunk with the others.

Jenny shuffles her feet, glances down at me. "I'm sure you have plans, but do you want to grab lunch?"

I close the trunk and turn to her.

I don't have plans right now.

Evan texted me earlier to wish me a happy Valentine's Day and that he'd see me tonight, so beyond going back to the studio, I'm free.

"I could do lunch," I tell her.

We had been going at it since seven this morning.

"What about the noodle house on Dunsmuir Street?"

"Yes, perfect! See you there."

Jenny waves and gets in her car.

My phone buzzes while I'm driving with a text from my sister-in-law with a bunch of heart emojis.

I hum as I drive, knowing that I'm going to have to tell my family about Evan sooner rather than later.

Nerves settle low in my belly, but it's the excited kind.

I know they'll be happy for me and Miranda will want all the details.

I can't help but grin huge, thinking of the details I'm going to keep to myself.

I park next to Jenny's car and get out.

"Thanks for doing this," Jenny says.

"Lunch is a good idea." I hold the door open for her and then step into the tiny restaurant.

It smells amazing and my stomach is rumbling, telling me I need more than a half a bagel and a yoghurt cup.

We find a table by the window in the back and sit across from each other.

A waiter comes over with water and menus.

"Matt is working late tonight. I guess I wanted to celebrate the first job I did that wasn't with the Wilsons."

"Cheers to that," I say, clinking my water glass against hers.

Jenny smiles, flipping her blonde hair off her shoulder. "I'm so happy for you, Mara. The new studio is incredible."

"Thanks." I smile back, but inside I still can't shake the feeling that

I don't deserve this, that it's too much.

We order and I check my phone.

"How are things with you and Evan?" Jenny asks with a smirk. "Oh, you don't have to tell me if you don't want to!"

"Considering I've seen you half naked, I think we're beyond that."

She covers her mouth with her hand and blushes. "True. So how are they?"

I laugh. "Good. Really good. I feel like I'm in a dream."

Jenny takes a sip of water. "I kind of felt like that with Matt. I couldn't trust that it was real. Do you know I've been married twice before?"

I shake my head. "No, I didn't know that."

"I'm surprised Sabrina didn't blab about it."

I knew Jenny was a year or two older than me, but ever since I first met her, she and Matt have been an item.

"Yeah, I swore I'd never be with someone again until I met Matt. Sabrina introduced us, so I have her to thank for that. To Sabrina." Jenny lifts her glass in a mock toast.

"To Sabrina," I echo.

"I kind of miss her."

I laugh. "Yeah, she has a kind of magnetic field."

Our food arrives and we dig in.

"What made you trust Matt?"

"When he kept trying. I don't know. I guess when he didn't do anything that I couldn't trust, you know? I kept waiting for him to be a jerk and it didn't happen."

"I kind of feel like that with Evan. Like it's too good to be true."

Somehow, saying the words out loud, it feels like a relief, but it also feels like what I have been telling myself isn't true.

I think back to seeing his ex in the café and tell myself that having money isn't everything. Emotional stability counts for a lot.

"I've seen how that man looks at you, Mara, and he thinks he's the lucky one."

"Maybe we're both lucky."

"That's the spirit. Thanks for giving me a job."

"It's not a proper job, at least not yet."

A wave of guilt washes over me because I still haven't chosen an assistant.

Jenny's great, but I know Suki really wants something new and before I ran into Jenny at Sinful Bites, I had Suki in mind.

"I am happy we pulled off these sculptures for Wendy. We'll see if the phone rings from her clients."

"I know it will," Jenny says.

We eat and finish and walk out with each other.

"Thanks for lunch," she says.

"It was nice." I smile.

I give her a hug. "Happy Valentine's Day. I'm sure you have plans for when Matt comes home."

"Beer and pizza. It's kind of our tradition."

She gives me a wave and I get in my car.

It's nice to have someone waiting for you at home and my butterflies flutter again, thinking of Evan.

23 EVAN

Celebration days, like Valentine's Day, are simultaneously easy and hard.

It's easy because it's a fixed menu. Everyone is excited to be here, and if ever there was a restaurant made to celebrate this day, it's Sinful Bites.

It's hard, because people, with all their imperfections, don't cease to stop being imperfectly human because it's a holiday and they've dressed up for the evening.

Customer expectations on a night like this are at an all-time high and sometimes impossible to meet.

"How can I help you?" I stop at a table in the middle row.

A woman has her sub's head in her lap and she's feeding him cherries while pulling on a nipple clamp.

"The table next to us? The man's ass keeps bumping into my sub's."

I school my face into a mask of calm but stifle a laugh.

The tables are so far apart that it's unlikely this is happening how she's describing it.

If she was seated at the communal table, she might have a case.

When I said we were going to have communal spaces, everyone thought I was nuts, but they have always been booked solid.

It's amazing how many kinky friend groups there are.

"Well, what do you suggest we do?"

The woman raises her eyebrows at me.

"Isla, you have to cause drama wherever you go," the woman at the next table says.

Her sub is kneeling beside her on a cushion, eating off of a plate.

"Ignore her. She just wants Liam back but he's never coming back to that old trash, is he?" The Domme at the neighbouring table says, lifting her sub's head.

"No, ma'am."

"Well, I don't want to see him," Isla says.

"Would you like to move tables?"

It'd be a nightmare for my head server Dawn, but we'd come up with a solution.

"No. I don't want to see him." The woman glances away.

"Ma'am. If I may?" Her sub says.

"Go ahead," Isla nods her permission.

"Maybe we could invite them to join us and then you can control what parts of him you see?"

"Why would I want to do that?" Isla's voice breaks.

The sub puts a hand on her leg. "You and him were together for seven years."

The woman's face crumbles and the other Domme rushes over. "Isla, we could have worked this out if you just admitted you wanted Liam and missed him. Cat told me you booked tonight after hearing we did."

I feel a presence behind me, turn with a smile to my server, Alli, and hand them a box of tissues

"Thank you…I'm sorry I just…today was hard."

"Please let me know if there is anything we can get you."

The other Domme nods and a second later, they are hugging each other.

I leave them to their conflict resolution.

The first seating is almost finished when Dawn comes and gets me at the bar, where I'm filling a champagne bucket.

"Mr. Brennon ."

I hear her, but my attention is entirely focused on the irresistible woman that walked in the door.

She's wearing the purple corset I left out for her and a matching leather skirt.

Mara glances around the room and even from here, I catch the deep blush on her face as something at the nearest table causes her to react.

She strides toward me and I step away from the bar and kiss her.

The patrons closest to us notice and we get a chorus of claps.

"Hello, princess."

"Hi Sir Evan. The place looks amazing."

"You look amazing." I kiss her cheek as she shakes her head at me.

"Mr. Brennon ."

Dawn is now standing at my shoulder.

"Apologies Dawn I got carried away."

She smiles. "I can see that. Alli had to leave. I tried calling our standbys and nobody answered."

"Either they had plans or found a shift somewhere else. With three more seatings to go, it's a tough night to be understaffed, but we can do it."

Dawn doesn't look convinced, but I know our staff can handle it.

"I can help." Mara squeezes my arm.

My heart legitimately flutters at her offer.

"Mara, it's going to get so busy here. This is the slowest it's going to be." I rub her shoulder.

She shrugs. "This is not a time to sit and look pretty. Put me to work."

"Great!" Dawn loops her arm through Mara's.

"Mara." I reach out for her arm.

Her brows furrow, her lips part, and I press a finger to them before she can speak.

"Thank you."

She gives me that smile I want to see every morning of every day. "I'm happy to help."

"I'll walk you through the seating plan and what you need to know. I hope you're a quick learner," Dawn says.

"I'll do my best," Mara promises.

I'm smiling so wide my cheeks hurt as I make my way through the restaurant chatting to guests, checking on everyone.

By the time all the whip cream bowls are empty and Isla is leaving with her arms around both subs, Mara looks like she'd been doing this forever.

She said goodbye to the guests, pitched in busing tables.

We all pitched in, clearing and resetting for seating number two.

This group were rowdy, high-spirited kinksters who had their subs crawl across the communal table.

Their antics had all of us in stitches. That table clean up took a lot of time, but it was worth it

It's nights like this where I am so grateful I rolled the dice.

Seating number three was more quiet, but everything would be after that and I got to steal a moment, kissing Mara before I checked on the guests in the dining room.

A Dom was using his sub as a table and eating off of her with a knife and fork. A couple across from them were locked into a hushed conversation.

"Is everything alright?" I ask, pausing at their table.

"Yes, it's fine," the woman says to me, but her lips press together in a thin line of disapproval.

"Tell him," the man urges, grabbing her arm.

"Is everything okay with the food?" I try to ease into it.

"Yes, the food is fine." The woman says.

"The food isn't the problem but the booze is—"

The woman ducks her head against the man's arm.

"Sarah, I had to tell him. In our booking we requested alcohol free and yet we have the champagne right here."

"I'm so sorry about that. Let me take it away." I grab the champagne.

I know the damage has already been done.

The man's face is red.

"Would you like to come back another, right?" I offer.

"Please Bay, can we stay? I'm fine, really." Sarah dipped her finger in the whipped cream. "I want you to play with me tonight" She sticks her finger in his mouth and he sucks.

"Please accept my apologies and let me know if there is anything I can do to make this up." I say, backing out of the room, but the couple is so entrenched that I'm not sure they've heard me.

Making my way to the bar, I stop. Dawn must have caught the look on my face and hurries over.

"What's wrong Mr Brennon ?"

"Guests requested that their table did not have alcohol but there was this—" I hold up the champagne, "—at their table."

"Oh no I'm so sorry!" Dawn's face pales.

I know how hard she works, and I'd be lost without her.

"It's okay. Don't sweat it," I say.

I spot Mara across, laughing with two women, and my heart skips a beat

"She's doing great." Dawn winks at me before rushing away to another table that needed attention.

The rush passed, and I took a moment, leaning against the bar, watching Mara flutter from table to table. She never stops, whether it was to get a package of baby wipes to a table, a drink refill, or to clear a plate.

You'd never know she was up so early.

I realize I've never had this kind of energy in a partner before.

The women I've been with have waited for me to do things for them or expected me to take care of them.

Partly because it's in my nature to care and protect but also, and most often, for my money.

Is it odd to say that seeing Mara work the restaurant reminds me of my mother and how she'd go to inventor conventions with my dad and help him work his booth?

I don't care, because I have never been more sure than I am at this moment that Mara is the woman I've always wanted.

I can't wait to tell her how I feel.

There's a small part of me, a tiny wobble in my confidence that wonders if she'll reject me, but she's worth the risk.

But I want to make it special

My pulse races, thinking of the scene I had planned.

Whatever it takes, I'm going to show her that she is mine.

24 MARA

"What a night." Evan drapes an arm around me as the elevator doors open to his floor.

"It was epic."

My feet are aching, my back is sore and my calves are screaming, but being part of the Sinful Bites Valentine's Day event is something I'll remember forever.

The restaurant was dripping with love and romance and consensual kink and I'm so happy I got to experience it.

"You're amazing," he cups my nape, pulls me in for a kiss against the door.

His kiss gives me a burst of energy and my body heats with desire.

I kiss him back, hungrily, feeling so dizzy with need.

Evan breaks the kiss and lets us inside.

He hangs up his blazer, unbuttons his dress shirt and I take off my flats.

"Thank you for helping."

"Your well-oiled machine would have been fine. It was fun."

He takes two steps and I back up against the wall.

"Mara, you pitching in means the world to me."

My breath catches in my throat as he drags the knuckle of his index finger along my jaw, over my neck, and brushes his lips against mine.

Never has a man made me feel so wanted.

So treasured.

"Can you help me get my corset off?"

He smiles, steps back. "It'd be my pleasure."

I turn around, giving him my back, gasping as he slides his hands up either side of my body.

With deliberate slowness, Evan unlaces it and I exhale, feeling the fabric lift from my breasts.

"There." He cups my breast, pulls me tight against him, and I feel his hard erection.

"I don't know how you are still standing, marathon woman."

"Pure exhilaration." I let out a little yelp as he squeezes my nipples.

"You deserve bed." His voice is deep and sultry.

My nipples pebble under his touch.

"I'm not tired." The yawn that stretches my face large enough to eat an octopus says that I'm lying.

"You deserve breakfast in bed." He slightly slaps my bottom. "Come on, time to tuck you in, princess."

"If you insist."

His arm slung around me makes me feel all liquidy inside.

In the bedroom, he unfastens my skirt and helps me step out of it.

He undresses, and I run my hands along his warm wall of muscles.

"You know what else you deserve?" He captures my wrists in his big hands.

"What?" I tilt my head to my shoulder.

"Orgasms."

"What about sleep?"

"I guess you could have some. Only after I give you an orgasm."

I kiss him back, loving his taste, loving the feel of his lips so familiar to me.

"You were phenomenal tonight, really Mara."

"It was nothing."

"You being there means the world to me."

He kisses me and lowers me to the bed.

"The bed feels good."

He flops down beside me, making the pillows bounce.

"Yeah. But I promised you a reward, princess. I will never break a promise to you. You're my Valentine today and always."

My throat closes up, I blink away tears. I know he means every word.

My heart beats like a steel drum.

I want to reach for him, to say something back that equals the magnitude of his declaration, but I'm too overwhelmed by the pure emotion that grips me.

"Sweet Mara." He braces himself over me, stares into my eyes and I turn my head, to escape his intensity.

I clench my hands at my side and swallow. What he feels, I feel it too.

There has never been a man where I have felt so comfortable being naked in front of.

Where I have felt free to share my thoughts and emotions with.

Where I know admitting my kinks isn't going to be met with a look of disgust but a wicked smile.

He leans down and sucks my nipple into his mouth.

It sets off a wave of need and a fresh pool of liquid between my legs.

His hot mouth is sealed around my nipple.

He sucks and laps. I squirm under him, almost ready to come right this instant.

He switches breasts, his dark stare never leaving mine.

He flicks his tongue against my nipple and just as I'm settling into that sensation, he lifts his head, and drops a trail of kisses along my stomach, gently across my folds, down to between my legs.

"Evan!" My hands are on his head as he licks my pussy, long and slow, as if we have all the time in the world. But I want what he's offering.

Even if it makes me selfish, I want all that he's offering.

I press his head down, urging him on.

His soft chuckle sends a fluttering vibration through my whole body.

I am so primed, that it only takes one more flick of his tongue, and I am sent soaring into an orgasm so strong, I feel like I am floating.

His mouth hasn't moved, and he's sucking my clit, his tongue moving so quickly, I am trying to catch my breath but before I can, another orgasm ripples through me, I drop my grasp from his hair and lay back, closing my eyes in the sea of hot pleasure rolling through me.

"Good girl, Mara." He gently covers me with a blanket and slips in beside me, laying his head on my shoulder.

"You don't know everything about me," my voice breaks.

"I know that you don't like mushrooms." He kisses my chin. "I know that you are a talented floral designer." He kisses my lips. "I know that you are grumpy without your coffee in the morning."

"Am not." I laugh, the protest ringing hollow.

"I know that you love your friends and family. I know that you work hard and you don't trust easily. I know that you have the bluest eyes I've ever seen." He laces his fingers through mine, bringing our joined hands to his lips. "And I know I'm going to spend the rest of my life learning what I don't know about you. You are mine, Mara."

I want to deny it, but I can't.

Because I want this so much and I can't deny that what is between us is good and solid and real.

"You're mine, too," I whisper.

His slow smile is like the sun breaking, it shows off his dimples.

He reaches for my hand and I snuggle against him, wanting to luxuriously wallow in this perfect moment.

In case when I tell him what he doesn't know, it shatters.

I watch his eyes drift closed and try to take this warm gooey feeling and hold it close, hoping it's enough to stop it from being shattered.

25 EVAN

FEBRUARY 15TH

Mara's alarm blares in the darkness at the usual ungodly hour.

I feel her shift beside me and I pull her back against me, her soft, curvy body all cozy against mine.

"You don't have to go anywhere, princess." I nuzzle her ear.

She giggles. "I have to shut off the alarm."

The alarm continues its blare with increasing loudness.

I brush my lips across her neck. "What do you have against sleep?"

She pulls away from me, to reach for the offending noise maker that is her phone, sets it down on the nightstand and comes back against my chest.

"We've talked about this before. I'm an early bird."

"But why deny yourself the wonderful option of the snooze button?" My hands roam along her back, over her soft rolls, sliding between her legs.

"You should thank my alarm," Mara says, arching her hips against my soft touch along her inner thigh. "If it hadn't gone off, we wouldn't be doing this,"

Slowly, I draw a circle on her inner thigh, then work my hand up to her breast. I give it a squeeze, loving the sharp intake of her breath.

Her nipple pebbles to a hardened point under my touch.

"And what is this?"

She turns her head to kiss me, her soft lips bruising against mine.

I fist her hair to deepen the kiss, and I groan at the sweet taste of her, the way she echoes my sound with a low gravely moan of her own.

"Waking up."

"It's an excellent way to wake-up." I toss the blankets off, to Mara's laughing protest, then I scoop one arm around her.

"What are you doing?"

"Putting you where I want you." I gently bite her shoulder, tumble her over and she catches on. A moment later she has her head at the bottom of the bed, and I'm straddling her hips, my erection rock-hard.

I look from her face to the mirror.

"I want to wake up like this every morning," I tell her, studying how her breasts spill to the side, her hair mussed from sleep.

"If you want to wake up like this every morning, I need to set my alarm earlier." Mara's fingertips dance down my pecs, to my waist, where she grabs my butt.

"Yeah? It'd be worth it."

I kiss her, hard and rough. I'm setting the tone for later and I want to see how she'll react.

She doesn't disappoint, kissing me back with the same roughness, pulling at my bottom lip with her teeth.

I laugh. "You get the game, princess."

"Yes." She raises her hips under mine, as if she's trying to dislodge me.

I grab both her wrists in my hand, pinning them above her head. "Don't move."

Her blue eyes widen, as I line up with her entrance, and glide into her scorching heat.

Her pussy flutters around my cock.

"Hold on baby, this is going to be hard and fast."

"Good." Mara raises her hips.

I close my eyes as her pussy clenches around my hard length and I rock my hips so quickly the bed bounces under us.

Cries rip from her throat, as I set the pace pounding and quick, sweat already breaking across my brow, my balls tightening so heavy and full.

"Oh god, Evan!" She grips me, almost scratching me, but I see how she bites her lips, as if she's trying to stop herself. My heart thuds as I pound into her, wrapping an arm around her hips, getting even more access to her pussy.

Her submission, her openness, her willingness to go where I lead her, all of these things are so damn precious to me and it's all there in the air between us.

It's intense, but it's mingled with a familiarity, an acceptance. I'm going to have my way with her and she's going to let me.

Her trust is so heady, and I know I am not going to last much longer.

"Give me your orgasm, you needy goddess."

I lean down, nuzzling the side of her neck with my teeth, feeling her pussy tighten around my cock. I see in the mirror her head tilt back, giving me that graceful neck. Her body tenses under mine.

She lets out a long mewl, the sound so sweet it vibrates through my body.

I see her toes curl. "Yes, now, baby."

Mara cries out as her orgasm breaks over her, making her eyes close, her body softening as pleasure ripples through her body.

"Good girl, that's it," I thrust through her aftershocks.

I thrust, and want to stay in her heat forever, but I can't hold back.

I come so hard my head swims in white fire, the room spins.

"Damn princess. Better than any workout." My lips fuse with her, and her hands glide down my back.

"I like waking up like this, too."

"Good." I kiss her again and her phone buzzes for attention.

With great reluctance, I withdraw from her heat.

"I'm going to grab a quick shower and make breakfast. I'll leave you to your phone."

"I guess someone wants my attention." She sits, reaching for her phone.

I catch the smile on her face, her eyes widening in amazement.

"I can't believe this. Wendy posted the pieces I did for her party on her socials and my phone is blowing up with all these tags. I have a request to meet with a friend of hers today."

I am super happy for Mara, but that's not why I am grinning huge. I wasn't sure what to do with her while I set up our scene, but this is perfect.

"You're going to take it, right?"

"Yes! I'm going to reply and tell them I'll meet them at the studio at one."

"Good. I'm happy for you." I drop a kiss on her forehead.

"Thanks, Evan. this wouldn't have happened if you hadn't given me the space."

"This success is all yours, princess." I whistle as I make my way into the shower, immensely satisfied that the little help I gave Mara has paid off.

***

When I'm dressed and out of the shower, I start making breakfast and once I have it nearly finished, I call Noel.

He answers after four rings. "Evan? Is everything okay?"

"Yeah. Why?"

"This is kind of early for you."

I smile at my older brother's dry tone.

"I already have coffee. Had breakfast."

"How did the Valentine's Day dinner go last night?" I hear Holly's voice in the background, Noel's mumbled reply.

A sharp pain of jealousy circulates through my blood.

I want what they have so badly; the passion and the mundane of the domestic.

Then I remember the shell of a brother I had after his first wife died and feel like a complete ass for being jealous.

"Fantastic. Sorry you guys missed it." I can't keep sitting down.

I stand, pacing in front of the windows.

"Evan, are you going to tell me what this breakfast phone call is about?"

Noel always knows when I have something on my mind.

"I am very serious about Mara," I say.

And I wince because it sounds like we are discussing the year-end reports.

"I like her so much, Noel."

"I'd be a hypocrite if I said that was fast."

"Much slower than you and Holly. We at least had one date before this week." I can't help but grin, remembering Noel's advice.

"So what are you going to do about it?"

That's Noel, right to the next point of action.

"I thought I'd put a ring on her finger." I glance behind me, even though I'm keeping my voice down and I know Mara's in the shower.

Noel whistles. "Congratulations. You're going to make mom and dad so happy and the other two are going to be seething with jealousy."

"I was kind of jealous when I heard Holly's voice," I admit.

Noel laughs. "Theo has to take a chance with this Callie girl."

I know Theo had a long term relationship that didn't work out and it nearly left him as wounded as I was but I didn't get all the details.

Our younger brother is private, but I've long suspected Noel knows what happened with Theo.

"I guess we're setting an example."

"It's our duty as the older ones," Noel says.

I hear the smile in his voice and I laugh. "I'm happy it worked out for you. I'm going to bring Mara to your wedding."

"I can't wait to meet her. We'll be there for your birthday bash."

"Yeah, I can't wait for the party."

Noel chuckles. "I got to let you go. I'm taking Holly to a matinee play."

"Talk to you later."

"Yep. And Evan? Go get your girl."

I laugh and hang up.

In the kitchen, I put the finishing touches on breakfast. Mara is a tidy person, which matches my style of things nicely. As much as the idea of breakfast in bed is a romantic one, I know that crumbs on the bed sheets would bother her.

I'm humming as I cook, and I am so happy, it's ridiculous.

I hear Mara in the bathroom and rush over to the door.

"Good morning, princess," I offer the tray.

She giggles. "A hairbrush in a vase?"

"It's for curly hair." There is a sudden ball of nerves in my gut as Mara sets the tray down on the bed and picks up the brush.

"Besides not being fond of flowers, I figure giving a floral designer a rose is like..."

"Giving a shoemaker shoes?" Mara says.

"Yes." I drop a kiss on her cheek.

She runs it through a part of her hair while staring in the mirror.

"Thank you, Sir Evan." She smiles, her eyes lit with pleasure.

"You're welcome. Come, let me feed you."

"You always want to feed me."

I grab her chin and crash my lips over hers.

As our lips touch, I sigh. The taste of her is so sweet, so familiar and one that I absolutely need.

"May I escort you to your post-Valentine's Day breakfast?" I dramatically offer her my arm.

Mara giggles. "You may."

"I love how this silky robe shows off your boobs."

"You really like my boobs."

"Yeah," I start nibbling her. She playfully swats me away.

"What about breakfast?"

"Fine, but you're going to be dessert later."

Mara's high musical laugh rings out as we make our way to the kitchen.

"You cooked all this?"

"Yep. French toast casserole, frittata, bacon and fresh orange juice." I mock bow.

"Perfect." Mara pours herself a glass of orange juice.

Her phone buzzes on the counter. She picks it up, frowns, sets it down.

"Still being inundated with how wonderful you are?"

Her sparkling laughter fills the space. "I can't believe the response."

"You deserve it, Mara."

She looks away from me.

"Hey, we've been over this." I grab her chin with my fingers, tilting her head to me.

"Say it."

She bites her lip, and long seconds stretch between us.

"I deserve it."

"Good girl." I reward her with a slow kiss.

Her phone buzzes again.

I break off the kiss, and this time her face has a worried expression that I don't like.

I think of how she said I didn't know everything about her and wonder if I should push her, if I should ask her who is calling her because it's obvious this one isn't from the positive feedback camp, but I don't want that to sound creepy or controlling.

"Sit, I'll plate."

She puts her phone face down and takes her cup of orange juice over to the island.

I concentrate on building out plates, but I want to take that worried expression off her face.

"So you want to be surprised when we do our primal play, you want to be captured, you don't want to know when it's coming and you want it to end in anal sex?"

We talked about it, yes, but it's important to go over the details again.

Mara makes this snorting sound and I turn.

I can't help but hide my smile as she covers her nose.

"Here." I pass her a box of tissues.

"Sorry. You made me snort orange juice out of my nose. That isn't sexy."

"It's adorable."

Mara sticks her tongue out at me and I cluck her under the chin.

"To answer your question, yes. You don't want to be scratched."

"And if you're going to kick, stay away from the face and testicles, please."

"I definitely wouldn't want to damage your sword." Mara raises her eyebrows and I don't know why, but I'm the one who is choking on my coffee now.

"How do you feel about clothing being ripped? I promise I'll replace anything that gets torn."

"I have no emotional attachment to any clothing I own. I can't wait. When are we doing this?"

"You said you wanted to be surprised. Do you want to know the day I have this planned, or do you want it to happen?"

Mara stares at me. "Real surprise. I don't want to know when it's coming. The anticipation is going to add to the experience."

"I agree."

"Do you want to wear any costumes?" I slide a plate across to her.

"Like animalistic stuff?" She digs into the food and moans around a forkful.

My dick twitches as I take the seat next to her.

"Or want me in a mask?"

"Maybe not for the first time. It's really the...element of surprise here I think that I want. Being tackled, taken down, knowing that I am helpless after I put up a good fight...that's what I want to experience."

My blood is roaring in my ears. "It's going to be great."

"I know. Thanks for breakfast." Mara takes the plates to the sink. "I'm going to get dressed and get going."

"Want some company?"

Her cheeks pinken and I grin. "Or are you needing some space?"

"No…there's just stuff in the studio I want to organize before people come over."

"Totally fair. I asked for five days and we've made it to day number six. I want you to know that I am all in, Mara. I want this next week. Next month. Next year."

She drags her palm down my chest. I grab her hand and kiss it.

"I'm not going anywhere, Evan."

I didn't know you could be so happy that your skin feels stretched because you're smiling so much.

"Get going, princess, before I tie you to the bed and show you what your words mean to me." I softly kiss her.

"I can't wait for you to tie me to the bed," she says over her shoulder.

I laugh and start cleaning up the kitchen, feeling like I am flying.

The primal scene I have planned is going to be so good and I go over the details in my head.

Mara comes out, dressed in a black skirt and a deep blue shirt.

"Do you want a ride?"

"It's okay. You rarely get a day off. Enjoy it."

"I will, but I'm going to miss you," I kiss her and wonder if she likes sliver or gold, but she wears a delicate gold chain on her neck, so I think I'm going to go with a gold band.

"I'll be back soon," she brushes her lips to mine and I walk her to the front door.

"Have fun with your new fame." I twirl a strand of hair around my finger.

"Thanks," she gives me a little wave and then she's gone and I'm in the apartment by myself.

After I call Julian to double check the details of the plan I need his help with, I leave the apartment to go see a man about a ring.

26 MARA

I pull into the underground parking lot, my head swimming with excitement.

This day has been wild.

First Wendy brought her friend, who wanted a flower sculptor for her daughter's wedding.

Just as I was wrapping up with her friend, the owners of a national baby convention buzzed at the door and then this afternoon, Wendy sent two more couples to me for wedding decor.

After everyone cleared out, I sat in the still mostly empty studio and started sketching ideas in my sketchpad

And daringly, I took a pencil to the wall and started to freehand a mural.

It's my place. I need to make it my own. I can't wait to tell Evan about how busy I've been

I'm confident that I can make this business work.

Pausing at the elevators, I consider which set to take. The ones that go up to the hotel, where I'll encounter guests, or the private one.

The private one is fine but I have to swipe the card through the readers and last time I did this it stuck and locked out and I had to use the other one. But what's the point of living in a private hotel if you don't use the secret elevator? I swiped my card in, and it lights green on the first try

I lean against the plush fabric, tilting my head back.

Only a week and this seems so normal. My mom is going to flip when I tell her about this crazy ride.

The elevator makes a clunk-clunk sound, stalling. My stomach drops to the floor.

There is only one button, no emergency stop button.

The elevator starts again and I exhale the breath I was holding. But the lights flicker off, leaving me in darkness. My palms are instantly sweaty and I wipe them off on my skirt.

I press my palm against the padded leather upholstery and fumble for my phone.

The lights flicker on.

And off.

But before I can press send on my text to Evan, the car whizzes back up, like normal, and the doors open.

It's fine, I tell myself, knowing that Evan is going to stroke my hair and reassure me and I'm going to nuzzle his neck and smell his good smell.

I step off the elevator, opening to the hall that leads to the apartments.

I notice the usual vase of flowers that's always on the table is missing.

The lights flicker, then go out, leaving me in darkness.

I hear a creaking door.

Then heavy footsteps.

The blood is roaring in my ears.

It's so dark, I can barely see my hand.

A scream is in my throat, but I force myself to move my feet.

I take a couple of steps, and I'm not on the usual floor, but something...harder? Firmer?

My mind whirls.

I hear footsteps again. My head is swimming with confusion. Ahead of me, something thumps, making a banging sound.

I scream.

My heart is thundering hard in my chest.

"Time to run," a deep booming voice says from behind me.

I am still frozen in shock. My mind is scrambling, and then footsteps are coming towards me.

I run.

Something thick crashes into my knee, I land on my stomach.

It's soft. Padded.

And then I giggle, because it's a relief to my fear.

Under me, I'm very sure they are gym mats. The thing that crashed into my leg is also a gym mat.

This is the take down scene.

An echo rustling sound comes from somewhere and it freaks me out

The unknown sound has my pulse racing again. I hear footsteps in front of me and I scramble to my feet

He's not going to get me that easily.

Nope, if he wants me, he's going to have to work a little harder.

Reaching down, trying to find the object that crashed into me, I grab it and throw it behind me and run, trying to picture the hallway in my mind

Heavy footsteps run behind me.

The unknown is crashing into my logic, the rustling sound cranked up and I keep running, hitting something with my feet. I tumble to the floor.

Gritting my teeth, I try to push myself up, and a hand grabs my leg, pulling me to them.

I furiously kick, tears falling down my face.

So many voices crowding my head, all the comments people made about my weight swirling through.

You're too fat to do that. My ex boyfriend's voice.

You're too fat to make anything of yourself.

My father's voice.

I kick furiously, my shoe comes off and I throw the other one behind me and run.

My breath is coming in short gaspy pants, adrenaline is firing through my veins and even though tears are streaking down my face, this feels good.

With a surge of adrenaline, I run, kicking an object that hits my foot.

But he was always going to catch me.

I scream as his hands come around my waist and push at him.

"I got you, princess."

"No you don't!" I throw an elbow, connect with his shoulder and break free again, a laugh breaking out through my fury of adrenaline.

"Damn, woman!" Evan cries.

I'm panting, breathing heavily, but I run to the edge of the mat, thinking I've outpaced him. When he grabs me around the legs, pulls me down to the mat.

He's on top of me, pinning my hands.

But I don't let him.

I twist under him, trying to get him off of me. I stop myself from scratching him, but using my knuckles, I try to get under his hold.

"You're mine and you're not going anywhere." Evan's breathing is hard too, and it makes me smile.

I keep turning and twisting, using my body to make this hard for him.

He leans forward to my shoulder and bites me.

"Ouch!"

It hurts, but combined with the adrenaline flowing through me, it arrows right to my pussy and I know I am soaked between my legs.

Using all my strength, I lean forward, get one hand out of his hold and head butt him in the chest.

He flies back, "Hey! That's it, princess, no more being nice about this."

I giggle as he wraps a leg around me, lets go of my wrist. He grabs the waistband of my skirt, trying to rip it off.

I'm covered in sweat, adrenaline heating my blood, but I don't care.

I grapple, kicking and twisting under him.

"Nope, I caught you."

My skirt is off of me and then he shoves aside my panties, shoving two fingers into my pussy.

"Drenched in zero point five seconds."

I flop down to the mat, loving how harsh his touch is, how he rips off my panties, and I grind against his hand, wanting more, needing him to claim me.

"That's it. You wanted to be captured, didn't you?"

His touch is so rough, making every nerve ending fire with anticipation.

"Yes."

There's no point in pretending otherwise. And I don't want to.

He's the only man I would let do this to me, trust in the dark in this way.

The only man who I'd run for, would submit to being caught.

His tongue plunges into my mouth, finding mine, not letting me up for breath. As his fingers work relentlessly, I squirm as he hits my G-spot.

Too rough, too fast, to be pleasurable, but an orgasm ripples through my body, making me scream.

"That's it, princess. You're going to give me another one." His hand snakes under my shirt, he gets it off over my head, and cups my breast through my bra.

My body is shuddering with the aftershocks of the pleasure.

I help him get my bra off with trembling fingers. He leans forward and takes my nipple into his mouth.

With the lick of his hot tongue, I see stars, the sensation so intense.

He sucks, and laves and doesn't let up, and I can't help but clutch him.

I want more and less, and I don't ever want him to stop all at the same time.

He switches to the other breast, his hand back between my legs. Heat blazes a trail through me. The pleasure already starts from my pussy, pushing at me to go under.

I spread my legs wider, giving him more access.

"Good girl." He rewards me by taking the tip of my nipple between his teeth.

The pleasure is so intense, so sharp, I can barely catch my breath.

He lifts me up and brushes my sticky hair from my face.

"Catching you is my new favourite pastime."

Oh, the husky way he said that has my heart beating even faster than it was when he was chasing me in the dark.

He kisses me, devouring my lips and I wrap my arms around him, wanting to be as close to him as I possibly can get.

I hear the whoosh of his belt as he takes it off, and reach for him, finding his waistband, getting his pants off of him.

"I am so hard for you, princess, and I can't wait to claim my reward."

I swallow hard.

Yes, I'm going to do this.

I want him to take me that way. I do because I trust him and I know he's not going to hurt me.

He rolls me over, sets me so that I'm on hands and knees. He kisses the nape of my neck, drags his lips over my back, right to my tailbone.

A shiver of desire, red hot and needy, drums through me as he presses his lips to my sensitive skin.

"Going to go nice and slow, baby. Ready?" I shake my head in the pitch black of the room.

"Princess, I asked if you were ready?"

"Yes Sir," my voice wobbles. "I like it when you call me baby."

Fear and excitement war with me and I don't know how to get comfortable on my hands, naked and waiting for him.

"I like calling you it," he rubs his mouth against my shoulder.

I hear a squirt, the sound of palms rubbing together.

"Oh!" I gasp as I feel Evan's finger circle my anus. Hot shivers roll across my skin.

"Breathe, princess."

I exhale the pent up breath I didn't know I was holding.

Evan's finger slides into my opening and it feels intrusive and hot and good.

He makes a circling motion and my mind goes blank.

A needle fine wave of pleasure, that starts from my centre, spreads out and threatens to take me down, I gasp and realize I'm making little mewling sounds.

I feel another intrusion, as Evan adds another finger, and I relax to the touch, closing my eyes as I am swallowed in this wave of pleasure.

My skin turns warm, then cool, and warm again and grows hot as Evan settles behind me, his hands on my hips, his cock hard and thick against my opening.

"Bare down. Breathe. That's it, that's a good girl."

His praise coaxes me to relax and I feel his hard length slide into me, slowly, until he's seated and I'm rocking beneath him.

The needling sensation is grabbing all of my attention.

My mewls are drowning out whatever Evan is saying as he starts to rock his hips, thrusting in and out of my most sensitive hole.

But I close my eyes, and give over to all the sensations, my thoughts stalling.

It's just a grouping of hot pleasurable sensations.

My breath coming out in gaspy mewls, Evan rocking above me in growly pants. It's wonderful and feels dangerous and hot and all too much.

I feel like I'm going to come apart from the inside.

"You feel so damn tight my cock never wants to leave this hole." His voice is like gravel and I claw at the mat. It does me no good but I move forward under him and he picks up his pace, pounding me, taking what he wants.

My head swims with the sound of roaring blood, pleasure too intense for me to ride, but it shatters me in little pieces, as if I am separated from my body. I love how his body feels above mine.

A muscled wall of heat, enveloping me. Keeping me safe. Ramping up my pleasure with every rock.

"Good girl," he moans above me, his hips thrusting, his cock pounding into my flesh. "Mara!" he yells my name and my heart explodes as he releases in me.

Both of us stay where we are, catching our breath.

Evan dislodges himself, rolls to my side, drapes his arm over me, and kisses me.

"You're amazing, princess."

I can't speak over the sobs in my throat.

So many emotions are coursing through my body, as if they all need to expel and those tears are back, rolling down my face.

I lay my head on his shoulder, and take comfort from his solidness.

"Next time, I think I want to wear a gorilla mask."

I love how he always surprises me. I giggle.

"Why?"

"Because I feel like beating my fists on my chest and telling the whole damn world how much I love you. I love you, Mara."

My hands in his hair, I pull his head towards me and kiss him. I kiss him hard, taking his lips between mine and finding his tongue, I swallow on it hard and sure.

"I love you, too, Evan Brennon."

The words are out of my mouth before I have a chance to over think them.

I'm a sobbing mess.

He sits up next to me and pulls me against his chest.

"I love you."

I nod against him, grabbing his arm. "I feel the same, Evan. I love you."

27 EVAN

My body is humming with the satisfaction of giving my submissive what she asked for.

Mara is mine to love, mine to protect, and mine to take care of.

I help her up off the mat and guide her back into the apartment, grateful that the only other occupant on this floor has given me privacy.

I leave the lights off, while I get us to the bathroom, the floor lighting comes on automatically as we walk.

In the bathroom, I start the shower and, with my hand on the small of her back, guide her in.

I take a puff thing, soap it up and start to wash her.

From her neck to her back, and I take my time with her breasts.

"These are very, very nice boobs." I can't help but to drop a quick kiss on her dusky areola, but this is aftercare and I don't want to ramp things up again, even though I'm tempted.

Mara laughs. "You really are a boob man."

"I told you. Spread your legs."

She does, and I soap between her thighs, then I cup her ass and make little circles with the puff.

Taking her from behind was so damn good. I'm going to dream about this scene for a long time.

That whole scene was amazing.

I loved how I could feel the moment when her fear turned to excitement and when her resistance turned to surrender.

Once I'm done soaping every part of her body, I gently some conditioner in my hands, and run it through her hair, massaging her scalp.

"That feels good."

"It's supposed to." I rinse her hair, find her lips and devour them.

Before she gets cold, I quickly wash myself and step out.

I dry her off and hold open her black, silky robe.

"Thank you."

"It's my pleasure." I'm smiling in that cheek aching way again, but this woman allows me to nurture her, to care for her and it makes the Dom in me roar in appreciation.

"My head is feeling all floaty."

"Time for aftercare, princess. You're a good girl. You're not dirty."

Her expression cools into something neutral. Her blue eyes are wide as she gazes at me, her fingertips brushing my pecs.

"You're the only one who has ever made me feel safe and brave and, like, the kink stuff is nothing to be ashamed of. That it's not some afterthought."

I hug her, kissing the top of her head. "I love doing kinky things with you. I like making you breakfast and taking you to work. I like watching you sketch and I like waking up next to you. I love you Mara."

"I love you."

I need her to keep saying it because I love hearing it and I'm going to spend every moment I have on this earth to show her how much I love her.

We go into the kitchen.

"How did you set the scene up?"

I smile. "That's a mystery."

"You can tell me. I won't tell a soul," Mara crosses her heart.

I laugh and take down two mugs. "Hot chocolate?"

"Only if you're having some."

"I'm manly enough to drink cocoa." I fill our mugs from the dispenser I had poured the hot chocolate in before I had started the scene.

I carry our mugs to the couch, set them on the coffee table and pull Mara's legs on mine.

"What did you like about that scene?"

She lays her head on the back of the couch. Her eyes light up. a small smile on her face.

"The fear...it was scary at first, but when I clued into what was happening, it was the fun anticipation kind. I liked that I stopped thinking and could fight."

I didn't see her as the kind of woman who struggled to give her submission. One of the things I adore about Mara is how self-aware she is and how well she knows herself.

"Do you need to fight?" I slide my hand between her legs, gently touching her, wanting to give reassurance.

"No. But being challenged and feeling like I can be physical is kind of fun." She reaches for her mug, takes a sip, and peers at me. "I don't think I would want to do that type of scene once a week. It's intense. What about you?"

I rub her leg, thinking it over. "I think next time I'd prefer to keep some light on. Being in the dark was a cool idea, but I didn't like not knowing where you were. I loved surprising you, pouncing and then claiming you."

I move my hand in between her legs with one hand and wrap my fingers through her hair with the other.

"Is there anything you didn't like about the scene?"

I gently massage her head, watching how she finishes her mug, sets it down.

She nestles up to my shoulder and grabs my arm, putting it on her stomach.

"It brought up a lot of emotions. In a way, it was cathartic."

"Is that good or bad?" I trace the curve of her stomach gently.

"I don't know. I was reminded of how people sometimes make comments about how I can't do something because of my weight. Like I can't run because I'm too heavy."

Her voice wobbles. I brush my lips against hers, fury rolling through my blood. I want to hurt anyone who said that to her.

"Who said things like that to you, your old bosses?"

"No...they'd make off-handed comments about my weight, but in my experience it's because the person saying it is being intentionally cruel."

She squeezes her eyes tight.

"Mara, I think you're perfect. I love you. You don't have to tell me, but I need you to know you can tell me anything."

"My dad," she bites out.

Her hair is soft and I twirl it around my finger, giving her space to fill the silence if she wants.

"He's not a good person. When I was a kid, he always tried to dare me to do something. Like, 'I dare you to run to the stop sign and back,' or he'd put my favourite candy on top of the cupboard and tell me if

I could do ten jumping jacks, he'd give it to me. Then he'd dare me to lose weight and then say things like nobody would take me to the homecoming dance because I was too fat."

Mara laughs. "Do you know a bunch of my friends and I skipped the dance to go to an art show? I'm still in touch with them. My mom and him split that year. But that's when I found out he'd been using my personal information to take out credit cards and apparently was in thousands and thousands of dollars of debt."

I shake my head, thinking of my scatterbrained, occupied father who was always in his own world but still made time for us. My dad is gentle and kind, and I couldn't imagine having a bully at home.

"That sounds awful. I'm sorry you had to experience that."

"I got through college with scholarships and my stepdad Bryan pitching in. My mom had been unhappy for years, trying to pay off my father's debts. She and Bryan had a quick romance of their own." Mara squeezes my hand.

"So. when you told me getting a business loan wasn't possible..."

"It's because my dad screwed up my finances pretty badly. And I didn't do anything about it."

My brain goes into high gear, thinking there must be a way I can help solve this for her.

If I had to spend every last cent in all my bank accounts to make her life easier, I would.

"If you hadn't given me the space and the funds for my business, it would have remained a dream."

"No." I squeeze her hands. "Maybe you wouldn't be sharing space with Steff, but you would be doing it, Mara. You're too determined and driven to have let yourself down."

"Thank you. I'd like to think that you're right.

"Believe me, princess, I don't think there's anything you can't do."

"It's a lot easier when your credit isn't wrecked."

"Through no fault of your own," I say. "Do you see him?"

"He comes around once a year or so and asks me for money. But I don't have a relationship with him and I won't." Her mouth is in a hard line.

I drop a kiss to her temple. "Good girl."

I'm so proud of her for telling me about her dad, but I want to ease us out of this heavy conversation.

"I got a bruise on my ribs from someone's elbow."

Mara giggles. "Sorry."

She kisses it and laughs. "I think my shins are bruised from falling and where you grabbed me on my hips feels sore."

"Yeah well, if you get some sleep, princess, I'll make it all better in the morning.

"Promise?"

"I promise."

"To bed, Sir Evan!" She grabs my arm and pulls me off the couch.

From the kitchen drawer, I find the arnica cream, and in the bedroom, I toss the cream on the end of the bed.

"Look at you," I tell her, kissing her neck. "You're beautiful."

She tilts her head against my chest, and I take the robe off her shoulders.

"Let's see those bruises."

Mara holds her arm out. "It feels like there is one here."

"I see it." I take the arnica and squirt some on that spot, then see one above her hip and dab at that.

"You're right about your shins."

Mara laughs, meeting my gaze in the mirror. "Even bruised, Sir, you make me feel beautiful."

My cock twitches. I quickly finish applying the arnica, then I cup her neck and pull her close to me, devouring her, kissing her as deeply as possible.

"I love you."

"I love you." Mara wraps her arms around me and yawns.

"Bed."

I pull down the bedsheets and pat the bed.

Mara gets in, and I pull the sheets up to her chin, then I shut the lights off in the bedroom and climb in next to her.

"How did you just happen to have mats lying about?"

I laugh. "Not giving it up, eh?"

"No." Mara yawns.

"I have a friend with customized mats to fit the hallway."

"Julian's into takedown scenes too?"

I take her hand in mine. "I'm not sure what Julian is actually into. He had mats customized to fit the hallway because he wanted to practice fencing, but then found a better space or something."

"Some people spend their money on fancy cars or customized gym mats." Mara giggles.

"He has plenty of cars, too. I'm grateful for the use of the mats, and he helped me flick the lights off in the elevator."

"How did you know I'd choose the private one?" Mara's eyes close, and she nuzzles against my arm.

"That was luck. If you hadn't, I would have chased you from the elevator. I saw on the security camera that you got into the private one."

"Spying on me?"

"Yes." I kiss her forehead.

"Good. I like you taking care of me like that."

I laugh. "I want to take care of you in all ways, princess. I love you."

"Love you." I can't stop saying it. And Mara's asleep in seconds, while I'm wide awake, feeling satisfied and happy in every part of me.

This woman makes me so happy. I can't wait to have more scenes with her and come up with even more ways to take her by surprise.

28 MARA

"I don't know if I like her calling you at a moment's notice," Evan grumbles as he parks outside of Steff's building.

"She's Steff Goldstein. If she calls and asks me if I can make her a floral sculpture with a two-hour deadline, I'm going to do it. You're just mad our lazy morning got interrupted."

"Well, yeah." Evan flashes me that smile that makes my pulse race. "You need to take off more mornings."

"I'll make this one up to you. Are you coming in?"

"Yep. There's Steff. I need to help her with that." Evan gets out of the car and rushes over to Steff, who is wheeling a cart that's stacked high with stuff and it looks like it's going to topple.

I reach for my to-go cup of coffee and take a sip, trying to centre myself to go and work. My body is still kind of sore from that takedown scene.

Evan and I stayed in bed till almost noon, having slow, languid sex, and I tried to get more details of his birthday bash from him.

"It's a party."

"Is it at Sinful Bites?"

"Yes."

"Do you play in front of your brothers?" The idea kind of horrified me, that I'd be meeting his brothers for the first time and end up half clothed or without clothes on at all.

He'd kissed my mouth. "No. Guests are welcome to play in the dining room, it'll be set up as a dungeon just like it was when you first came to Sinful Bites and I guess if my brothers wanted to. I know Hunter and Theo won't play. I was thinking of taking you to Shivers after dinner. If we don't do it for my birthday, I want to take you soon. You need to meet Nevie and Griffin. Everything I learned about BDSM and kink, I learned from them."

"Then I definitely need to meet them." I kissed him back, long and slow, and couldn't believe how much had changed since I had come to Sinful Bites with my former bosses that night.

Steff had called me as we'd just finished our shower, asking if I could make a sculpture for a special client of hers and I'm not going to say no.

Just because Evan has made my life easier, it doesn't mean I'm going to stop taking every opportunity that comes my way.

I watch Evan, helping Steff steady the pile of stuff, makes me all fluttery.

I can't believe this man loves me and we're together. I can see a future with Evan.

As I open the door, I run my inventory through my head and I know I am going to need another cooler in the space. With the business Wendy has brought me, it's not going to be hard to achieve.

"Hi Mara! Thanks for coming in. I have a picture of what I'd like."

"You're welcome." I close the door and follow behind them.

"Leave it there, Evan, thanks," Steff says and almost trips over the cart.

I hide my smile as I open the door to the studio.

"Thanks."

He hadn't been in for a while and my stomach twists into a nervous knot as he circles the room, looking at the mural.

"I appreciate this Mara," Steff sets her bag down on the counter and opens up her iPad. "Here's what I was thinking. Is this enough time?"

The sculpture is an open mouth bass meant for a table display, thankfully, and small enough that I could do it in this time frame.

"What colours are you thinking?"

Steff shakes her head. "At this point, anything you have. I'd love something bright."

I know I have some dusty pink amaranth, orange hibiscus and carnations to finish it off.

"I can do this," I reassure Steff.

She claps her hands together. "I knew you could! Thank you! Text me when you're done."

"I will." Steff wrings her hands standing there.

"Steff?" I raise an eyebrow at her.

"Right, I'm going!"

Steff waves by and I start pulling flowers out of the cooler, set them on the counter and then I go over to my cart of supplies.

"I love watching you work. Am I going to be in your way if I sit over here?" Evan gestures to the other bench.

"Nope, I'm going to be pretty focused on getting this sculpture done."

"I promise not to interfere with you, but I have to say you look very sexy holding that tool."

"Pilers?" I shake my head at him. "I know you know what these are."

"Are you sure?"

"You showed me a picture of your dad's workshop."

"Hunter's the one who knows his way around tools. But okay, you're right. I just like that you know how to use them and that thing."

I roll my eyes and start cutting the wire I need, trying to estimate as accurately as I can because I don't like wasting materials.

Evan's phone rings and he brushes by me, taking the call outside.

I'm thankful for the interruption, because apparently having him in my space is a distraction after all.

I get to work on sculpting the shape of the bass.

It's finicky and my fingers are cramping by the time I have it done.

Reaching for the amaranth, I start twisting the delicate strands around the frame, careful not to destroy the petals.

With how it spills everywhere, it's perfect for the base of the fish.

I'm lost in covering this sculpture when Evan slides back into the room, sets a bottle of water down on my bench.

"Thanks." I nod.

He quietly takes his seat again and I reach for the alliums. They're going to form the bulk of this fish.

I cut the stems as needed, wrapping them around the body of the sculpture and as I work, everything floats away, including Evan, who is reading something on his phone.

I know how lucky I am to be doing this for a well-known designer. I know many of my friends dreamed of opportunities like this and even though I know Evan did it because he wanted to and I give him what he needs, there's no way I can ever pay him back.

I ignore the ache in my fingers and keep going, vowing to make an appointment for a good hand massage. It was Sabrina, my old boss, who told me to get hand massages by a massage therapist to protect longevity in this field.

I kind of miss Sabrina and Kyle, even though they were toxic.

But you can miss someone even if they aren't good for you. I know that from my dad.

Thankfully, I have Arthur and Miranda for Evan to meet, well properly, and my mom and Bryan. I can't wait to tell my mom the story of how we met and I know she'll laugh and say that instant love, whirlwind romances are hereditary.

Lost in putting on the finishing touches of this fish, I have no idea what time it is but see that it is darker outside.

I'm covering the last eye with an orange hibiscus, when I feel Evan at my side.

"That's the prettiest fish I ever saw."

"Yeah?"

"Oh yeah. You're very good at this, Mara."

I am blushing to the roots of my hair.

"Thanks," I whisper, concentrating on getting the last of the mouth covered.

I put down my tools, circle the fish and take a picture. It's an array of colour and I love it.

I text Steff a picture and five minutes later my door bursts open.

"This is better than I could ever have imagined! Thank you! My client is going to be so impressed!"

"I'm happy you like it."

"I love it! Is there a way to pack this up for transport?"

"We can find something."

I have a couple of utility shelves that aren't all that organized, but I rummage through and find some cardboard and foam.

"Can you hold that piece there?" I ask Steff.

Evan comes around and between the three of us, we've wrapped this awkwardly shaped sculpture.

"Open it from the sides and you'll be good,"

"I can't wait for them to see it! I'll tag you in all the photos."

"Thanks." I smile.

"Got to get this to them! Have a good night." Steff dashes out the door, holding the box away from her.

"It's going to make it, right?"

Evan laughs. "Yeah. Steff always comes through for her clients."

"Good." I'm smiling wildly at him and I don't know why, other than it feels very good to have him in my workspace. I giggle and Evan raises a cool eyebrow at me.

"I was thinking that I like having you in my work space. But I might like you being here better when I'm not working."

"Oh yeah?" He pulls me against him and kisses me, his tongue twirling with mine.

"Hmm-hmm."

"What do you say to dinner?"

"Yes, please. Sinful Bites?"

"No, I'm taking the night off. I have something else in mind." The smile on his face makes me feel so adored, flutters burst low in my stomach.

I tidy up my workspace, turn off the lights and we're exiting the doors, when I see a man with a ball cap and a leather jacket walking past.

There's something in me that recognizes him and I stiffen.

"Mara, what is it?" Evan asks me, pressing his hand to the small of my back.

"Nothing."

But the man turns and my mouth goes dry as my dad jogs over to us. "Mara! There you are. You keep ignoring my calls. I went by your old apartment and I guess you're not there anymore."

This man is going to wreck everything. I stare at my father, not believing that he is here to wreck everything, but of course he is, and bile rises in my throat. Evan reaches for my arm, but I can't.

"I got to get away from here," I take three steps away from Evan. "Leave me alone. Please."

I see the angry expression on my father's face and I don't think, I just take off, walking briskly, then jogging.

At the entrance to the park, I run left, down a windy trail and finally stop to catch my breath, my hands on my knees.

What am I going to do now?

I don't know how I am going to face Evan, knowing that my dad probably asked him for money.

Evan had a little luck yes and a lot of privilege but he's worked hard for everything he has and someone like my dad could make a mess of his life

I had tried to put my father out of my mind, convincing myself I could have something good and happy with Evan. Taking out my phone, I see two missed texts from Evan.

I ignore them and dial Suki.

"Princess."

The phone slips from my fingers to the ground. I close my eyes.

"Mara, look at me."

I shake my head.

I feel his fingers under my chin, tilting my head to his, and I bite my lip. "Come on, princess. Open those beautiful eyes."

I can't resist him. Evan picks up my phone. I shove it in my pocket, wipe away my tears.

"Why did you run?"

My stomach tightens and I feel like I'm going to throw up.

"I don't like seeing him. But I was afraid he was going to ask you for money. I don't know. I felt overwhelmed and ashamed."

Evan pulls against his chest is the only place I want to be.

"Princess, if I have to capture you a million times to prove to you that there is nothing you could ever do that'd make me not want you, I will. I'm going to take you back to my kingdom and punish you for leaving."

More tears fill my eyes. "But did he ask you for money?"

Evan chuckles. "People ask me for money all the time. Brennon Consortium has a whole staff that deals with donation requests or financial aid requests. It wasn't a big deal, Mara. You decide what you want to do with your dad, but if you want help in finding a way to help him, I'm here."

"I don't know what I did to deserve you, Evan, but I love you so much."

"I love you. You are thoughtful, caring and kind. I love you so much. I'm the lucky one. This has been the best week of my life. You are amazing, and anyone who doesn't think that? Forget about them. I'll banish them from our kingdom forever. I'm going to work every day to be the kind of man you deserve."

I'm wiping tears away from my eyes and gasp as he stops in the middle of the path and kneels.

"Evan?" I don't know what to say and I'm trying to wipe the tears out of my eyes.

"Mara Cotter, will you marry me?"

He is holding out a box with a ring, and I can't believe this is happening. My pulse gallops.

There is only one answer. My heart leaps.

"Yes, Sir Evan, I will."

He takes my shaking hand and slides the ring on my finger, stands and kisses me.

I melt under his kiss. It's a kiss of promise and want, a kiss that makes me tingle, a kiss I don't want to end.

He breaks off the kiss and touches his forehead to mine. "I love you."

"I love you."

"I love you too. I can't believe you did that."

"I can't wait to keep surprising you."

I laugh, and it feels good.

He takes my hand in his and we walk out of the dark park together.

"What else did you say to him?"

"I told him to leave you alone, and if I saw that he was on that property again, I'd take legal action."

I exhale. For years, I had resisted taking any action against my dad because...well, he's my dad, and I thought it would be fine if I just avoided him, and I didn't want to put my mom through any stress.

But Evan, taking care of it for me, makes me safe. Nobody has ever stood up like that for me.

"Evan, thank you."

"Not a problem." Evan holds the car door open. "Get in, princess. I can't wait to have my way with you, wife-to-be."

"I'll go wherever you do. I love you."

His lips come down hard on mine, and I open, giving him all the access he's demanding. We kiss, long and slowly, out in the middle of the street, and I don't care where I am as long as I am with this man.

"I love you, too."

I know I'm the luckiest woman in the whole world, and I can't wait to see where loving Evan takes me next.

EPILOGUE – EVAN

I knew they would, but seeing Noel and Theo dote on Mara and welcome her, makes my heart soar.

Julian presses another drink into my hand. "Whose idea was the flame eater?"

"Logan's. Not that I've seen him, yet."

Julian raises a cool eyebrow. "Speaking of little brothers, mine has it in his head that he wants to live here. I'm not kicking you out but wondering about your future intentions."

Across the room, Mara is laughing with Holly and Holly's friend Patricia.

"Tell your brother he can have it. I need to find a home with a garden."

And I'll learn to like the scent of flowers if that's what it takes.

"No rush. I prefer you as a neighbour." Someone calls Julian over, and he claps me on the back.

Speaking of little brothers, Hunter's striding towards me, a huge grin on his face that reminds me of my father, his blond hair curling at his collarbone.

"Hey you old man."

"Watch it you young punk. I'll tell mom that it was you who destroyed that car."

Hunter steps back. "It's your birthday? You don't look a day over twenty.

I laugh and man hug my little brother.

"Happy you're here tonight."

Mara comes up behind me and wraps her arm through mine.

"I wouldn't miss it for the world. And this must be Mara, the woman you convinced to be yours somehow."

"Car."

"Hey, it was only that one time."

Mara laughs, her blue eyes glow as Hunter takes her hand.

"The restaurant industry must be good for the size of that ring. I can't wait to get to know you, Mara. Welcome to the family."

"Thank you"

"Oh cool, I see Griffin, he's always a good laugh." Hunter claps me on the back. "I'm going to enjoy your party now, see you later."

"He's fun," Mara says.

"He's a pain in the ass" I grumble but then I catch sight of the little pearl earrings I gave her and pull her close to me.

"I love that you're here tonight. I'm going to dance with you so I hope those heels are comfortable."

"What, these old things?"

Holly, Noel's fiancée, gives me a smile and laces her hand through Mara's

"I have something I need you to see," she says.

"Do you mind?"

"I guess I can spare you for a few minutes." I pull her down to me and kiss her, tasting red wine on her lips.

"Okay!"

I grin. Holly and Mara had met earlier to go shopping.

I got to spoil my girl with the new dress, and new heels that make her calves go on for ages.

"How are you liking your party?" Theo says, ambling next to me.

"Thanks for throwing it together. The band is a nice touch."

Theo smiles and raises his glass to me. "I'm thrilled you found Mara, Evan. You deserve to be happy."

"If I can forget about my ex, you can forget about yours."

Theo lifts his shoulder in a shrug. "Maybe."

"Any decision on a kinky bed and breakfast?"

"I don't know." Theo frowns. "But I'll do anything I can to make Callie happy."

"Good."

The whole room starts to sing, "Happy Birthday," and my head chef is pushing out a cake alight with candles. Mara's bringing me over to it, smiling.

"Happy Birthday, Sir Evan. Make a wish."

"You're all I could ever wish for, princess."

She squeezes my arm.

I blow out the candles, then kiss my princess as if she's the cake, and I'm tasting her all over again for the first time.

***

To keep up with the Sinful Delights Series join Mercy's newsletter here

https://mercydenton.substack.com/welcome